PENGUIN BOOKS

The Truth Must Dazzle Gradually

'A compassionate portrayal of love, support and grief . . . filled with hope . . . There are many strengths to this novel, not least of which is the author's decision not to fill the pages with anguish . . . A writer whose skill is matched by an ability to surprise with each new work' *Irish Times*

'Cullen's beautifully observed novel charts a family across thirty-seven years, living through a tragedy on a remote island; portraying mental health and the fall-out around it with enormous humanity and integrity. Tonally reminiscent of recent Colm Tóibín' Caoilinn Hughes, author of *Orchid and the Wasp* and *The Wild Laughter*

'So wonderful on the Irish family and the utter complexity of motherhood, family entanglement and love. I was full-on weeping at the end' Elaine Feeney, author of *As You Were*

'A beautiful novel – Helen Cullen writes with such deft care and attention about the things that hold us together when everything falls apart' Rónán Hession, author of *Leonard and Hungry Paul*

'An extremely moving read. Handles the complexities of love, grief, family life and mental illness with sensitivity and depth. A truly gorgeous novel' Ali Land, author of *Good Me, Bad Me*

'Such a tender read. Astute and compassionate, it made me cry. It's full of love. And it's quietly magnificent' Tor Udall, author of *A Thousand Paper Birds*

'A perfect combination of deeply felt tragedy with great hopefulness' Anne Youngson, author of *Meet Me at the Museum*

'A beautifully observed saga of abandon~~ed~~ loss and self-discovery. A fabul~~ous~~

'An intriguingly titled story that tackles weighty themes with an epic reach', The RTÉ Guide

'Absolute poetry and a love letter to family and to the arts. Such a gift in these times. The depiction of depression is as accurate as any I've read and the empathy in this book is beautiful' Maggie Smith, poet and author of *Good Bones* and *Keep Moving*

'Cullen's writing is precise, haunting and, above all, beautiful. Her depictions – from the minutiae of the Moone's home to the mood of the nearby sea – are masterfully constructed . . . a book of rare quality' *Independent*

'Cullen's atmospheric novel captures beautifully the continuity of life even at times of deepest grief. If we avoid tragedy in literature, we're closing ourselves off to some of the most powerful and moving writing, as exemplified here' *Business Post*

ABOUT THE AUTHOR

Helen Cullen is an Irish writer living in London. She is the author of *The Lost Letters of William Woolf* which has been optioned for television. She was shortlisted for Newcomer of the Year at the Irish Book Awards.

The Truth Must Dazzle Gradually

HELEN CULLEN

PENGUIN BOOKS

PENGUIN BOOKS

UK | USA | Canada | Ireland | Australia
India | New Zealand | South Africa

Penguin Books is part of the Penguin Random House group of companies
whose addresses can be found at global.penguinrandomhouse.com.

Penguin
Random House
UK

First published by Michael Joseph 2020
This edition published by Penguin Books 2021

001

Typeset by Jouve (UK), Milton Keynes
Printed and bound in Italy by Grafica Veneta S.p.A.

The authorized representative in the EEA is Penguin Random House Ireland,
Morrison Chambers, 32 Nassau Street, Dublin D02 YH68

A CIP catalogue record for this book is available from the British Library

ISBN: 978–1–405–93517–3

www.greenpenguin.co.uk

Dedicated to those who always leave a light on,
and Demian Wieland in particular.

And from the record player, through the crackling, Henry Mancini's orchestra began to play. The opening notes of 'Moon River', at once so familiar and yet newly revelatory, broke through the cracks, and with them came the light.

Contents

ONE

Queen Maeve

Inis Óg: 2005

It was Christmas Eve.

Murtagh wore tan sheepskin slippers, broken down at the heel.

He shuffled to and fro along the well-worn floorboards in the shadowy hallway of the Moone family home.

Smoothing unwieldy fair hair back from his forehead, he gently touched where his temples throbbed. Still damp from the rain, he hugged his cardigan tighter and the wooden robin brooch on his lapel turned upside down.

The ticking of his wristwatch was amplified in the silence, its pearlescent moon face catching the streetlight through the window and winking back.

The door to the living room remained firmly closed.

Christmas waited inside.

The branches of a lopsided fir tree – the one he had dragged home across the Gallaghers' field seven days before – were weighed down by decades of tinfoil garlands the children had clumsily stitched together with red wool. None would ever be thrown away, however tattered they became. Every year, as the Moones assembled to transform their island cottage into something akin to Santa's grotto, each child claimed their own creations with jealous possession. With ceremonial grace, their mother carefully unrolled their handiwork from the fraying white tissue paper that protected it for the other forty-eight weeks of the year. One by one the decorations were placed on the tree.

Over these festivities, as with all others, Murtagh's wife reigned supreme.

His Queen Maeve.

None of the children challenged the traditions; their mother had sewn them so meticulously into the fabric of their being.

Stitches that could not be outgrown.

How he loved her for this gift she bestowed upon the family: permission to remain childlike in their enthusiasms; never to become embarrassed by what they had once loved. 'You never have to lose anything, or anyone,' she often said, 'if you just change the way you look at them.'

And yet he had lost her.

Even while he held her close.

Even with his eyes wide open.

Murtagh had woken that morning, once again, to an empty bed; the sheets were cool and unruffled on Maeve's side. He had expected to find her sitting at the kitchen table, wrapped in her hound's-tooth shawl, pale and thin in the darkness before dawn, a tangle of blue-black hair swept across her high forehead like a crow's wet wing, her long, matted curls secured in a knot at the nape of her neck with one of her red pencils. He had anticipated how she would start when he appeared in the doorway. How he would ignore, as he always did, the few moments it would take for her dove-grey eyes to turn their focus outward. For the ghosts to leave her in his presence. The kettle would hiss and spit on the stove as he stood behind her wicker chair and rubbed warmth back into her arms, his voice jolly as he gently scolded her for lack of sleep and feigned nonchalance as to its cause.

But Maeve wasn't sitting at the kitchen table.

Nor was she meditating on the stone step of the back door drinking milk straight from the glass bottle it was delivered in.

She wasn't dozing on the living-room sofa, the television on but silent, an empty crystal tumbler tucked inside the pocket of her peacock-blue silk dressing gown, the one on which she had painstakingly embroidered a murmuration of starlings in the finest silver thread.

Instead, there was an empty space on the bannister where her coat should have been hanging.

Murtagh opened the front door and flinched at a swarm of spitting raindrops. The blistering wind mocked the threadbare cotton of his pyjamas. He bent his head into the onslaught and pushed forward, dragging the heavy scarlet door behind him. The brass knocker clanged against the wood; he flinched, hoping it had not woken the children. Shivering, he picked a route in his slippers around the muddy puddles spreading across the cobblestoned pathway. Leaning over the wrought-iron gate that separated their own familial island from the winding lane of the island proper, he scanned the dark horizon for a glimpse of Maeve in the faraway glow of a streetlamp.

In the distance, the sea and sky had melted into one anthracite mist, each indiscernible from the other. Sheep huddled together for comfort in Peadar Óg's field, the waterlogged green that bordered the Moones' land to the right; the plaintive baying of the animals sounded mournful. Murtagh nodded at them.

There was no sight of Maeve.

As he turned back towards the house he noticed Nollaig watching him from her bedroom window. The eldest daughter, she always seemed to witness the moments her parents had believed – hoped – were cloaked in invisibility, and then remained haunted by what she had seen. Ever since she was a toddler, Murtagh had monitored how her understanding grew, filling her up, and knew it would soon flood her eyes, always so questioning, permanently.

He waved at her as he blew back up the path. Later, he would feel the acute pain of finally recognising the prescience his daughter seemed to have absorbed from the womb.

'How long is she gone?'

Nollaig was now standing before the hallway mirror, her face contorted as she vigorously tried to wrangle her frizzy mouse-brown hair into shape. She scraped it together into a tight ponytail that thrust from the back of her head as if it were a fox's brush.

'Ach, you should leave your gorgeous curls be, Noll,' her father cajoled, 'instead of fighting them.'

She smiled at him but slammed the mother-of-pearl hairbrush down on the sideboard.

'I don't have curls, I have Brillo pads,' she sighed. 'Did she say where she was going?'

Murtagh squeezed his daughter's arm as he continued into the kitchen. 'I'm sure your *mother* is just out for a walk. Happy birthday, love. *Lá breithe sona duit.*'

He placed a small copper saucepan of water on the range to boil and waved the invitation of an egg at his daughter. She nodded begrudgingly and curled into the green-and-gold-striped armchair that sat in front of the stove.

'With your white nightdress, you could almost pass for the Irish flag,' he joked, and was gratified with her snort of glee.

He watched the clock hand count three minutes in silence. Expected any moment to hear his soaked wife splash through the door. He was poised, ready to run towards her with a towel and hushed reprimands for her careless wandering, but the boiling, cooling, cupping, cracking and spooning of each egg passed uninterrupted. Nollaig yawned, stretching her arms and legs before her in a stiff salute.

'Why don't you go back to bed for an hour?' Murtagh asked. 'We'll all have proper breakfast together later.'

She eyed him with suspicion but acquiesced. 'If Mam's not back soon,' she said, sidling away, 'come and wake me. Promise? We'll go out and find her. Remind her what day it is, for God's sake.'

Murtagh nodded, ushered his daughter out of the kitchen and watched her climb the stairs.

Born on Christmas Eve, Nollaig was the only one of their children who came into the world via Galway Maternity Hospital and not into the impatient arms of Máire Ní Dhúlaigh, the midwife of the island. She resented it; how it made her feel less of a true islander. What was more, the specialness of her own day for individual attention, her birth day, was irrevocably lost in the shared excitement of Christmas. In retrospect, it had been a mistake, perhaps, naming her Nollaig, the Irish for Christmas, and further compounding the association. No nickname had ever stuck, however. She wasn't the sort of child who inspired others to claim her for their own with the intimacy of a given name.

'Born ancient,' her little sister, Sive, always said of her, with bored disdain.

Nollaig carried the weight of being the eldest with pained perseverance, heavy responsibilities that were self-imposed. Her mother harboured a not always silent resentment of it, and it seemed only natural, if unfair, that Maeve and Sive gravitated more towards each other; the baby of the family shared her mother's wit and wildness and often expressed the irritation her mother tried to hide at Nollaig's sense of duty.

As soon as he heard Nollaig's room grow still, Murtagh pulled on waterproof fishing trousers over his pyjama bottoms, and wellington boots. He struggled into a heavy jumper of itchy grey wool, impatiently yanking the sleeves of his nightshirt down from where they were caught at the elbows and shrugged on the duffel coat that remained his favourite, though long past its prime. It was eight in the morning now; the sun would not rise until closer to nine. As he reached into the cupboard under the stairs for a torch, he was relieved to find only one waiting on the shelf.

At least she's taken a light.

The beam from his flashlight showed him little but the safest path for his own feet, but he was glad of it as he waded through the inky blackness.

8

Come meet me, Maeve.
Show yourself.
Come meet me, Maeve.
Show yourself.

As he marched a beat down the long, narrow lane towards the pier, trailing his left hand along the stony walls covered in moss, he repeated his mantra.

Not another soul stirred.

What would call them from the warmth of their homes to be drenchèd in this storm?

When the weather enveloped the island in an angry embrace such as this, the isolation became almost unbearable. The elements made prisoners of the islanders, who could be convinced they had been swept out to sea, lost and untethered, never to reach the mainland again.

As Murtagh leaned against the weather-bleached clapboard sign that shouted ferry times in bright orange paint, the sky became diluted with the first strata of light.

The rain eased.

The darkness slunk away, but only by as little as it had to for dawn to be officially considered broken.

Perhaps Maeve was already at home, she in turn now worried for him.

In the weak winter light he trudged through the sand to retrace his steps, willing with each breath for his home to have sprung to life while he'd been gone.

The sound of the twins arguing in the kitchen heartened him as he wiped his boots on the back-door mat. Eighteen now, they occasionally loomed before him as fully-grown men. At other times, they were still the small boys who hadn't liked sharing the same supermarket-trolley seat and let their objections be known.

'How hard is it to make toast, Mossy?' Dillon said, scraping the charred surface of a cremated slice of soda bread into the sink. 'Every. Single. Time.' He enunciated each syllable with a violent scratch of the butter knife.

Mossy, indifferent, stood drinking orange juice straight from the carton, ignoring the rivulets that dribbled down his chin. His face lit up as his father peered around the door.

'Da! Where were ye? What's the story with breakfast?' He shoved the carton back in the fridge, its lid discarded on the countertop.

'Yeah!' Dillon chimed in. 'Where's the feast Mam promised? We're half-starved waiting!'

Murtagh swivelled his head around the kitchen. 'She's not back, then? Your mother?'

The twins caught each other's eyes, before their gaze fell back on their father as he wrestled off his boots.

'Was she not with you?' Mossy asked, dragging his floppy fringe across his forehead and plastering it behind his ear.

Son Day, his mother called him. Tomás Moone, the pale, blond, waifish bookworm who inherited not only his paternal grandfather's name but his colouring and temperament, too. Son Night, his brother Dillon, with ebony-black curls and high cheekbones, was unmistakably his mother's son. Named in honour of two of her heroes, Bob Dylan and Dylan Thomas, the artistic mantle lay heavily on his shoulders. He had the dream to be an artist, but not the driven determination. Dillon was never interested in struggling, only in enjoying what came easily. Mossy was the one who worked hard, persevered conscientiously with any task until it was complete. Sometimes Murtagh wondered how each would have developed if their names had been swapped at birth, or if, with the naming, their fates had been sealed.

Nollaig reappeared in the kitchen, dressed now in the white velvet pinafore and red polo neck her mother had bought her to wear on Christmas Day. 'Has Mam not resurfaced?' she asked, her face flushing.

Murtagh absorbed the questioning expressions of his three children and shook his head. 'I'd better wake Sive,' said Nollaig, and pounded back upstairs.

Sive had turned sixteen that summer and relished her new, more mature-sounding number. Obsessed with the Manic Street Preachers, Suede and Placebo, she wore fandom like a uniform, a jet-black bob curled under her chalk-white-painted face like the Lego hair of the figures she'd played with as a child. Eyeliner rimmed her eyes in rivers of kohl-black, the same dove-grey eyes she saw mirrored in her mother. Blood-red lipstick emphasised how little she smiled, although the melancholy music elated her. She revelled in the secret world inside her headphones and fantasised about escaping to London. Discovering her musical tribe had made her feel less alone, more optimistic for future connections, romance and inspiration. For now, she advertised for her ilk through her clothes, usually striped, always sooty black, battleship grey or midnight blue, that she wore in layer upon layer, with garlands of silver stars draped around her throat. A full-length fake-leopard-print fur salvaged from a charity shop on Eyre Street in Galway city was her most prized possession. It was this she wore over her night-dress now as she reluctantly followed Nollaig into the kitchen. She pulled the coat tighter around herself upon detecting the tense cloud that lingered in the air, observing the private smoke signals her brothers passed from one to the other. Her father was busily burning sausages in the pan. She was surprised to hear him curse when the sizzling oil spat at him.

'So, what's the plan? Is Christmas cancelled, then?' Sive asked, checking the temperature of the coffee pot with the palm of her hand.

Murtagh poured her a mugful and scoffed. 'Don't be daft! We're going to have a little fortification and then perhaps we can all take a stroll and go and meet your mother. She's lost track of time, that's all.'

Sive reached for the mug and they both held it for a moment. 'So, a search party. That's what you're saying. Great.' She slumped in a chair at the kitchen table and elbowed Mossy to give her more room.

Her father turned back to the hob, his voice strained. 'That's not funny, Si. And it's nothing of the sort. I just think we'd all like to start the day together and, you know your mam, she'll be having a great time walking the roads and will be delighted to see one of us coming to meet her.' He put the ham that Maeve had prepared the night before in the oven and set the timer for noon.

Not long afterwards, as the rain started again to pour, the

brothers forged ahead towards the rusty shipwreck on the east of the island.

Nollaig and Sive elected to walk past the chapel, on to Tigh Ned's pub, and agreed to then carry on to the castle ruins if they hadn't found her first.

Murtagh set out for the lighthouse, convinced if Maeve was gone this long that must be the road she had taken. Although, the thought struck him, he did not know how long it had been since she left the house.

Why hadn't he insisted she come to bed with him? She was too restless, she'd said. Too full of the moon for sleeping.

After they reached their destinations they would reconvene back at the house instead of continuing on; the chances were their mother would be waiting at home when they came back, wondering where they had all gallivanted off to.

Nollaig and Sive returned empty-hearted first. Nollaig scraped the ashes from the grate in the living room then Sive set the kindling for a fire. They stood in front of the mantelpiece in silence, waiting for the others, warming their hands near the flames without feeling the heat at all.

The twins burst in next, drenched, Dillon's fluorescent trainers squelching as he walked. When they saw the sisters were alone they backed out of the living room without a word; Mossy climbed back under his duvet, fully clothed, his brown brogues dangling over the foot of the bed, and pretended to read a book of poetry by Keats. Dillon drained the tank of hot water in the shower, his discarded clothes a steaming pile outside the bathroom door.

★

When Murtagh's arrival wasn't accompanied by the fluttering sing-song of their mother's voice, Sive's eyes flooded. Nollaig snapped, told her to pull herself together and hurried towards the kitchen to speak to their father alone. The aroma of roasting ham percolated throughout the silent house, as if in spite. When the electric beeps heralded its readiness, Nollaig turned off the oven without even looking inside. She hoped her mother would be home soon to reprimand her for not taking greater care. Dinner was sacrificed to a god she wasn't sure she believed in as her father prepared to face the elements once again. Nollaig called her brothers and sister together and they divided up the island paths between them for a second search. Nobody spoke as they marched out of their cottage in single file, back into the storm.

Minutes of acute expectation bled into hours of increasing anxiety. By mid-afternoon Murtagh and his four children were wet, exhausted and turning on each other. In vain, their father encouraged them to eat bowls of lukewarm vegetable soup that he ladled out slowly. He choked his own down, spilling some on his cardigan, dropping his spoon on the floor tiles with a clatter. Nollaig caught his eye and he nodded.

'We need more help,' he said as he eased himself up from his chair. 'I won't be long.'

Murtagh walked to Tigh Ned's, where the islanders were gathering before evening Mass for hot whiskies and shepherd's pies amidst the owner's begrudged festive decorations; a lime-coloured plastic Christmas tree on the windowsill wore a Galway jersey and was circled by pint glasses holding beeswax candles donated by the parish priest, Father Dónal.

The *RTÉ Guide* bumper Christmas edition stood on display by its side with a small laminated sign perched against it: *Not to be removed from the premises.* The air was heavy and moist as a result of the condensation rising from damp clothes and human bodies huddled together.

Murtagh spoke to Father Dónal, whose white denim jacket sat stark against his black shirt and slacks, a sprig of holly pinned to his breast pocket. With head tosses and clicking fingers, Dónal summoned a semicircle of islanders before draining his tumbler in one, crunching an ice cube with his back teeth as he delivered instructions. The Moone children would come to the pub, eat some dinner there, no objections entertained. Murtagh himself was to wait at home for Maeve.

'In case,' Father Dónal said, before correcting himself, 'I mean, for *when* Maeve comes back by herself.'

In groups of twos and threes, they dispersed, half-consumed pints of Guinness left resting on the grille in the hope of a speedy return.

And so Murtagh found himself pacing the floorboards of the hallway, fingering rosary beads in the pocket of his cardigan out of superstition more than faith. What little light had broken through that day had once again dissolved into darkness.

Through the small window in the hallway he watched the streetlamps flicker into life in quick succession as the cuckoo clock chirped four with inconsiderate glee. He shouted at it to stop and then found himself apologising to the little yellow bird.

A knock pounded the front door.

Murtagh hid in the study for a moment, covering his ears. He didn't want the news a knock like that would bring. What he wanted was a hand to reach for that door that belonged to someone who could unlock it, walk herself in and wrap her arms around him.

He blessed himself with the ruby-red beads and opened the front door a crack. Father Dónal stood on the doorstep, his denim jacket soaked through, his hands wringing a tweed peak cap. Over the priest's shoulder, Murtagh saw Seamus McCann and Áine O'Connor waiting outside the gate, huddled under a huge canopied umbrella advertising Tayto crisps, their eyes focused on the laneway beneath their feet.

'Why don't they come in, Dónal?' Murtagh opened the door wide and beckoned them with his arm, but the priest reached for it and held it in his own.

'Tell me, Murtagh. Your currach, is it still in the boat-yard? When did you last have her out?'

Murtagh took a step back, the priest a step forward, still holding his arm.

'Only yesterday, sure where else would it be? No one would be out in this weather. No one. What are you asking me that for?' He shook himself and stood up straighter.

Dónal squeezed Murtagh's arm tighter, his frozen fingers exposed in black fingerless gloves. 'There's a currach caught in the rocks by the westward cliff. A few fellas are climbing down now to release it. Could you come with me, Murtagh? Just so we know it's not yours. To eliminate it.'

Murtagh shook away the priest's hand and pushed past him without stopping for his coat.

Dónal hesitated before pulling the door closed behind them and followed Murtagh up the path, his hands clasped together.

Murtagh threw his shoulders back as he repeated his walk from that morning to the pier. His name designated him protector of the sea, and now he pleaded with the melanoid Atlantic for his own protection.

Father Dónal, Seamus and Áine rushed behind him in silence, but no one tried to match his step.

At the boathouse, he found the door unlatched, and the discovery stuck the soles of his boots to the sandy ground. Áine stepped forward, gently swung the door wide and pulled the string to light the bulb that dangled from the ceiling. With a glance, she quickly knew what Murtagh's eyes would not believe, however hard they scanned and searched.

The boat was gone.

From the distance, Murtagh heard voices calling from the shore. Ignoring protestations from the priest to wait until he had learned more, he staggered down the sand dunes to where a cluster of men stood in a half-moon around a currach, their hunched shoulders turned away from him. As he approached, Peadar Óg, owner of the whining sheep, moved towards him. His clothes were saturated, his face red raw and freezing, eyes wild.

'I'm sorry, Murtagh,' he croaked. 'It's Maeve. We have her. She was tethered to the currach by a rope. Her pockets.'

His voice broke.

'Her pockets were full of stones.'

He stood aside, and Murtagh dropped on his knees in the wet sand beside the boat. In the silver light, blue veins traced delicate pathways across Maeve's face, like tiny cracks in a porcelain vase. He traced a line over each one with his little finger while the islanders turned their faces away.

Father Dónal began a decade of the rosary and, in quiet voices, each person joined in, even the ones who weren't believers.

In fact, theirs were the loudest voices of all as, with each 'Amen', the darkness crept closer.

TWO

Days of Crow

Dublin: 1 May, 1978
Noon

It was the shoes he noticed first.

Tomato-red suede platforms tied with white ribbons for laces.

Double knots.

Loopy bows.

Feet crossed at the ankles.

Black-and-white striped stockings stretched over the knees.

An inch of milky skin.

The rest of the woman who would one day become his wife remained hidden behind the stone campanile at the centre of Trinity College. Her left foot beat a determined rhythm, the right foot carried along in lopsided surrender.

Murtagh smiled.

Stepped forward.

Hesitated.

He transferred the weight of his leather satchel from one shoulder to the other. Wiped his nose once again in vain (it had not stopped running for days) and fingered the fraying blue handkerchief in the pocket of his new brown duffel coat.

Later Maeve would describe it as 'Frank Sinatra-eyes blue' but he could not know that yet.

Nor how the big toe of her left foot poked through a hole in one of those pedestrian-crossing stockings.

Nor that she had spray-painted those tomato-coloured shoes herself, with an aerosol can she found abandoned, next to an unfinished graffiti portrait of Lady Madonna, on Francis Street that morning.

All he knew for now was his compulsion to discover who owned those shoes, those stockings, those knees. He nodded at Sir William Lecky, eternally patient upon his green granite perch, and stepped on to the grass.

Murtagh grimaced as the soles of his Chelsea boots squelched in the soft earth. The hems of his corduroy flares were trailing in the mud from that morning's summer showers. Scanning the silver skyline for nimbus clouds to prophesy whether another downpour was in the post, he was relieved to detect only a hazy veil of stratus.

Too much time with his head in the clouds.

Or so his mother, Teresa, had always said. As a consequence, he learned to name every one and became an official cloud-spotter.

Not all children were fortunate enough to have their very own Mother Teresa.

His hand reached automatically to smooth his messy mop of hair, as if she had just appeared before him, but he resisted the impulse. Instead he wrapped the emerald-green scarf she had knitted him tighter around his throat.

Murtagh circled the campanile.

Stood silently for a moment piecing a little more of the puzzle together.

Her slender frame bore the burden of an over-sized denim rucksack. It was covered in dozens of embroidered patches: yellow roses and purple stars, green-and-orange concentric circles, two crows perched on a branch, a white lighthouse with a red flag flying, rainbow stripes, slogans for anti-apartheid and anti-Trident, badges shouting Led Zeppelin and The Ramones.

A coil of blue-black braid was pinned loosely under a scarlet beret as her head rested against an army surplus jacket she had crumpled against the wall as a pillow. A low-pitched whine got louder as he inched closer.

Was she in pain? What on earth was wrong with her?

He tentatively tapped her beret with his forefinger, cringing to see the potting clay embedded still under his nails. She swiped sideways with her bare arm, so pale that blue veins traced fragile lines beneath the translucent skin. Her fingers clenched his arm in a surprisingly vice-like grip and he stared at the plum nail polish perfectly applied to her round fingernails. She turned her head to look at him; suspicious dove-grey eyes peering out from beneath a thick fringe. Her face was that of a bird in human form: the point of her nose, the angles of her bones and jaw, the heavy eyebrows for protection.

'What do you think you're doing?' she asked, releasing his arm and clambering up into a stand as she rested her backpack on the ground.

An American!

She was tall, thin, threatening, wearing short red velvet dungarees and a shimmering ivory vest; it looked more of her than on her.

Murtagh held his hands up as if she were the police. 'You sounded – that noise you were making – I thought you were sickening from something.'

She emitted a dirty, guttural cackle. 'That *noise* was me singing a Patti Smith song. Well, trying to. I guess I'm a little outta practice.'

He watched her waiting for him to speak, but when nothing was forthcoming, she filled the silence herself.

'Do you go here?' she said, stretching into a yawn. 'I'm waiting to get into my dorm, but reception doesn't open until two. I almost fell asleep there, my bag coulda grown legs.'

Murtagh found his voice, a croak though it was, and mustered up a question that felt unworthy of the effort it took.

'Whereabouts have you travelled from?'

She leaned her head to one side, cocked one leg behind her like a flamingo and squinted at him.

'Can't you tell?' She waited a beat.

Murtagh nodded, his head light as he struggled to hold her gaze, blinded by the beams of silver sunlight scattering from her vest.

'I'm from Williamsburg, Brooklyn, to be precise.'

He began to ask her how similar New York really was to how it seemed in the movies but stopped mid-sentence. '*Mother of God!*' he yelled as he held his head, swaying back and forth, moaning, cursing and stamping his feet.

Maeve reached out to him then took a step back, 'What's the matter? Are you having a fit or something?'

He looked up at her, his eyes red, streaming.

'A bee.

'I've been stung by a bee.

'On my ear.

'Like a hot poker in the side of my head.

'It *stings*.'

Maeve stifled a snort as she rustled in her backpack, extracting copper tweezers, a miniature tincture bottle and a crumpled orange paper napkin with numbers written on it in blue ink.

'Here, let me.' She pulled his hand away from his face and inspected the wound. 'Sit down, I'll get the venom out.'

She sat on the stones beside him, curled her army jacket into a ball on her lap and patted it in invitation for him to lie down. He slid forward so he could place his head in her lap, the offended ear turned towards her, his nose buried in the folds of her coat.

It smelled of apples.

He took a deep breath and sighed.

So, this is what all those songs are about.

He clenched his fist as she extracted the sting from the back of his ear with the tweezers, washing the wound with water from her flask. It trickled down the collar of his shirt, but she stemmed the flow with her hand. Every nerve in his body was focused on the tiny intersection between the burning skin of his ear and the cool touch of her finger-tips. He heard her twisting a cap loose, her silver bangles shaking, and felt the press of a handkerchief to his ear. 'What can I smell? What is that?' His eyes squeezed tightly against the sting.

'Chamomile,' she replied. 'I carry all sorts with me. My grandma is a naturopath and has taught me a lot. Not for nuttin' but I'm not a big fan of modern medicine.'

Murtagh sensed a story but was too wobbly to pursue it; he would have happily lain there all day listening to her

American drawl. It was like being inside a movie; a feeling entirely unfamiliar but utterly seductive.

With a little push from Maeve he sat up, shielding his eyes from the sun with his hand.

'Well, I guess I'll say goodbye, then, and go crawl under a rock somewhere and die of embarrassment,' he said. 'I'm so sorry for the trouble.'

She stood up, laughing, and held out her hand to help him up in turn.

'I've seen worse. Trust me. Let's go find coffee and a doughnut. Maybe you can keep me company while I wait.'

'Are you sure?' he asked, still holding on to her. 'I'm not convinced that I have the powers to redeem myself.'

'I *think* I'm sure,' she answered, still holding his hand. 'That's as good as you get with me, I'm afraid. I'm Maeve, by the way. Maeve Morelli.'

'Murtagh Moone. Moone with an E.'

Murtagh carried her rucksack on his back and Maeve criss-crossed her body with his satchel, resting her hand on it as they walked to Ma Reilly's, the ramshackle café at the back of Finnegans Wake bookshop. 'No apostrophe,' she said. 'Good work.' Only three tables clustered together consti-tuted their dining emporium: one pine, one oak, one teak. The seats had been salvaged from a clear-out of the Shan-non Hotel; red upholstered dining-room chairs with gold lacquered legs. Dusty second-hand paperbacks lined the wall of bookshelves behind them and lay abandoned on the bare tabletops. A teenage boy, red hair cut tight to kill the curl, swimming in a creased yellow shirt several sizes too big for him, lumbered over to take their order. His hand shook a little as he rested the nib of a plastic Biro against a spiral notepad; two kissing giraffes, necks entwined, graced the cover.

'So, tell a girl, what coffees have you got?' Maeve asked him, arching her brow.

His eyes widened. 'Er, Nescafé? You can have it with milk or no milk? Or sugar?'

'Ness-caffay? What is that? French?'

Murtagh leaned across the table and touched her sleeve. 'It's instant. You'll hate it, but it's the best you'll get.'

She wrinkled her nose but smiled at the waiter. Murtagh was transfixed by the whiteness of her teeth. Like someone on the telly. 'Two instants, then, please, sir,' she said, but Murtagh interrupted: 'I'll just have a tea, thanks.'

She looked at him in horror. 'You don't drink coffee?'

He shook his head. 'Too bitter for me.'

Murtagh stirred three spoons of sugar into a floral china teacup that looked much too delicate in his strong hands. When he poured from the teapot the lid slipped and hot brew splashed across the table. He pushed a pile of Flann O'Brien novels out of the way and stood up to brush the scalding tea from his lap. Maeve snatched a tea towel from the rear pocket of the waiter's jeans as he passed and mopped up the mess without pausing the flow of her story. 'So, I won the scholarship and I'm here representing my theatre class for the summer at the Trinity Drama School. Eleven weeks. Six plays. And, first up, I'm doing a scene as Desdemona. Can you see it? Me as Desdemona?' Murtagh could, and nodded in fervent agreement. 'What about you?' she asked, sipping her coffee with a tight grimace. Murtagh pined for another wrinkle of her nose.

'I'm at NCAD, studying ceramics. I want to be a potter, some day.'

'NCAD?'

'National College of Art and Design. It's on Francis Street, near the Liberties.'

'Francis Street. That's where I found the paint for my shoes! It looks like a fun part of town. A potter. I like that. It's soulful. Meditative.'

'Hang on,' he said, feeling the tightness in his chest relax a little. 'What do you mean, *paint for your shoes?*'

She laughed and stretched out one leg to rest her foot on the table beside them, her dungarees sliding upwards to expose more of her leg; the waiter dropped a tray and Murtagh smiled at him.

'Do you like?' she asked. 'I did them myself.'

'I do,' he answered as he lifted his foot up to sit beside hers. 'Maybe you can do mine.'

A dusty Chelsea boot and a tomato-red platform shoe kissed.

And that was that.

At five minutes to four o'clock the waiter began hovering around Murtagh and Maeve, shoving discarded paperback books haphazardly on to the shelves, half-heartedly spritzing the tables with furniture polish and dragging a dirty dishcloth across them. 'Is it closing time?' Murtagh asked, checking his bare wrist for a digital watch that lay on the windowsill of his college practice studio. He could picture it there, its neon-green numbers flashing in the emptiness, beside the half-eaten Granny Smith apple he'd also put down in order to scrub his hands of clay.

The waiter nodded. 'The boss does his Tarot reading here on Monday evenings, and it doesn't work with other customers in, 'cause they're always earwigging.'

Maeve perked up. 'Tarot reading? Well, who can blame them? Is he any good?'

The waiter looked over his shoulder as if expecting his boss to appear. 'I'd save your money, miss. I've heard him say the same thing more than once, if you know what I mean. He calls himself Marcello Pollo, but his real name is Marky Platt. Says it all, eh?'

Maeve laughed. 'Still, might be good fun. I wouldn't mind knowing what Dublin has in store for me. We'll clear out – give me a minute while I pop to the powder room.'

While she stepped away Murtagh settled the bill and carried her rucksack outside to wait for her. He added an interest in the occult to the list of interesting things he'd learned about her over the course of the afternoon and counted them on his fingers:

- How when she was anxious she liked to lie on the grass and feel the earth beneath her.
- That she loved listening to opera, *Carmen* in particular, but had never been.
- That she distrusted vegetarians and thought it an affectation boring people adopted to give them something to talk about. He couldn't wait to hear

what his best friend, Jeremy, a vegetarian since primary school, had to say about that.

- That she'd never owned wellington boots but coveted a pair, preferably red, with a tartan lining.
- How she hated the smell of lilies, because they reminded her of funerals, and the sight of any flowers at all wrapped in cellophane, because it looked as if they were choking.
- That she liked writing poems in pencil because the mistakes were impermanent that way.
- How sometimes she had trouble sleeping but lavender on her pillow helped.

The pieces of the Maeve puzzle were intriguing and unnerving in equal measure. He felt so grey in the shadow of her Technicolor. If he were to hold her interest, he knew he would have to shake off the ennui that so often dogged him, that he'd need to achieve more than just getting by. *Mediocrity would not the heart of Maeve Morelli win.*

While Murtagh's fingers moved in acknowledgement of each revelation, Maeve stood in front of the mirror in Ma Reilly's toilet cubicle and splashed cold water on her face. The towel draped over the basin was soggy, so she dabbed her skin dry with a clutch of toilet paper and tossed it into the overflowing wicker basket by her feet. She paused, deciding if it was sensible to encourage this Irishman to walk her home. Surely she could spend twenty-four hours in the city without meeting a man already. Wouldn't it do her good to be on her own for a while? She smoothed the velvet of her dungarees with the palms of her hands and hoisted up her stockings. Loved the smack of elastic against her skin when she released the band. Snapped it once, twice, three times. A future version of herself might be strong enough to walk away, but Maeve recognised she hadn't become that woman yet. She frowned, wondering for a moment if she would ever become that person if she remained afraid to be alone with herself. 'Stop it, Maeve,' she whispered to her reflection, and pinched some colour into her cheeks. Instead of seeking out excuses to run, she threaded the little beads of knowledge she'd collected about Murtagh together and wore them like a talisman around her throat. Unbuttoning a purple moleskin notebook from her pocket, she extracted a little red pencil from its spine and rolled it between her fingers before writing:

Dear Diary,

I don't have much time but, before I forget, or sense robs me of them, here are the reasons why I cannot let this man disappear:

- First of all, he's a potter! That's like being a poet with your hands. And his hands, well, they look like poetry, but secondly, he never makes pots when he's out of sorts because he thinks the toxic energy spoils the clay.
- He collects old recipe books and loves cooking for others but never for just himself.
- He's an only child, like me, but has never minded it, unlike me.

31

- Two different-coloured ink stains on his shirt pocket from leaking pens – didn't learn his lesson the first time. He needs some looking after! It would be nice to be the one doing the looking after for a change.
- Writes to his mother every Sunday without ever telling her anything about his real life; just pretends to be the son she wanted – his 'specialist subject'.
- Hasn't talked about his father yet, other than to say he is still alive, an Irish teacher and captain of the county hurling team. Not a fan of hurling but does love taking black-and-white photos of the matches. 'Ballerinas in another life,' he said. 'So swift and graceful were the players.'
- In his company, I feel my edges soften. Maybe I could stop bumping into my own sharp corners if I spent more time with him.
- Those hands, have I mentioned the hands?

The lead snapped on her pencil. She cursed. Dropped it back into her bag with the notebook. At least she couldn't pretend later she hadn't thought it through. It was written down, even if only in pencil.

In the short time they had been apart, long distances were travelled. And so, when Maeve looped her arm in Murtagh's, the satchel he had almost forgotten draped over her shoulder, it felt entirely natural. It was only a few minutes' walk back to Trinity College, but they dawdled along Grafton Street to postpone the ending of the afternoon.

'I'm so excited to finally be here,' Maeve said. 'Ma used to sing that song to me all the time, you know the one. *Grafton Street's a wonderland, there's magic in the air.*

There's diamonds in the lady's eyes and gold-dust in her hair.'

She looked at him expectantly and, despite himself, he shyly joined in.

'And if you don't believe me, then come and meet me there.

In Dublin on a sunny Sunday morning.'

She put her hands on his shoulders and stood before him. 'You *do* know it,' she said. 'Ma would be beside herself to see this.' The sudden thought of her mother so far across the Atlantic Ocean tripped her up, and she withered like a kite when the wind unexpectedly drops. 'Would you like to call her?' Murtagh asked. 'There's a telephone in my flat you can use.' She squeezed his arm. 'Are you sure you wouldn't mind? I'll pay you back.' He waved the suggestion away, suppressing a niggling fear of how expensive a transatlantic call might be.

'How about I check in, we go to yours to make the call, and then I'll treat us to a beer somewhere?' Maeve held out her hand to Murtagh and they shook on it.

Murtagh couldn't know that Maeve's mother, June, was pacing her Brooklyn hallway, willing the telephone to ring, her father repeatedly moaning that they should have never let her go.

He had no idea just how far Maeve had really come when she crossed the ocean to make peace with herself in Dublin.

Or how temporary that calm might be.

Not that he would have cared.

In that moment, he couldn't have contemplated any

reason not to initiate an immediate surrender to this woman who fizzed beside him; it was as if his heart had been patiently waiting for her to arrive and the hesitation he'd felt before about other girls was now entirely justified. As if he had unwittingly been training for Maeve's arrival for years. He pledged to do all he could to hold her interest, as tightly as she held his hand.

And as she held it, Maeve loved the solid way he moved through the world in that scratchy duffel coat, the kind she'd only known small boys to wear in the past, but which suited him so perfectly. Her feet had never been more grounded and yet felt so light.

Those heavy boots were left back in America, she was sure of it.

So, in the doorway of Brown Thomas on Grafton Street, a deal was done.

Dublin: 18 August, 1978

Maeve's mother and father were expecting to greet her at JFK in two weeks' time. It choked her up to think of Hank wearing a suit for the occasion, his silver cufflinks winking at him as he drove his gleaming white Oldsmobile Cutlass to the airport, turning the steering wheel with his hands fixed in the ten and two o'clock position; to imagine how June would have spent the morning readying her old room, baking the cheese scones Maeve loved as she sang along with Roy Orbison playing on the tiny yellow record player that she treasured.

If she posted the letter today, it would hopefully arrive before her mother called Murtagh's flat on Sunday week for their fortnightly appointment – June thought her daughter stopped in for tea on Sundays after she and Murtagh had taken Mass together. Or at least she pretended to think that, and Maeve didn't spoil things by ever confessing the truth.

Maeve sat at her desk and tore a sheet of pale blue notepaper from the pad her mother had optimistically sent, and rested it on top of *The Country Girls*; she hated when words were imprinted on the pages underneath. In her left hand, she held the fountain pen her father had gifted her at graduation; in the right, a pure white pebble in the shape of a triangle that Murtagh had found for her on the strand in Bray. The record player whirred softly, having reached the end of *Live and Dangerous*, but she didn't switch it over. Instead she closed her eyes and listened to the satisfying thwack of a tennis ball against the strings of a competently yielded racquet in the courtyard below her, the hateful flapping of two pigeons arguing on her windowsill, the muffled vacuum cleaner from Dorothy in the flat above. She was waiting until she knew how to begin, but as is so often the case, it was only when she began to write that the best way to express how she felt was revealed. Slowly the words came.

18 August, 1978
Trinity College, Dublin

Dear Ma, Dear Pa,

As always, I hope that the pair of you are healthy and happy as you open my letter. You'll be pleased to hear that I am healthy as I write it and will be happy when I'm done.

Ma, I can picture you sitting straight as a ruler on the living room sofa reading this aloud to Pa like a radio announcer; Pa, I can see you in your armchair, a saucer resting on the armrest with two vanilla biscuits poised for dipping in your cocoa. I know how you both love to receive these letters, and that's why I have waited so long before writing this one, for I hate to spoil it for you with news I know you don't want to hear.

Maeve paused and looked around her dishevelled room. Before any more writing could be done, she drank a pint of elderflower cordial over the sink and dipped her flushed face under the cool running water. It still shocked her that there was no air-conditioning in Ireland. 'Not worth it for the few sunny days,' Murtagh had said as he fanned her with a copy of *Hot Press* magazine with Rory Gallagher on the cover, his face floating in and out of her vision as she ate banana ice-cream straight from the tub.

A little cooler, she crouched on the floor and began cutting encrusted lumps of candle wax from the carpet with nail scissors. Why hadn't she listened to Murtagh and cleaned it up immediately when it happened? Because it would have meant turning the lights on, that's why. It would have meant the end of their dancing, the rinsing out of glasses, sobering up, when she'd really wanted him to stay. Despite her nerves; in part, because of his.

She reached over her head and felt around the unmade bed for the strap of her blue leather handbag; the mirrors that were glued all over it caught the hot, white afternoon sun and reflected miniature rainbows around the room as she pulled it towards her. It spilled its contents into her lap and she riffled through the debris; a blunt kohl eyeliner, honey-and-lemon cough sweets; a mix-tape from Murtagh he'd named 'Sounds of the Summer'; two ticket stubs from the Stella Cinema for *Sgt. Pepper's Lonely Hearts Club Band*; and the journal she'd started on the flight from JFK. Only a couple of blank pages remained.

She opened it at a random date from a few months previously:

8 May
The boxes arrived!
Finally!

I had begun to nurse a creeping paranoia that they were lost in transit and that I'd never forgive myself for risking my most beloved worldly possessions to the international postal system. My records are all here now, and I love Ma so much for indulging me in sending them over, even if it's only for a few months. I kissed the covers like old friends, and they are all here now, like ghosts from past lives come back to haunt me.

To think of that schmuck in Fibbers last night, shouting at Murtagh for wearing a Horslips badge at a Blades gig. I hate that we are all supposed to pick a side, march in just one musical tribe and scoff at anyone who plays for a different team. 'Music is a whole universe,' I shouted at him, 'and you're stuck in one spot listening to the same song on repeat.' I thought he was going to slap me for a second, felt Murtagh tensing beside me, but then he screamed and poured a pint of cider over his own head and dived back into the mosh pit.

Poor Ma, if she could have seen me.

She tried to hide a Mary Immaculate statue of holy water in the pocket of my tuxedo jacket that she sent me. I think Ireland is the one place she doesn't have to worry about a shortage of holy water. I hid Mary I. on the bookcase behind Edna O'Brien. I don't want her judging me and know Edna would understand.

For Maeve, music wasn't entertainment. It was an ointment, a lighthouse, a hot-air balloon. When she sang along with Ian Curtis, she felt legitimate. Like the rage she felt wasn't unique to her alone; that others suffered, and others survived. The songs allowed her to articulate what she felt but often struggled to find words to express.

She shivered to think of what might have become of her in the past if she hadn't incubated her troubled mind with the songs of Nina, Bowie and Leonard. They made her feel less alone, when no one knew what to say to her, the right questions to ask or advice to offer; inspired her to perform; made her long to get better. Eventually the fear of never creating art herself somehow became more powerful than the fears of facing the world again. They could never know it, but on many nights these musicians saved her life.

It gave her such pleasure to see the albums from home integrated now with those she'd collected that summer; records she'd found trawling markets with Murtagh and those that had been for sale at gigs and signed by the band themselves. *TV Tub Heart* by The Radiators from Space was signed by Philip Chevron and Pete Holidai with a red lipstick Pete had found in the pocket of his leopard-print fur coat, and Bob Geldof and Pete Briquettes had scribbled across *The Boomtown Rats* in a barely legible blue pencil. The albums were stacked now in a red crate in alphabetical order. To be handled with care. She changed the record on the player to The Rads and continued the letter to her parents.

Don't worry, nothing bad has happened. Only good things. But, those good things do mean I will be away from you a little longer. I applied to transfer my final year to Trinity and they've accepted me, and honoured my scholarship too, so I've accepted. I know you will feel I should have discussed this with you first, and I'm sorry that you haven't had more warning, but I didn't want us to spend hours discussing something I know I have to do. You couldn't have changed my mind and I didn't want the pain of us arguing while you tried – especially when I didn't yet know if I'd been accepted.

There are so many reasons I want to stay. You know about Murtagh, of course, but I promise, much as I love him (and I'm convinced that I do), he's not my only motivation for staying. I feel like, in three months, I've settled down here in a way that I could never manage at home; I'm more grounded, peaceful, in control. It helps that everyone expects me to be that way. At home I feel like my personality is all wrapped up in how sick I was.

People looked at me and saw that first.

And it's not their fault.

Here, people see the theatre student, the vinyl collector, the poet, Murtagh's girlfriend, the American, the actress; so many different things, and none of them are the sick girl, or the other far worse things we know some folks called me.

I can't express how free that makes me feel. My body now is a vehicle for me to live and be happy in; not something I inhabit resentfully, judging it based on how I see others judge it.

Maeve lay down on the bundle of clothes that sat on her bed and considered how to proceed. She flicked through the pages of her journal, pausing every so often when a date, or a doodle, or the tone of her handwriting caught her eye.

Murtagh is still sleeping, curled on his side, both hands tucked under his pillow. I didn't notice last night that his pillows are covered in tiny daisies. Sweet.

I can't resist leaning over to kiss that strange little tuft of blond hair that grows on his right shoulder blade, but he doesn't stir. Such a deep sleeper, when I awaken at the slightest thing. He's so close, but couldn't be further away inside his secret, private dreams while I wait for him in the waking world.

I hope things won't be strange between us when he wakes up, that last night wasn't a disappointment to him. It felt to me like all the electricity that had been crackling between us somehow imploded when we touched.

It all suddenly became very quiet.

Maybe we were both just nervous.

I hope I hadn't imagined the sparks.

She smiled, remembering how moments later Murtagh had woken up and, without saying a word, took the notebook from her hands, dropped it on the floor and pulled her to him. And what came next was the opposite of silence.

Later she had read Keats to him while they both lay naked in bed.

> Darkling I listen; and, for many a time
> I have been half in love with easeful Death,
> Call'd him soft names in many a musèd rhyme,
> To take into the air my quiet breath;

And from that day on he often called her his darkling, whenever what he really wanted to say was *I love you*.

25 June

Murtagh met his mother for afternoon tea at Bewley's on O'Connell Street today. He didn't invite me along. Too complicated, apparently. It seems you don't get introduced to the folks here until wedding bells are ringing. That's what Finola tells me – I'm so lucky to have made a friend like her. I never dreamed I could build these connections in such a short space of time. That I could create my own family here.

I guess the fact that Murtagh didn't invite me to meet Mammy means he has doubts about me.

I guess I can understand – the ticket for my flight home is pinned to the noticeboard over my bed like a warning sign not to get too close. We don't talk about it, but the question lingers between us, especially when friends discuss plans that are happening after our expiry date. Sometimes I wish he would ask me to stay, or admit how he feels about me leaving at least, but he shies away from that sort of chat.

I couldn't resist getting a look at his ma, though; Finola and I crammed into the phone box outside to watch her arrive, her heavily hairsprayed perm giving me compulsive sneezes. It was strange seeing Murtagh standing waiting, how lost he looked when no one was watching, and then witnessing the smile that turned on like a flashlight when the woman we assumed was Mother Teresa bustled over to him.

She was all sewn up in a navy two-piece suit, cream blouse with a pussy-cat bow and pillar-box hat firmly secured over tight silver curls. A formidable grey leather handbag was tucked under her right arm; it matched her shoes exactly and there was no doubt she was wearing pantyhose, despite the heat. They didn't kiss, or hug, but she immediately fussed with the tie he'd grudgingly worn and pulled his chin towards her to frown at the golden beard he has started to grow. I had thought it would be funny to see them together, but it just left me sad for how much time we spend pretending to be what others want us to be. Does Mrs Moone's behaviour make her happy? Or is she behaving the way she believes a mother should? Has she been trained to behave like that by another unhappy mother before her?

Maeve never told Murtagh that she'd spied on him; in advance she had presumed she would but, in reality, it had felt like a betrayal that she didn't want to admit to.

What she didn't know was that he had seen her and Finola hiding in the telephone box but had pretended not to notice. He assumed she had her reasons, and reasons for the silence that followed, but he didn't ask.

Maeve closed the diary without reading any more; the entries from the recent weeks were too familiar to hold any surprises or nostalgia for her. With a sigh, she returned to her letter.

So, you know Finola? Well, she and I are moving into lodgings in Rathmines; what Ms Hoskins, the terrifying landlady, calls 'respectable accommodations for respectable ladies'. The university scholarship covers my board there, and you would love her — it's still the 1950s in her house — so you've nothing to worry about.

I'll be so nervous before speaking to you on Sunday, but please don't be too disappointed in me and please don't try to change my mind. I am so happy with how things have evolved, but I would love your blessing.

She signed off, leaning heavily on the pen nib, as if it were possible to impress all her love on the page with it, and then rested her head on the desk, exhaling slowly. She folded the letter carefully into an airmail envelope and sealed it.

Maeve turned her face towards the wall and picked at the remnants of Blu-Tack that remained following the removal of her Zeppelin and Ziggy Stardust posters. What she told her parents was the truth; this summer, she had metamorphosed. Six days out of seven, her legs worked perfectly fine. She could shower, get dressed, crimp her hair, buy bananas, catch a bus, go to rehearsals, make small talk, walk past two wild cats fighting over an abandoned sausage roll, use a public toilet, queue in the post office, stir sugar in her coffee without her hands shaking, keep some food down.

Maybe even nine days out of ten. But expectation of a slip prickled her skin like the tag left inside a new dress.

On the windowsill sat two red ceramic wellington boots that Murtagh had made for her in his workshop; each held a cactus: Spike and Mike. It gave her so much pleasure to sit quietly in the studio watching him work at the wheel, always self-conscious at first but slowly connecting with the clay to the point of forgetting she was there. Observing his deep concentration was meditative in itself, as if she were in the company of grace.

She placed the letter between the cacti for safe-keeping and tied the curtains up so she could clear the windowsill of the miscellaneous objects she had assembled there: eggshell-blue eggcups, lavender candles, a tiger-print pencil case, a cellophane bag of costume jewellery, Polaroid photographs. She would miss those ugly green-and-white curtains, she decided; they had set the stage of a whole new world.

Dublin: 18 September, 1978

On an unseasonably warm Tuesday Maeve came undone. Like so many times in the past, it wasn't a major obstacle that triggered her, but a tiny wrinkle.

Rehearsals finished early and she lagged behind, foraging in the kitchen for a piece of fruit while she waited for Murtagh. A strawberry yoghurt slipped from her hands on to the yellow tiles and, in that moment, she could not stand up to herself any more.

Watching the sticky pink puddle spread and coagulate in the grout caused her knees to weaken. A dampness to form on her hairline. Her heart to pound. A dry mouth. Trembling hands. Her vision blurred as the fluorescent light bulb seemed to grow as large as the sun.

Maeve crouched in the corner on a pile of old newspapers, counting backwards from one thousand, her eyes squeezed tight.

Nine hundred and ninety-nine.

Nine hundred and ninety-eight . . .

Clasping her hands between her knees, she stamped her feet on the tiles to stop herself from floating away.

Nine hundred and sixty-six . . .

The thought of Murtagh arriving and waiting outside made her shoulders heave.

Eight hundred and forty-two . . .

She counted louder, beating out the rhythm on her thigh with a clammy fist.

Eight hundred and twenty-seven . . .

Eight hundred and eleven . . .

Eight hundred and one . . .

Seven hundred and ninety-nine . . .

Voice scratching.

Seven hundred and thirty-three . . .

Her breathing slowly steadied.

Heartbeat settled.

The dizziness in her mind calmed and she risked opening her eyes.

The room was still, and she felt numbness tingling in her fingers and toes.

Questions buzzed around her mind like angry wasps.

Why? What? How? When?

In the new light, she felt ridiculous as she cleaned the tiles, and reprimanded herself for losing it over something so trivial.

Where the yoghurt had been, the yellow tiles gleamed, exposing how dirty the rest of the kitchen floor was. So, she remained on her hands and knees and kept on scrubbing. Tried not to think of Murtagh still waiting.

When she was done, her purple nail polish was faded and chipped, her hands red raw from the detergent. She plunged them deep in the pockets of her leather jacket as she walked home.

Reluctantly, Maeve acknowledged the warning to herself and prepared a mental checklist of what must come next.

Rest
Nourishment
Exercise
Peace

If she was careful, things might not progress. Sometimes she found a way through before the fog completely descended. She would listen to music, read, get out into nature, practise her yoga, sleep, eat well. It was not always enough, but she could try.

When Murtagh collected her to go to the pictures the following evening he didn't comment on her absence the previous day. His eyes asked the question, though, and there was a soft hurt there, but she chose not to answer it, glad that in the cinema they wouldn't have to talk as they focused on *The Buddy Holly Story*. He walked her home after the film, as usual, but unusually, she didn't invite him in. 'A small headache,' she offered, and he accepted it with a sad nod. She sat up all night at her desk, rehearsing lines she already knew by heart, afraid to look out of the window, unable to close her eyes.

She hated herself for the doubts she gave him, but wasn't ready yet to tell him the truth.

To test the depths of his feeling for her.

And she already loved him too much to lie.

Thirteen weeks and two days later

Murtagh stood under Clery's clock on O'Connell Street. He shuffled a few feet to the left and tilted his canopied grey umbrella back, craning his neck to see how many degrees those golden hands of time had swept through since he had last looked. The department store was adorned in white lights for Christmas, with festive scenes painted on the window-panes and garlands of tinsel stretching between the doorways. A statue of Santa Claus leered at him from atop a green papier mâché sleigh: *How long are you going to wait, you silly fool?*

Murtagh gazed at the GPO, trying to imagine the scene at the post office when from its steps the Irish rebellion declared the country a republic. He remembered his father pushing his fingers into the bullet holes in the stones: 'Can you hear the gunfire, son? Close your eyes and picture what it was like.' He pretended he could to show his father he loved him. The memory drew a terrible loneliness upon him as the droves of shoppers, buskers and tourists jostled past. It was six o'clock now. The whole city was ready for its tea. Himself included.

A punk, dressed top to toe in black leather and studs, nodded to him as he maintained his own impatient vigil at the next window. He clutched a bunch of wilting snow-drops wrapped in tinfoil, the flower's hue echoed in the white stripe running through his Afro. When his date turned up, resplendent in what appeared to be a pink lace wedding dress, Murtagh gave him a discreet thumbs-up and the punk winked in return. It was gratifying that his own floral Led Zep-inspired blouse and corduroy flares hadn't come between them.

The arms of his brown leather mac squeaked when they brushed his sides. Aggravating. It called attention to how many times he turned to look at the clock. He squeezed and released his toes inside his brogues.

Tap right foot.

Squeeze toes.

Release.

Maeve was late again.

Tap left foot.

Squeeze toes.

Release.

But this was particularly bad. Even for her.

Turn to look in the window.

Rotate to face the GPO again.

And repeat.

Annie Hall had started twenty minutes ago. He wondered if they could use their tickets at eight o'clock instead. Not that it mattered if they were late; Maeve had already seen it so many times she could recite most of the lines by heart. She had been so excited to hear it was running at the Ambassador again. Tentatively, he poked the brown paper bag of chocolate peanuts squashed in his pocket. Where was she? If she hadn't arrived by seven o'clock, he would telephone her lodgings. Brave speaking to Ms Hoskins.

She didn't approve of gentleman callers.

Or gentlemen at all, it seemed.

The dread of it gave him patience.

At seven fifteen, he bundled himself inside a telephone box on the corner of Henry Street. On a little silver shelf, plastered in stickers for club nights, pornography and taxis, he counted out a pile of five ten-pence pieces, dialled the number committed to memory – 2272111 – and counted the rings as they echoed down the line. He could picture the receiver of the glossy black Bakelite telephone where it sat outside Ms Hoskins' room, trembling with the attention of his request. Positioned anywhere else, she wouldn't have been able to eavesdrop on every call her tenants received. In his mind's eye, he saw her oak-panelled door opening wide, exposing the floral chintz calamity of her busy living room, and Ms Hoskins emerging with a self-importance that belied her lilac paisley housecoat, furry pink slippers and fading auburn hair set in curlers.

And yet, the door didn't open.

The call disconnected and his coins clattered back to him.

Could he risk it a second time? He would! He would eat the peach.

Ring ring.

Riiiinnnng riinnnnnng.

Ring ring.

A girl's voice answered shyly.

'Hello?'

What luck!

'Finola, thank God it's you!'

'Murtagh? Was that you a second ago? You're brave,

ringing twice. Hoskins is gone to the pictures. I was hoping you were Fiachra.'

'Still nothing from him? Well, he's a fool, Finola. Don't be sitting in waiting on him now, girl.'

'S'pose not. I presume you're after Maeve?'

'Is she there?'

'Well, she is, but I don't think she's feeling well. She hasn't got up today.'

'What, at all?'

'I knocked in earlier to check on her, but she was asleep with the curtains drawn.'

'She was meant to be meeting me. Would you mind trying her again?'

'Hang on.'

Murtagh fed the telephone three more coins while he waited on the line, knowing already the answer that would follow.

'Murtagh, she says she has a migraine. She'll call you tomorrow. I'm sorry, love. She wasn't up to coming to the phone.'

'Ah, that's okay. Thanks, Fin.'

'Don't worry, she'll be grand. I'm sure you'll hear from her in the morning.'

'I'm sure I will. Goo—'

The line disconnected before he could finish his sentence.

A lingering worry tangled in his mind as he made his way home, about how much more there was to all of these migraines, but he hadn't resolved yet how to broach the subject with her.

The episodes were impossible to predict and all-consuming.

'Maggie is here,' Maeve would say before she retreated to the cool darkness of her room. 'I'll call you when she's left town.'

And while he waited, he worried.

Thinking of the times his own mother took to her bed, and the silence that engulfed the house. While he was elsewhere, did his father sit on the edge of her bed and stroke her hair? Pleat the woollen border of their embroidered eiderdown and speak soft words to her?

He doubted it.

Waiting things out, that was his father's modus operandi.

I can do better than that, surely. Can't I?

But it was hard for him, he who couldn't remember the last time he'd hugged either of his parents; or ever said aloud that he loved them. Maeve was teaching him how to love in a different way, but he hadn't fully learned the lesson yet and wondered if he ever truly could.

He struggled to find a voice for his fears, to pull stubborn threads.

Instead, he nursed bruises like babies.

Allowed another voice to whisper in his ear.

Maybe she was just avoiding him.

Perhaps the migraines were an elaborate ruse and muggins here fell for it.

Could there be someone else?

That awful Malachy with his put-on accent and pathetic moustache.

Or lanky Paul of the cottage in Brittas Bay that was so lovely for a night swim.

★

Murtagh walked halfway to Rathmines before he noticed the rain trickling down the collar of his coat. His long blond curls were matting like dreadlocks in the downpour; a mocking reminder of his umbrella that perched abandoned in the telephone box on Henry Street. The rain made the squeaking of his jacket even worse. When he reached his bedsit, he peeled it off, flung it in the back of the hall cupboard and slammed the door closed. Two wine glasses, and a plate of cheese and biscuits covered in cling film, anticipated Maeve's arrival. He ate every morsel standing up, wiping away the crumbs from his beard with a tea towel, and then fell asleep on the couch in his wet clothes. An envelope with two tickets to *Carmen* remained hidden under Maeve's plate.

The next morning, he woke with a crick in his neck and the aftertaste of his solitary feast unpleasant in his mouth. Under a hot shower he rotated his shoulders and lathered his body in Maeve's apple shampoo until the water ran cold and the strain behind his eyes cleared. It would soon be Christmas; just four days until he presented Maeve to his parents on Christmas Eve like an extravagant gift they would be embarrassed to receive. Before then, they needed to be at peace with each other. One way or the other.

When Maeve opened the front door of her lodgings, Murtagh was standing on the doorstep holding a bottle of milk and a carton of eggs. He realised he had never seen her without make-up before and marvelled at what lay beneath the kohl, the blusher, the powder. How had she managed that on the mornings they awoke together? Her face flickered from shock to frustration to acceptance like a traffic light changing to the green he was waiting for.

'You'd better come in.'

Ms Hoskins looked surprised to see Murtagh appearing in her kitchen so early in the morning, but she demonstrated some uncharacteristic restraint and scuttled out without asking any questions.

Maeve slunk into Ms Hoskins' knitting armchair and hugged her knees. Her toenails, hot pink, looked mocking.

Murtagh took his coat off, rolled up his sleeves and started making scrambled eggs and coffee without speaking a word. Methodically he worked, carefully mixing the eggs and milk in a glass measuring jug, grinding the pepper just so. There was no sense of urgency; now that the time for the conversation had arrived, he was scared of how it might end, unsure how to proceed.

What if forcing her hand pushed her away?

He set the breakfast neatly on the table, placing a sprig of holly from his buttonhole on Maeve's plate, and waited for her to join him.

The flower dissolved her annoyance at being ambushed.

She squeezed his hand, warm despite the cool kitchen air, and sat across from him, her back straight, palms flat on the table.

'This isn't a confession,' she began. 'I hate when people say that – how they want to *confess* to a problem they've had. Because nobody *confesses* to having a broken leg, do they?'

Maeve pulled her hair into a knot on the top of her head and made a few attempts to start:

'The thing is, well, it's not one thing . . .

'I'm afraid that once I tell you . . .

'There isn't an easy way . . .'

Murtagh reached across the table and touched the tips of her fingers with his own.

'If there's someone else, you can just say it,' he said. 'I'd prefer to know.'

She pulled her hands away from him and jumped up, leaning over him as her voice rose.

'Good God, Murt! How can you even suggest that? After all the time we've spent together! The very idea that you could even think such a thing makes me wonder what the hell I've been doing . . .'

He dashed around the table and she stood stiffly as he wrapped his arms around her.

'Maeve, sssshh, love, I'm sorry. I didn't mean it. I've been so worried about your disappearances, and the migraines, and . . . I feared the worst. I should've known better. Please, go on. Forget I said anything. Please.'

She sat back down, stabbing at her breakfast with a fork while he pulled up a chair beside her.

'Seriously? You thought I was capable of that? And it's not that I didn't want to explain, but it never seemed the right time. I couldn't bear –'

'Bear what?'

'To change the way you looked at me.'

She measured out her words carefully in spoonfuls of egg. Rewarded herself with a small bite after each sentence.

Murtagh only ate when she ate; they were in this together.

'I swear there is nothing you can say that will make me leave this room,' he said.

'Apart from that I'm seeing someone else?' she snapped back, with an arched eyebrow.

Murtagh swallowed, said nothing, but his eyes were kind; he was determined to get out of the way of her telling. So, like a burst pipe, her story spilled out on the floor around their feet.

'I sometimes think it would be easier to understand all of this,' she explained, 'if there had been one terrible, traumatic incident that set all of it in motion, but there wasn't.'

She waved her hands around her head and then flopped them back on the table.

'Nothing bad has ever really happened to me and so I have no excuse. But I realise now that this – this *thing* – was always in me from when I was a little girl, but I didn't know that was peculiar then. I thought all children worried the way I did.'

'Ach, worries can get in on you. Sure, I can understand that; we all feel that way sometimes. I don't know why people always say schooldays are the happiest times of your life. So many people hated school.'

She sighed. 'Most kids don't worry like I did.'

Murtagh urged her on with the shy smile her earnest face always summoned, a lightness that she fostered in him, even in the blue moments. 'You'd be surprised,' he said. 'What troubled you?'

'Everything,' she said. 'World wars in general, and my father being conscripted in particular. My mother dying, or losing her mind. Kidnappers. Leukaemia. Aliens. Cracks in the sidewalk. Sponges. The Devil. Drowning in the bath. My parents getting divorced, even though they never argued. The basement. The attic. Old people. Babies. Amber traffic lights. Jellyfish. Nuclear power. Stuff getting in my ears. Stickers. That I'd lose my memory. Failing exams. Homeless people. Getting fat. Dying – that was a major one, of course. Falling asleep. That if I fell, all my bones would crumble. That if I cut myself, all the blood would go rushing out of my body. Questioning if I really existed. If everyone around me was an actor.'

He nodded slowly. 'I was always afraid of crucifixes and electric fences.'

Maeve looked at him in confusion. 'I'm not sure it's quite the same. My parents were amazing, but, well, I don't know how seriously any adults take children's fears. They described me as sensitive and a little nervous, but I think they thought I would grow out of it. I used to have a stammer – did I ever tell you that?' she paused, her eyebrows a question.

Murtagh shook his head. 'No. How did you lose it?'

'The same way I learned to cope with all of the other things I was scared of. Ma sent me to drama classes, and it helped a lot. When I was pretending to be someone else I lost my stammer and I could be someone who wasn't afraid of everything for a while. Gradually I started playing that character all the time, a version of me who wasn't afraid, and the appearance eventually became a new kind of reality.'

Murtagh clasped her hands in his own. 'Sure, isn't that brilliant? And now look at you! You're fearless up there on that stage.'

Maeve levelled her gaze at him. 'It didn't all just vanish,

though, Murt. It just evolved into a more considered way of catastrophic thinking. I wasn't terrified of particular things so much as I was of potential consequences, and I would become utterly convinced something awful was going to happen if I did X, Y or Z.'

'How do you mean? If you made a mistake you'd get in trouble – that sort of thing?'

'Not exactly. More, it was an amplification of potentially reasonable fears, like I was convinced that I would fail an exam and then end up having to repeat the school year and maybe end up never getting my high-school diploma at all. Or if I missed the school bus, that I'd have to walk home and would probably get abducted and never see my family again. I always thought small goodbyes would be last ones, so I was upset whenever my folks went out at night; I was convinced they were going to be killed in a car accident. I would jump from a minor anxiety to the worst-case scenario and then become paralysed by fear.'

Murtagh stirred more sugar into his coffee then flinched at its sweetness when he tasted it: 'I think we all have a bit of that, though, don't we? Fearing the worst? You just have to not let it get in on you, my love.' The lino in the hallway squeaked. Maeve stood up and turned on the radio, spinning the dial until she found some classical music. 'The walls have ears,' she said. 'And yes, but it's not that easy for me.'

She rearranged a salt cellar, a sugar bowl and a milk jug into a triangle formation on the table and sat back down.

'So, my troubles became threefold,' she explained. 'The anxiety evolved into bouts of, well, some seriously dark moods. I sometimes get so overwhelmed by the worry that

I end up shutting down. Sometimes it works the other way too; I feel this black mood coming in like a cloud over my mind and it summons the anxiety, but the two are often, if not always, linked for me.'

'And the third?' Murtagh prompted.

The kitchen door flew open and Maeve shrunk in her chair as Ms Hoskins sidled in, made up in a shiny canary-yellow dress. 'Oh, don't mind me,' she said. 'You can carry on your conversation. I'm paying no mind to you.' She started riffling through a drawer stuffed with papers, occasionally holding one up to the light, before discarding the document for another.

Murtagh cleared his throat, 'So, as I was saying, I'm going to try and pick one pattern to focus on now, instead of trying lots of different designs, try to develop a signature collection, and then . . .

Ms Hoskins released a long sigh, 'There's lovely crockery in Woolworths now, you know, for next to nothing.'

She edged towards the windowsill and turned down the radio. 'It's blaring into my room,' she said, 'and I can barely hear myself think.' As she clicked in her heels towards the door Maeve called after her, 'Aren't you forgetting something?' and she nodded to the open drawer.

Ms Hoskins pulled her shoulders back as she returned, snatching up some papers and knocking the drawer closed with her hip before exiting into the hall, leaving the door ajar.

Murtagh closed it softly behind her and pulled his chair closer to Maeve's so they could lower their voices. 'And the third?' he asked again, his stomach doubling as he watched her fight to retain her composure.

'Problems with eating,' she said, her voice cracking. 'I spent a long time in hospital.'

'Oh, Maeve, my love,' he whispered. 'I'm so sorry, but that's all behind you now, right? You have to try not to think about it so much – we have so much to look forward to!'

She started to clear away the plates and Murtagh saw her hands were trembling.

'Actually, that was what ended up saving me because, when I was eventually discharged, I found a new psychiatrist, Dr Goldman, and he had a totally different approach. He understood that the meds only worked for some folks and didn't push them on me. We talked and talked and talked and he helped unlock the patterns in my thinking so I could try to reprogramme my brain. He helped me believe in a more holistic way that I had to love and heal my body so my mind could be healthy too. He saved my life.'

Murtagh came to stand beside her at the sink as she did the washing-up, carefully drying each knife, each fork, each plate she handed him. When they were done, she leaned into his body and he held her tight for a few minutes before he spoke again.

'So, tell me about now,' he said. 'The migraines?'

She pulled back from him and dried the sink with one of Ms Hoskins' Vatican City tea towels, polishing the aluminium surface with slow circles.

'That was an easier explanation, but not really a lie, because the feeling is not dissimilar to one of my spells. I've worked out what helps me – working, but not too much, avoiding the things I know cause me stress, meditating, exercising, but not too much, eating well, getting enough sleep, writing in my journal, talking to a counsellor. There's no magic remedy, but I feel I have some tools I can use. And I can recognise the warning signs. Sometimes it starts with feeling like I'm getting the flu; other times it's a headache that grows more and more intense. Some days I don't get any warning at all and can barely crawl out of bed. Sometimes months pass when I don't feel any symptoms at all. Dr Goldman says, as I grow older, the spells might become years apart, and may one day stop coming altogether, or . . .'

'There is no or,' he finished for her. 'That's what will happen, love, I know it. We're in this together, and I bet now you've let it all out you'll start feeling better.'

Maeve rested her head against him once again.

'I'm not sure you understand,' she said. 'I don't know how this will all . . .'

Murtagh shushed her. 'My love, I look at you and I see the light of my life. The darkness is behind you. I'm sure of it.'

Maeve frowned as he kissed her forehead, smoothing her hair away from her face, and found a small smile for him.

By the time Murtagh left the house that evening the frost had started to settle like silver dust on the street.

The soles of his shoes sounded different to his ears as he trod carefully.

He could smell the cold as he breathed in the night air and felt his lungs expand.

The city had transformed while they were talking; now, instead of houses, traffic and shopfronts, all he could see was nature: a fox nuzzling a discarded takeaway, dandelions peeking through cracks in the pavement, a robin that perched on an electricity line; the trees that lined the avenue appeared to be the rulers and no longer just aesthetics.

Maeve had told him her story, and now the world seemed more beautiful and brittle than ever before.

He was so relieved that what ailed her hadn't come between them.

Her truth had cracked his heart and, immediately, a new love spilled from him to fill the gaps.

He would be a better man because of her trust, and she would be a happier woman for having trusted.

Their love could be complete.

Dublin: March, 1981

In the basement of Fibber Macs, Gavin Murphy crouched on his knees as he wrestled an overloaded adaptor plug into the socket. The bleached tips of his Mohawk stabbed a red-brick wall with every thrust, before a micro pyrotechnic display of blue sparks exploded, plunging the venue into darkness and silencing the speakers that blasted David Bowie into the shadowy venue. The audience enthusiastically groaned, barely drowning out Gavin's cursing as he shouted for the barman, Barry, to trip the switch. Again. The first karaoke night to hit Dublin City wasn't launching with the aplomb that had been advertised, but the false starts only contributed to the giddy anticipation in the room.

Maeve flicked open a fluorescent yellow lighter and held the flame above the list of songs. 'Careful.' Murtagh nudged her elbow. 'Your fringe is about to get singed.' She brushed it back, calling out songs to their group of friends, who sat on white pleather beanbags in a tight circle, knees and elbows touching, as if they were huddled for warmth around a campfire: Isaac, a sculptor from Murtagh's class, wore blue denim dungarees and stared at Murtagh all evening, for he was a little bit in love with him; Evelyn from Maeve's theatre company, perspiring with nerves in pink Lycra leggings, was terrified that everyone would be forced to sing and kept insisting that they couldn't make her, while hoping that they would. Finola wore her dad's ivory Argyle jumper stretched over the red mini skirt that Maeve had insisted she borrow. She tugged at it incessantly in a hopeless effort to make it reach her knees. Maeve was always so persuasive and, ultimately, Finola always so remorseful for how susceptible she was to her influence.

They were in high spirits, corralled as they had been by Maeve, though she was the only one who intended to sing. The names of the songs rolled off her tongue like a teacher checking attendance: '"Upside Down" – Diana Ross. Not a chance . . . "Call Me" – Blondie. Yes, definite potential . . . "Crazy Little Thing Called Love" – Queen. Don't think I could pull that off . . . "The Rose" – Bette Midler. Hardly . . . "Dearg Doom" – Horslips. Oh, Murt you *have* to do it . . ."Mull of Kintyre" – Wings. Seriously, are they trying to kill the mood altogether? . . . "Wuthering Heights" – Kate Bush. Oh, Kate, I love her too much to murder that song at karaoke . . . "Bette Davis Eyes" – Kim Carnes. Yes! Yes! That's the one. I feel like my whole life has been building up to this very moment.'

The lights burst back on and David Bowie picked up exactly where he'd left off in 'Five Years'. Gavin, glowing a hot pink inside his three-piece white polyester suit, scrambled up on to the ramshackle stage constructed of black-painted wooden pallets. The microphone squealed as he blew dust from it, and the speakers crackled but, undeterred, he persevered. Red, blue and green disco lights danced across the canvas of his suit as he welcomed everyone to the inaugural Karnage-aoke, a 'working title', and encouraged everyone to sign up on his gold glitter clipboard. To get things started, however, he turned to the karaoke machine balanced precariously on some beer crates in front of the stage and cued 'Bridge over Troubled Water' as his own backing track.

Finola squeezed Maeve's hand under the table to stop herself laughing out loud. 'That is the last song I would have expected him to choose,' she whispered.

'And probably the last one he should have gone for, too,' Maeve answered, hiding her face in her friend's shoulder to stifle her laughter. Gavin had tears in his eyes, so moved was he by his own performance; a song that seemed considerably longer than when Simon and Garfunkel sang it.

While Gavin worked towards his big finish, Murtagh handed their friends a powder-blue postcard each – an invitation to an open evening at NCAD: Murtagh was displaying a collection of bowls he had created for his final-year project that were inspired by the clouds he loved so much. Maeve had named each one: *Nimbus*, *Pileus*, *Fractus* and, her favourite, *Altostratus*. They all promised they would come, and Murtagh beamed, smoothing his curls as he talked of the exhibition, and how he still had not found a permanent job. Most of his classmates had started scattering across the globe in search of employment. He and Maeve knew he would probably have to follow suit, but for now he paid his half of the rent by working as a teaching assistant in NCAD on the course he'd completed himself. In exchange for his time and labour, he received a minimal wage but could still access the studio and kiln to continue his work, which he would never have been able to afford to do otherwise. He had written dozens of letters to potters across the world, seeking a position, or an apprenticeship, but had received nothing in reply. 'Chin up,' said Finola. 'It's only a matter of time, and we're not ready to lose you both yet.'

'Hopefully, we can stay here,' Maeve answered, squeezing her hand. 'It feels like we're only getting started with *Shake the Spear* – it took us so long to get our Arts Council funding organised that we haven't even had a chance to think about our first production yet.'

Sheila and Aliaj jumped from behind the bar and abandoned service to duet on 'You're the One That I Want' in homage to John Travolta and Olivia Newton-John. With their matching green Fibber Macs polo shirts and hair-sprayed quiffs, they cut quite the idiosyncratic picture. Nonetheless, they had clearly been practising, as they performed a synchronised dance routine to complement their number. It was a shame they hadn't anticipated having only one microphone; Aliaj hogged it even during Sheila's parts, which he also performed with gusto, leaving Sheila to sing inaudibly into her fist, as she had done in rehearsals.

'I get it now,' Isaac said. 'Karaoke gives a backing band to people who would never, ever be allowed to sing with a real one.'

Murtagh snorted. 'I can't see it catching on. Wouldn't you rather be listening to the jukebox? No one's enjoying themselves apart from the singers.'

Maeve stood up and shook out the legs on her black tuxedo trousers, tucked in her mother's white silk blouse and released her hair from the knot piled on top of her head.

'Exactly,' she pronounced. 'So, I'm next.'

She kissed the top of Murtagh's head as she clambered past him; he nuzzled her side as she wriggled by. 'Has anyone heard her sing before?' Isaac asked, his eyebrows arched in a question. Murtagh shook his head. 'Not properly, but she seems pretty confident, so . . .'

Finola winked at him. 'Don't they all, Murt? Don't they all? Look!' she pointed. 'There she goes.'

Maeve's four friends stood up, whooping and stamping their feet on the floor. She waved at them, despite being only ten feet away, then turned her back on the audience while she waited for the backing track to play out over the tinny PA. She had somehow procured a tambourine, which she now shook in time with the music, one arm stretched over her head, her body frozen like a statue, illuminated from behind by a single spotlight that cast her in silhouette. The audience began to nudge and point as she commanded their focus. For the first verse, she kept her back turned, her breathy voice booming out with hypnotic power.

'Is that the record playing?' Evelyn asked, her eyes wide and locked on Maeve's figure. 'No,' Murtagh replied, shushing her. 'That's Maeve.'

Maeve slowly turned as she sang of New York snow and Gavin erupted into applause from his perch beside the machine.

While Maeve sang, the dingy pub basement took on the ambience of a downtown jazz club, electric and transformative. The light tangled in her blue-black hair, scattering prisms of colour around her head like an aura. Murtagh felt everything inside him bend to her power.

As the drunken revellers clapped along in time to the music, Maeve's eyes turned to each face in the crowd in turn, drawing them in. When the song ended, a stunned silence filled the room for a beat before everyone was on their feet, slapping her on the back as she returned to her friends on the beanbags. It no longer seemed appropriate seating for her, down there on the floor among the mere mortals. Unfazed by the attention, she sat cross-legged and rested her hands on her knees while Evelyn and Finola threw their arms around her from either side. Murtagh smiled at her, not sure of what he had witnessed, or what he had learned.

He caught her eye, reading him, and looked away.

Later that night, while Finola, Isaac and Evelyn caught the bus from the quays, Murtagh carried Maeve on the crossbar of the blue Dutch bicycle that he'd spent most of his student grant on. 'A great steed for a daydream,' Maeve said as she tried to find a comfortable perch. They wobbled to a stop at the traffic lights on O'Connell Bridge and Maeve rocked back and forth to regain her balance as he clutched the handle-bars. She leaned against him and her hair tickled his nose, causing him to sneeze loudly thrice. Each time, Maeve shouted, '*Gesundheit!*'

They pushed on across the bridge and Murtagh bellowed over the noise of the traffic, 'Maeve, Maeve, can you hear me?'

She turned her head to look at him and almost toppled them over.

'Eyes front! Eyes front!' he called.

She laughed and held on tighter.

'Maeve, I think.'

'Maeve, the thing is.'

'Maeve, will you marry me?'

'What did you say?' she called over her shoulder.

'Will you marry me?' he whispered into her ear.

'Stop the bike! Stop the bike!' she cried out, slapping the handlebars.

Murtagh yanked on the brakes as they careered into a lamp post on Grafton Street. Maeve jumped off just in time and turned to grab Murtagh by the lapels of his corduroy blazer and tugged them hard as her eyes searched his face.

'Are you serious?' she asked him. 'Do you really think you can handle spending the rest of my life with me?'

He placed a hand on either side of her face, wiped away a smudge of red wine from the corner of her lip with his thumb. 'The rest of my life, you mean. And I do. Could you bear it?'

She paused a moment before answering.

'I couldn't bear not to.'

And then they kissed.

Across from the gates of Trinity College, where it all began.

The following morning Maeve lay on the sofa with slices of cucumber pressed on her eyelids and a cold flannel laid across her brow. Murtagh was feeding her segments of mandarin orange while watching a VHS recording of *Bracken* with the volume turned down. 'Let me know when Gabriel Byrne appears,' she croaked. 'That man fell from Heaven.'

'What were we thinking, dear fiancée of mine?' he whined. 'I'm not sure I can feel my face.'

They were dozing in their hungover languor when the doorbell disturbed their recovery process. Maeve swung her legs off Murtagh's lap and he reluctantly staggered to the door, pulling a jumper on over his pyjamas.

Dennis, their local postman, who was driven by a constant low-level resentment of his duties, shoved a heavy brown cardboard box into Murtagh's arms more roughly than he needed to. 'Another one came for ye,' he said. 'From the U, S, Ah. Has she not enough stuff by now? There can't be much left in America, at this rate.' Murtagh sighed and reversed back into the hallway with his arms full as Dennis tossed a letter on top of the box.

'Oh, and this one is for you, too. From Galway.'

'Thanks, Dennis.' Murtagh snapped. 'We're well able to read who it's from ourselves, thanks all the same.'

He nudged the door closed before Dennis could reply and tore back into the living room.

'It's a Ma Morelli Care Package! Your mother is a saint,' he called. 'Open it for us, love.'

Maeve jumped off the couch, rejuvenated by the thoughts of Jell-O Pudding Pops, Caramellos and maybe her ma's baked pretzels. 'It's like she knew we'd be celebrating. Imagine if there was champagne in here! Although I don't think my liver would take it.' While she ransacked the contents Murtagh sat on a kitchen high stool and stared at the letter from Galway with its unfamiliar minuscule handwriting. He opened the envelope and slowly read its contents through. He stood up, sat down, and read the letter once again.

'Maeve?'

'Yes! Captain Crunch cereal. Ma, I love you.'

'Maeve, are you listening?'

She looked up while tearing the top off the cereal box and

pouring some straight into her mouth. 'What is it? Who's the letter from?'

'I've been offered a position. With this amazing potter. He has no one to pass on to . . . doesn't want the business to die with him . . . I know his work. We even have one of his bowls here – let me find it.'

He opened the kitchen cupboard and started lifting bowls out on to the counter.

Maeve walked over and took the letter from his hand.

'Where's the studio, Murt? Where would we be living?'

He turned and watched her read, her eyes darting over the page as she searched for the information she needed most.

'Inis Óg?' she asked, her eyes searching his face for answers now. 'Where is *Ines Ogg*?'

'In-ISH OH-G,' he corrected her. 'It's an island off the west coast of Ireland.'

'How far away is that? Is it a big island?'

'Not exactly, but this man, he's a master craftsman, and such a wonderful potter –'

'You said,' she interrupted, 'Let's talk about it later, okay? I have to go to rehearsal.'

Murtagh listened to her movements in the bathroom while he tidied up the living room, composing in his head what he would say when she re-emerged, but she darted across the living room to their bedroom without even glancing his way and the moment passed. Before he could speak again, she had fluttered past him already wearing her coat and vanished through the door with just a kiss blown over her shoulder.

72

He spent the afternoon hunched over the kitchen table, sketching designs for his work, grazing from a little bowl of almonds, wiping his fingers absent-mindedly on his pyjama bottoms after each mouthful. All the time imagining what he would do if Maeve didn't come home; was such a thing possible?

Had the letter exposed to Maeve what the reality of marriage to him might mean?

Had it all suddenly become too real?

Should he really have proposed before he knew where his life was going?

Work expanded to fill the time allowed for it and little progress was made on the page despite the electricity volting through his mind.

When Maeve eventually burst through the door that evening, Murtagh closed his eyes for a moment, offering up a silent prayer of thanks to whom he knew not. The news from that morning seemed completely gone from her mind and Murtagh wondered if the obsession had been his alone all day. He stood up, suddenly self-conscious to still be in pyjamas, kissed her on the cheek and washed his hands in the sink, cautious as he read her mood.

'I'm probably flammable from all the setting solution and hairspray,' she said. 'One of the girls wanted to practise on me. She's giving up acting to be a hairdresser. It's a bit grim.'

'How was the rehearsal? Is it still *Once a Catholic*?' he asked, watching her primp her hairdo in the mirror.

She sighed, her shoulders slumping. 'Abysmal. It was as if Fiachra had dragged us in off the street to read the lines cold.

Mary O'Malley would be mortified if she could see how we're butchering it. Davina doesn't even pretend to like me any more, but it's easier that way than enduring the false compliments and platitudes. I don't know why she's so touchy – she has the lead, after all, even if it is a little beyond her. She cares too much about what she looks like on stage, that's her big mistake. She can't act properly for fear it makes her look ugly or she might forget to suck in her stomach.'

Murtagh nodded. 'Davina's a strange fish, all right. Comedy wouldn't suit her. Sure, she's entering the Rose of Tralee, for God's sake – doesn't that say it all?'

Maeve snorted. 'I'm happy to play the other Mary, though – there's a few great lines to work with there.'

'No small parts, eh?'

She caught his eye in the mirror and smiled at him: 'Exactly'; and he turned his back to fiddle with the coffee filter his fingers could never master. It slipped from his grip and skidded across the countertop as Maeve came up behind him. She covered his eyes with her hands and whispered in his ear, 'I broke the news to Fiachra. Told him what was coming. That this would be my last play with them. For now, anyway.'

Murtagh spun around to face her. 'Do you mean . . .?'

She nodded.

'So, we'll take it?' he asked, scanning her expression for confirmation. 'Shouldn't we discuss it properly first, or weigh up our options?'

She stood back, holding him at arm's length, looked him straight in the eye, and said, 'We'll take it.'

Inevitable decisions are best made fast.

Somewhere over the Atlantic Ocean: April 1982

On the flight home from their wedding in Brooklyn, Murtagh woke in the middle of the night to see Maeve staring out of the aeroplane window, tears trickling down her face, with her hands clasped in her lap as if in prayer.

'Maeve, my darkling.' He wiped her face with the back of his hand. 'What is it? Please don't tell me you have regrets.'

She twisted her neck away from him and rubbed her eyes with the sleeve of her jumper, a new one her mother had knitted, white with a red zigzag across the front.

'No, no regrets,' she said. 'Not for things done, anyway.'

'What does that mean?'

'I do feel we've made all the right decisions, like sensible people should, but –'

'But what?' he asked, his hand on her knee.

'But, nothing, I guess. We're moving to the island because you have a real opportunity there – we couldn't sacrifice that for me to stay in *Shake the Spear*, not when we have no *real* prospects. I get it. It's fair.'

She looked out of the window for a moment then turned back to look at him.

'I'm worried, though, that I gave up too easily, that maybe something might have happened if I'd held my nerve.'

Murtagh fidgeted into a new position, careful not to disturb the priest sleeping in the seat to his right.

'But we talked all about this.' Murtagh started counting on his fingers. 'You're going to get involved in the theatre scene in Galway, for starters, and if the chance of a tour or a movie ever comes along, you'll take it! Dublin's only a train-ride away.'

He paused, waiting for her to agree, before hesitating and beginning again.

'Maeve, we are not going to that island if it makes you feel like it's all over for you. That's not happening.'

Murtagh's skin prickled under his clothes.

In the unnerving manner Maeve had of seeming to read his mind, she threw a dark look at him that made him squirm.

'Don't make promises you can't keep, Murtagh,' she said, her voice catching in her throat. 'You know it's too late for that now. Don't pretend you can walk away, because you're only saying that now so, later on, if I hate it there, you can insist you gave me the option not to go and I didn't take it.'

The priest started coughing and silence fell between Maeve and Murtagh while he drank from a glass bottle labelled *Holy Water*. Murtagh rested his head on the back of his seat and closed his eyes, swallowing continuously. Maeve put her hand on his and the heat of her touch felt like it was radiating through him.

'It's okay,' she said. 'I'm in. I promise you. I know that there is more than one reason to go. But please can we be honest about how hard it's going to be? You don't have to always pretend you're fearless about it, that it's all going to be wonderful. I'd be so much happier if we could admit it whenever we think it was all a terrible idea, which we will, without that having to mean we're not going to stick it out. Do you get it? Let's just be real about it. Otherwise, I know I'll lose it altogether.'

He put his hand on hers. 'I do. I'm sorry.'

'Don't rewrite history so that I was the one who decided we should go. We have to both take responsibility, agreed?'

The priest leaned over in his seat and smiled at them. 'Word of advice to you both,' he offered, his head a shining pink snooker ball atop his black shirt and slacks. 'The family that prays together, stays together.' He made the sign of the cross, excused himself to go in search of a nip of whiskey from the drinks trolley. 'There's no hope for us, so.' Murtagh laughed as Maeve curled in under his arm. He stroked her hair, willing the worries to leave her with his touch, trying to suppress his own.

Would his mother ever forgive him for getting married abroad? Would Jeremy?

His stomach seemed to double upon itself as he pictured himself waiting for Maeve at City Hall on their wedding day, the blank space beside him where his best friend should have been. How could Jeremy not even like, let alone love, the woman he was besotted with? It didn't sit right with him at all. *What am I missing?*

He thought of the night Maeve and Jeremy had finally met. It was New Year's Eve, the one night of the year when he believed no good ever came of hitting the town. And that occasion was no exception. Instead of joining Finola at her new man's masquerade party in Maynooth, Murtagh and Maeve had decided to spend the night alone, to avoid the crush of drunk strangers squashed into student digs and the inevitable last-minute panic to catch a night-bus back to the city. Their relationship had found a state of bliss; Maeve had been walking on air since their engagement was announced and Murtagh was happy to be the one with his feet on the ground. Now everything felt different and they were happiest when alone together, secure in the intimate knowledge that only they shared of the promises made between them.

Maeve was concocting a punch from the remnants of various bottles of alcohol when the telephone rang. She heard Murtagh's muffled voice from the hallway but couldn't quite catch who he was talking to. His head popped around the door, the telephone receiver smothered in the lapel of his cardigan.

'It's Jeremy,' he whispered. 'He wants to meet for a drink. Something happened with a girl. I should say no, yes?'

'No way!' Maeve mouthed back. 'This is my chance to finally meet him. We're going!'

Maeve sensed that Jeremy had been avoiding meeting her before now but from all the stories felt as if she knew him already; how he and Murtagh used to sneak into town to visit the record shop during PE; that their first big concert had been Leonard Cohen at the National Stadium in 1972; how, in reality, most of their adolescent firsts had happened together. Jeremy was an exciting piece of the Murtagh puzzle and Maeve was intrigued. So, on Lower Baggot Street, they waited in one of Toner's infamous wooden booths; it was Jeremy's favourite drinking emporium. 'He always says the privacy promotes bad behaviour,' Murtagh explained. They sipped cheap red wine and eavesdropped on the conversations around them as folks reflected on a year that saw six thousand people march through Dublin to protest the building of civic offices on a Viking site, Maeve and Murtagh amongst them, a year when Ireland launched a brand-new television channel, RTÉ 2, and mourned the death of Jack Doyle, 'the Gorgeous Gael', famous for being a boxer, an actor and a tenor, and the thought of whom sent Murtagh's mother to confession. Talk of the Troubles in the north bubbled up and faded away while Maeve strained to catch more understanding. She'd asked Murtagh to take her to Belfast, but he declared it 'an unnecessary risk to his well-being' and instead bought her *Troubles* by J. G. Farrell to read. In the corner, a trad session was gaining momentum and Maeve loved watching the organised chaos of the musicians finding time with each other as they looped through the old, familiar songs. It was a warm cocoon in the midst of a black, wet night as the rain poured down, cleansing the old city anew once again. They'd heard a rumour The Undertones were playing a secret gig in town tonight but, for once, they didn't feel the need to chase down the buzz.

Jeremy appeared: androgynous, pristine and stylish in a vintage pinstripe suit. He hugged Murtagh tightly, mumbled something in his ear and then stood back, noticing Maeve for the first time.

She was perched in her seat, ready to jump up to greet him, but he looked away from her towards Murtagh. 'I thought it would be just the two of us,' he said, and Murtagh flushed.

'But it's New Year's Eve, I couldn't . . .'

Jeremy brushed past him and elbowed his way to the front of the queue at the bar, while Maeve slunk back into the booth.

She gripped Murtagh's hand under the table with her own. When Jeremy eventually sat with them, she overcompensated, trying harder and harder to make him laugh, and as each anecdote collapsed between them he retreated further and further away.

While Murtagh and Maeve slowly drank their wine, Jeremy wasted money he did not have buying shots of Jameson whiskey that barely touched the glass before he swallowed them whole. When he staggered off to the bathroom, Maeve insisted on following him. 'This isn't on, Murtagh,' she said. 'He needs to get a grip.'

She found Jeremy squaring up to a man twice his size wearing a Limerick football jersey. Before Maeve could reach him, Jeremy was pinned to the wall. She squeezed herself between them, pushing the other man backwards, and he laughed at them both.

'Is your little girlfriend going to stand up for you, eh?'

Jeremy ran at him and aimed a punch that was easily deflected. Instead he received one hard and deep in his own stomach. He doubled over with a low groan and Maeve tried to help him stand, but he shook her off and snarled in her face: 'Get away from me. I don't want you anywhere near me.'

She stepped back, shocked, and watched him shove his way through the bar to the exit. Maeve never told Murtagh what had happened, just that she saw him leave.

By the time the bells of Christ Church had chimed midnight, Maeve and Murtagh were already at home and in bed together. As Maeve's breath steadied beside him, Murtagh lay awake, staring at the ceiling. He couldn't shake the image from his mind of Jeremy's back as he'd leaned over the bar, how the fabric strained across his shoulder blades. He recognised the clouds that lingered around him as similar to those that had hovered before, when Murtagh told him he was leaving for art school in Dublin. *Leaving Jeremy behind in Sligo.* That was how he had taken it.

'It's six hours on the bus, ya know?' Jeremy had said in despair as he paced back and forth in Mrs Moone's kitchen, rapping his fingernails along the kitchen counter in contrary rhythms. It took six months of Murtagh coaxing and cajoling before Jeremy would come to stay in his bedsit in Rathmines.

'I don't want all your new posh *arty* friends looking down their noses at me,' he'd protested – he hated telling Murtagh's classmates that he worked making bathroom scales in Hanson's Ltd, much as he loved the camaraderie there, and the celebrity that his unexpected star performance as the team's striker for the MacArthur Cup had brought him.

Once Jeremy had tested and tasted the fruits of the city centre for the first time, however, Murtagh could barely keep him away. He was a country mouse destined to be a city dweller; he just hadn't known it yet. Before long, not a weekend passed that Jeremy didn't turn up at his door after taking the last bus from Sligo town. Every Friday night between midnight and one o'clock, Murtagh was sure to hear the dilapidated doorbell ring and his name being whispered through the letterbox.

'Murt, are you awake? It's me, Jer.'

As if it would ever be anyone else. Until it could be Maeve, of course.

And then Jeremy stopped coming.

Was it really four months since they'd last seen each other? How had he let that happen?

Now, Murtagh breathed in the smell of Maeve and stayed awake, watching over her while she dozed, until they landed in Shannon Airport with a gentle bump.

'Blessed be the pilots,' the priest said, mopping his bald head with an Aer Lingus napkin.

'Amen,' said Murtagh, and nudged Maeve awake.

'Are we home?' she said, rubbing her eyes with the cuff of her jumper.

'I hope so,' he answered, as she stretched within the confines of her seat and shrugged off the sleep.

Maeve beamed the confidence at him that she knew he needed her to feel.

The seatbelt light pinged off and they were released into their new life.

'Amen,' Murtagh said again, under his breath, twisting the new band of silver he now wore on his finger and shaking off the guilt he felt for Jer.

They disembarked the aeroplane, hands held tight.

They were the Moones now and a whole new life awaited them.

Inis Óg: July, 1984

It was two years, three months and five days since Murtagh and Maeve had arrived on the island of Inis Óg, growing the population from 197 to 199 as of 11 May 1982.

They were relieved to have finally finished renovating, and extending, their thatched stone cottage. Now so firmly embedded in the perfect imperfections of their dwelling, it was strange to recall how, stepping off the ferry on that glorious sun-drenched day, in clothes unfit for purpose, they had not yet seen the ramshackle house that would become their home.

Murtagh was busy flattening cardboard boxes in the back garden, the last debris of their home improvements. Maeve watched him carefully fold each one as she wrapped potato and carrot peelings in newspaper for Christy Moore. The contrary donkey they had adopted upon his retirement, and that now grazed in the adjoining field, had drawn their wooden cart with all of their belongings on that first day on the island.

Maeve could picture herself sitting up front with Liamie, his owner, a scarlet crocheted blanket across her knees, gripping the side of her seat, with rust-coloured seaweed bunched by her feet, excited but wary of what awaited them. Liamie had explained that the donkey was named in honour of his favourite folk singer, and that he reckoned the real Christy Moore would be proud to know of his namesake.

Murtagh perched precariously on the rear of the cart, his legs dangling over the edge, one arm around the waist of her dressmaking mannequin as the wind whipped his hair about his face. The smell of the sea, cut turf and damp grass overwhelmed him as a hot April sun scorched the stones they clattered over making them sizzle.

Maeve had flung her head back and filled her lungs with a deep breath. 'The air feels different here,' she said. 'Like it's got magic in it.'

'Folks say it's healing,' Liamie replied. 'They come over from the mainland, ailing and weary, and leave here transformed. It's the three S's.' Maeve stared at the grooves in the leathery skin of his hands as he held up one finger at a time to list them off. 'Sea salt. Soil. Stones. That's the Holy Trinity right there.'

The moment Maeve stood before their cottage, she recognised it as their own immediately.

Those thick whitewashed stone walls overgrown with ivy; the dirty golden-thatched roof it wore like a heavy toupee. The black wrought-iron gate that squealed each time they passed through; an affliction they would soon stop noticing and never repair. It was clear to her that the front garden had once been much loved. Empty wooden windowboxes, painted a sky blue to match the sills, remained and flower baskets hung on brass hooks from the thatch gables, with some blooms still surviving. Dandelions and weeds were breaking through the cobblestoned pathway that led to the red front door, and the grass needed cutting, but all along the garden perimeter rose bushes flourished: yellow, white, blush pink and the deepest burgundy. Although the rest of the garden had fallen into decline, the roses remained triumphant. Maeve crouched down to breathe in their scent: 'I declare myself the newly crowned rose queen.'

'Queen Maeve,' Murtagh bowed. 'I am but your loyal servant.'

In time they would realise how much they were indebted to Seamus O'Farrell, the retiring potter to whom Murtagh became an apprentice, for what, in the end, was only three months. Murtagh had inherited an already established studio, with loyal customers and a shopfront for tourists in the summer holiday season. It was more than he had ever dared dream of; the letter that arrived from Galway had accelerated his life from student novice to professional potter almost overnight. And yet, Seamus's gift was not solely one of commerce. In his own quiet way, he lifted the veil off the island for them and helped them understand the islander ways. Although walking, for him, had become a feat of gargantuan effort, he liked to link his arm with Maeve's and shuffle to the end of the lane, where they would sit on a low stone wall as he trickled truths to her.

'Don't be afear'd of the direct way they have of looking – sure our eyes have been trained to scan the horizon for the boats coming in. Makes us all good at seeing.'

'That explosion of colour in the flora and fauna, you'll not see the likes of it anywhere else on God's great Earth. Once May is in, Mother Nature starts showin' off, and where all was barren the flowers bloom; four climates all integrating here – the Mediterranean, Arctic, Alpine and Temperate.'

He gave her a book with glossy photographs so she could learn all of their names: the Irish harebells and Ox-eye daisies, the red clover and saxifrage, the *Dryas octopelata* from the Arctic and the Alpine *Minuartina verna*. To hear him murmur their names, it sounded like a prayer.

The secrets of the clay that he passed to Murtagh were seldom spoken of. The apprentice learned by witnessing his master at work, sometimes in silence, sometimes while Seamus taught him to read the sea and how his beloved clouds were in a never-ending dance with the waves. The challenge was daunting, but Seamus demonstrated discipline, commitment and endless experimentation in a manner that emboldened Murtagh to take more risks with his work, not to shy away from what seemed too difficult, and to seek balance between creativity and productivity. The rhythm he found in the studio was soon emulated outside of it as the philosophies his teacher had developed over a lifetime were slowly delivered to him. And with Seamus's open-hearted invitation to the Moones, he gave the islanders permission to accept them also.

They learned that Maeve's roses had been the pride and joy of Seamus's deceased wife, Alma. In the end, as his energy waned, it was the roses he had used his depleting resources to maintain.

When the day came that the funeral procession passed by the cottage, with Seamus's coffin carried on oars by men who would miss him but seldom speak of it, the mourners paused outside his former home for a decade of the rosary while children wriggled impatiently to move on; there was no shielding them from the reality of death. One of their own was gone, and all the island would mourn. Maeve snapped a white rose that stretched through the iron gate and placed it on top of the coffin. An elderly woman, her head covered in a black woollen shawl, nodded her approval, and the procession moved on.

While Murtagh was reconciling his practice with the ghost of Seamus, Maeve found satisfaction in the design and execution of their decorating. The interior of their cottage had proved better and worse than expected, but she revelled in deciding what to nurture and what to replace, which elements were characterful and which just caused unnecessary suffering.

The original floorboards in the hallway remained, their shine illuminated when sunshine flooded through the small glass window.

Maeve immediately claimed a cuckoo clock perched on the wall as her own.

The framed Sacred Heart picture hanging over the door, however, was removed immediately; Murtagh avoided the eyes of Jesus as he gently lifted it down and tucked it out of sight.

It was still hard to shake the all-encompassing guilt impressed upon him since childhood; shame borne of the knowledge that the omniscient God could see inside his heart and mind, that just thinking of sinning was as damning as acting upon it. Coveting, resenting, dreaming, avoiding, tempting, looking: all slippery slopes that only abstinence, penance and the strictest policing of self could save him from. Of all the blessings Maeve had brought to his life, her gentle mocking of his eternal guilt was a salvation. Her teasing undermined its power and made him, if not fearless, more confident that, if God existed, his intentions had been woefully misunderstood. They were both adamant that when they had children of their own they would hand down a different quality of faith, and the time was drawing closer for them to translate their values into behaviour, for Maeve was four months pregnant.

Now, post-renovations, the rear half-door of the original cottage remained; freshly painted royal blue but still swinging with the same joy as when first hung by Seamus fifty-four years before. Only now it opened to reveal the Moones' modernised kitchen and the stone archway that led to their new bathroom off to the right. This was a big improvement on the first facilities that they had discovered tucked into the corner of the garden, a miniature stone shed with its corrugated door ajar, a tail of white toilet paper fluttering under its frame. They had paused, giving each other a long look, before slowly picking their way across the soggy grass to peek inside: a claw-footed white tub, toilet and sink all squashed into the five-foot by five-foot box, tiled from top to toe in beige. 'So, we have to come out here in the middle of the night if we need the loo?' Maeve had wailed. 'What if it's raining?'

'You could try holding on?' Murtagh suggested, struggling to keep a straight face. She shoved him, harder than she intended to, and he lost his balance, toppling right into the bathtub. 'Oh, Murty, I'm sorry,' she said, leaning over to kiss him where he lay on his back, his feet sticking out over the end. He pulled her in on top of himself, and as they lay there laughing, a cough at the door made Maeve scream. It was Liamie, squinting in at them. 'The rest of your boxes are here,' he'd said, 'whenever you're done.'

88

To think of it now still made Murtagh smile as he turned back towards the house, his hand pressed into the ache in the small of his back. 'How did we ever manage at all?' he asked Maeve, leaning on the lower half of the door, his arms resting naturally in the grooves worn in the wood by the arms of so many others who had rested there before; some to speak to neighbours, others to commune with their own loneliness in the comfort of the black canopy of stars that hung over the island. Maeve smiled. 'Naivety about how long it would all take, that's how!'

Queen played on the radio, and Murtagh watched Maeve shimmy in time to the music as she unpacked the crockery he had made and arranged it in neat rows inside their new yellow cupboards. A green-and-white striped vinyl wallpaper coated the interiors, like the silk lining of a summer suit. Maeve had sewn curtains to match; they weren't dissimilar to the loathed ones that had hung in her room back at Trinity which she now remembered so fondly.

The window ran almost the full width of the back wall, so their view extended to the lowlands of the island below them: the patchwork of green fields dissected by stone walls, expanses of limestone so similar to that of the Burren, and islanders' cottages that spread across the earth before the island met the sea. With no forestry, tall buildings or lakes, the flatland rolled out endlessly before her. A teacup slipped from Maeve's fingers, but she caught it in the crook of her elbow before it could hit the shining tiles of their freshly laid black-and-white chequered floor. 'Very modern,' Áine O'Connor had said, after calling in on behalf of the Irish Countrywomen's Association, ostensibly to offer help, whilst enjoying a good look around so she could report back elsewhere on the result of 'the great expansion plan'. Maeve unpacked jars of preserves and a tin of cocoa from a parcel on the counter. 'Why is your mother still sending us food, Murtagh?' she asked, laughing. 'We're not students any more!'

Murtagh stacked them in the cupboard and smiled at his wife. 'How else would we know that she loves us?'

He remembered how he and Maeve had huddled over a map of the island in their flat in Rathmines before they moved, him tracing the roads with his forefinger, following the path that led from the pier to their house on Bóthar An Chaisleáin, the Castle Road, on the hilliest part of the island, in the shadows of the ruins of the ancient Norman castle. Now they were standing where once a red drawing pin marked the spot, and it was hard for him to reconcile what the map appeared to show and the land he now called home – an island that felt less of the modern world and more of an open-air museum of medieval times. The map didn't identify any of the landmarks that mattered to him: the tangle of blue twine and sheep wool that marked one mile to the lighthouse; the dry stone beehive hut where the road ended and island wilderness began; the moss-covered tombstone in the graveyard where Maeve was shocked to find the barely legible name of Morelli – was one of her ancestors buried here? She liked to visit that grave sometimes, to pull the weeds from its borders, secure a posy of flowers with a smooth stone at its base. Whenever they had a trouble, Maeve would suggest they go ask Morelli what he thought and drop their worries in the cemetery well. The weight they carried on the way home was invariably lighter.

Sometimes Murtagh worried if Maeve visited the well more than he knew.

As he watched his wife work, Maeve fiddled with the length of green gauze she used to tie the curtains open. She planned to cover every inch of the terracotta-tiled windowsill with Murtagh's pots, filled with herbs and the cactus plants her mother sent her from Brooklyn. These were a great novelty on the island. 'Nothing wrong with a pot of chrysanthemums,' she'd heard more than once. 'And you give them names, I hear? How peculiar. Sure, haven't they the names God gave them? Not that you'd know them, I suppose. Maybe if you lived in Mexico.'

'Why are they so afraid of me having a cactus?' she had demanded of Murtagh as she spritzed her spiky friends with frustrated urgency.

'They take it personally,' he answered, shrugging his shoulders. 'If you don't do the same as they do, *they* think it's because *you* think you're better than them. Basically, notions.'

Maeve filled her spritzer at the sink, water overflowing on to her hands as she looked at him over her shoulder, her hair escaping from a loose braid she'd tied with a strip of fraying white cotton. 'But that's madness. They can have anything they want on their windowsills – what do I care? What are they so afraid of?'

Murtagh stood behind her and turned off the tap. 'You asking those questions, that's what they're afraid of. No one wants to have to defend choices they made without ever thinking about it. Why do you think they all go to Mass every week, get their children baptised? How many of them do you think ever even considered whether it was what they wanted or believed? It's automatic, learned behaviour. But you didn't get indoctrinated in the same way, so it's not implicit to you.'

Maeve leaned into him and nuzzled her cheek against his. 'It's not like I wasn't dragged to Mass back home,' she said.

Murtagh kissed the top of her head. 'But you knew plenty of people who weren't, saw lots of folks making alternative decisions, and that's the difference.'

Now, as Maeve fussed with her curtains, she admired the new view of their garden with its sapling apple trees and vegetable beds and ignored the tomato plants awaiting her attention. All she could feel was a sense of achievement that they had reached this milestone; it had been a long time coming. It was a relief that their home had expanded to accommodate not just their new family but the idea of how life might be if they stayed here, permanently. Murtagh's pottery business was thriving, and the studio had quickly become his own.

Situated behind their little shop on the seafront, Makes of Moone, the studio retained many of its original features. A slab of sandalwood, six-foot long, lay on top of black iron supports in an uneven rectangle, carved as it was from one tree by Seamus himself. His pottery wheel sat in the window, venetian blinds pulled to the top of the glass, overlooking the ocean. 'Where else would you put it?' Maeve had said while she helped him to settle in, leaning out of the window to breathe in the sea breeze. Now, a record player also sat on a three-legged table in the corner, a battered wooden fruit box beside it crammed with vinyl discs.

On the walls were noticeboards covered in photographs of

work and pictures cut from magazines. Inspiration seemed to strike him from the strangest of places – war photography, vegetables in the soil, the aquatic world, human faces, animals, fashion, architecture, pop stars, the Seven Wonders of the World, the Amazon. He was obsessed with ceramics as stories and loved to compare what pots they were making in Ireland, Japan, Israel, Germany, Africa, Australia, India at the same moment in time of ancient history. He examined how they were all so different, and yet how often their stories were the same; the universal human truths of existence.

Maeve still loved to sit with him while he worked, to help him mix the glazes, trying to anticipate the secrets that the kiln would reveal. It was because of small comforts such as these that Maeve remained grateful for the particular peace the island gave her. Her plan to commute to Galway every week for rehearsals with the Salthill Players had proved futile when her ability to travel was controlled by the elements; a definite decision to stop was never made but slowly her life evolved away from this as an essential plan. With each passing season, the stage she had dreamed of seemed further away, but she found she was relieved not to endure the intensified anxiety that also accompanied the adrenaline of performance. Was it a fair exchange? She thought so. Most days. And on the days when the injustice of it penetrated her resolve, she walked it off, stamped it out of the soles of her feet as she wound around the back roads of the island until she collapsed exhausted at the foot of the lighthouse and watched its beam sweep across the craggy rock she'd learned to love. When she was out walking, Murtagh always left the porch light on, their own beacon to call her home.

With Maeve's manner that was so atypical of the traditional island women, she carved out a place for herself in their society. She joined a Saturday-morning knitting circle, sitting amongst the women unravelling their yarn, and refused to indulge the silence that fell as she entered, until they slowly thawed. Maeve loved to ask questions that mortified them but that they all relished hearing the answers to, whispered as they were into sleeves and with one eye on the door. When Maeve learned that many of the island women couldn't swim she was shocked; so many families had lost people at sea and had become afraid. Immediately she ordered inflatable rings from Dublin and started lessons on Sunday mornings before Mass and cajoled them to join her one by one. Father Dónal couldn't understand why the parish women started arriving for Mass so giddy and flushed; it was the Maeve effect. The ease with which she made real human connections, how naturally she found fun with others despite their differences, remained a mystery to Murtagh. He envied her open mind that his shyness couldn't always replicate, but the island made them both more patient, less concerned with meeting like-minded friends, and more appreciative of how the diversity in their community helped it harmonise.

In the summer, Maeve taught drama classes to the young people of the island; releasing their inner demons, helping them connect with their bodies in the loving way she never could at their age.

Let those magic fingers dance, look at them move, they're electricity! Dance, faster, faster, FASTER and shake, shake, shake. Love your limbs, let them feel your blood racing through your veins!

In the afternoons, she sold Murtagh's ceramics in Makes

of Moone. She sat in Seamus's old rocking chair under the shade of a blue-and-white striped awning and read two books a week, waiting for the custom of their island neighbours, or the tourists stepping off the ferry to experience what they called 'Ancient Ireland', where children could still be found running barefoot and no cars were driven. She kept her camera on a shelf under the counter and always asked if she could take a photograph of each new customer; most agreed, and she usually got her best shot while they were busy preparing themselves for it. She had the black-and-white films printed in Galway city and placed them all with their names and the date of their visit in blue photo albums that she lined up on a shelf in the shop, some open and on display, so visitors could flick through. Occasionally folks wanted to buy one, but they weren't for sale. 'Purely a private collection,' she explained, before asking if they would then pose for it. Sometimes holiday-makers returned years later and would find themselves in an album; sometimes they teared up to see themselves even just a few years younger. A lot can happen in two years. Or two months. Or two minutes.

With the last of their unpacking now done, Maeve, bored of her own domesticity, retrieved her journal from the cutlery drawer and considered whether she could scribble a few lines. A thought struck her as she found a blank page. Perhaps she would consider rousing the adult islanders into doing a play with her; a winter performance to break up the shock of the dark? Could she convince them? She felt the flicker of inspiration spread through her before rational thought could douse it. Murtagh slipped out of the front door and returned with one of Síle's yellow roses. He placed it in one of Seamus's old sea-green vases on the kitchen table. 'In honour of the great people who invited us to make this our home.'

In years to come he would look back on those days and realise they had just experienced their longest period of uninterrupted happiness and yet, while they were living it, they thought there was so much to worry about.

As he watched Maeve hold Alma's flower to her nose, laughing at the series of sneezes that followed, loving the slight swell of her belly as she stretched, he could never know how in times to come he would pine for something so simple, so sweet, as this.

Inis Óg: December, 1984

'Oh, you're carrying to the front, it's definitely a girl, so.'

'Is it ice-cream you're craving? You need more calcium.'

'I hope you're not thinking about breastfeeding. Sure, you'll never know if it's being fed enough. Put it on the bottle and none of that messing.'

'Breast is best – it really is your motherly duty.'

'Don't be jumping up now every time the baby cries, or you'll spoil it rotten.'

'Babies need their mammies. Keep the cot right beside your bed so you can reach it whenever it stirs.'

'I hope you're not taking hot baths, you'll scald that baby inside you.'

'There's nothing better for you now than a long soak with a drop of chamomile.'

'You're tidy all the same, only for the bit of bump you'd never tell.'

'A glass of stout is what you need now, to thicken your blood. Full of iron.'

'You're mad to be out swimming in your condition! You should have your feet up. You'll get a cold in your kidneys.'

'A bit of gentle exercise now will do you the world of good.'

'Have you a name decided on yet? It'll be *American*, I suppose.'

'I heard you've terrible heartburn, that baby will have a grand full head of hair, so.'

Maeve couldn't move for all the advice that was thrust on her every time she ventured out into the island. Women who had barely nodded at her before now felt compelled to put their hands on her belly, lean in close and offer nightmarish tales of their own terrible labours, or beloved old wives' tales. Where were all the old husbands' tales, she wondered. Maeve had been initiated into a club that she didn't remember applying to join and this secret society was dedicated to educating her on how to become the perfect mother. The island was suddenly too small; there was no escape, but she had unwittingly found the golden ticket for acceptance amongst the inhabitants. It was a pity they all contradicted each other; or that no one acknowledged how scared she was; how sometimes she felt as if her body had been invaded by an alien that drained her of all her resources.

It made her miss her own mother dreadfully and miss her in ways she'd never before felt. She read and re-read her letters, committing her advice almost to memory. 'There's nothing more special than a boring pregnancy, remember that' and 'Don't forget to take care of you. A happy mammy is a happy baby.' What Maeve really wanted, though, was to sit across from her mother in Romano's deli, look her in the eye, and speak to her woman to woman. Instead she sat on the floor in the pottery shop, closed for the month of December, and spread before her the photos she had taken since September. The baby kicked her bladder repeatedly until she surrendered and hoisted herself up to the bathroom at the rear of the shop. Sometimes the baby frightened her; as if she could tell her mother had doubts and was trying to kick them out of her. Maeve was sure it was a she, and not because she craved sweet things, or because, as Áine O'Shea said, the grey in her face was her daughter stealing her beauty. She just knew, the same way she knew she was pregnant before any real evidence presented itself.

Maeve pulled out the high stool in front of the counter and sat on it with her back to the window so as not to catch the eye of any passer-by. She reached under the counter for Murtagh's good fountain pen, the one he was always losing, despairing over, and finding again, and began a letter to her unborn baby.

Dear daughter, hello, it's me, your mama,

And what a shock it will be if I am wrong and you come kicking and screaming into the world insulted that I thought you were a girl. How could your mammy get it wrong? Well, if that comes to pass, I'm sure it will only be the first mistake of many. I think, though, on this point, I am correct, and we will know for sure soon.

Your father is so excited; any nerves he has are drowned out by the joy he has that we've created you, a little human who will be a strange mix of him and me somehow mingled together. At night we lie in bed and fantasise about which elements of us will be passed down to you in genes or blood. I play along, pretending I care if you have my grey eyes or his golden hair, but really all I pray for is that you'll have your Daddy's peace of mind, and not be tormented by the old crow that sometimes sits on my shoulder, squawking in my ear.

Don't get me wrong, I am longing to meet you, too, but I'm scared. Scared of how loving you will change me. I remember my mother telling me that when I was three months old, Papa took her to Manhattan for lunch in Bergdorf Goodman's for a treat, and my cousin Carletta babysat me. She said she spent all day feeling as if she'd left her handbag behind her until she realised it wasn't her handbag that was missing. It was a part of herself. It was me. And it dawned on her that she would never be the same again, that she could never again be alone in the world with just her own mind, independent of me, even when I was somewhere else.

How does that change you?

Friends say to me nothing else will ever be as important again, that having a baby gives you purpose, puts things in perspective. Well, can I say, I find that quite tragic. I don't want to not care about all the things I'm passionate about, and my former childfree self is insulted at the implication that I was merely filling time, waiting for you to come along to give my life meaning. Does saying that already mark me out as a bad mother? I'm sure you think I deserve a good, hard kick, but I can't be the first mother to feel that way so why aren't we allowed to say it? Is that one of the rules of membership of the secret society? If we aren't delighted all of the time, we're broken? Well, maybe hesitation, doubt even, is good. It just means our minds are still open, questioning, curious, awake to inspiration.

And one more thing, and then I promise I'll stop panicking. I am so tired of everyone saying this is a magical time, because I have never felt anything so physical, so real, in my life.

My body is transformed, irrevocably.

I will feed you at my own breast, hold your skin against mine night after night and breathe in the smell of you.

Maybe we have to believe in a type of magic to help us get through the sleepless nights, but I don't think it helps to call it that. The mothers who feel exhausted, inadequate, anxious . . . should they be made to feel worse if this very real, very physical experience doesn't also dance along as a magical experience of infinite joy? It seems there are only two types of mothers allowed: the perfect mother, and the bad. How can that be when nobody is pure perfection or pure badness? Maybe the perfect mothers are lying, and the bad mothers are too hard on themselves.

I hope that this is my hormones talking, my sweet thing.

You deserve a mama who believes in magic. Can I try and go one better and just believe in you instead?

Hurry up and come along now, little one.

We're ready for you,

Your loving mama

She ripped the page from the pad, cursed the raggedy edge and folded it into a tidy square to slip inside her journal later. When she turned around, she jumped to see young Father Dónal staring in at her, his forehead pressed up against the glass. He waved her over and so, with a deep sigh under her breath, she waddled over to the door and unbolted the lock.

'It's yourself, Maeve,' he said. 'I'm glad I saw you there. I've something for you.'

She hoped it wasn't another St Francis medallion or

booklet of prayers for a new mother but smiled at him none-theless. 'The suspense is killing me!'

He grinned at her and made two rings around his eyes with his thumb and forefingers as if to impersonate an owl.

'Dónal? I'm not sure −' And then it hit her, and she mirrored the same action back at him. 'Murtagh's binoculars? Tell me you got them!'

'I did,' he said, patting his black shoulder bag. 'I was just scheming about the best way to get them to you on the sly, and sure then I saw you in the shop as if you were expecting me.'

'Come in, come in,' she said, bustling him inside.

Father Dónal stepped around the neat piles of photographs she had arranged on sheets of newspaper on the floor. He laid a white tissue parcel before her on the counter. Impatiently she tore the string off before gently revealing a brown leather case with gold stitching and silver hardware; inside were the Swift Skipper, Model 789, binoculars of Murtagh's cloud-spotting dreams. 'I'm afraid to even take them out of the case,' she said as she breathed in the aroma of the fine leather. 'Thank you so much, Dónal. I would never have been able for the ferry this week, and they still hadn't come in the last time I was in Galway.'

He patted her on the arm. 'It was my pleasure, dear. And hopefully it won't be the only present he gets this year, eh?'

She wriggled into her raincoat, which now only barely snapped closed across her bump.

'To be honest, Dónal, with tomorrow Christmas Eve already, I hope she hangs on a few days. I think we could do without that drama until the holiday's over.'

'We'll leave it in God's hands, so. Shall I walk you to the corner?'

But they didn't make it that far; not four feet from the door of the shop Maeve's waters broke and drenched Father Dónal's black patent shoes. With all the dignity he could muster, he wiped each foot on the back of the opposite leg in turn and held up Maeve as he guided her towards the pier. 'Come on now, Maeve. You'll get the last ferry to the mainland if we're quick.' A great bellow of pain filled the air and she doubled over on the path. Two girls in matching red cloaks came skipping around the corner and froze when they saw her; a chocolate biscuit fell from the hand of the taller of the two. 'Sinead and Aisling Brennan, just the girls. You know Mr Moone the potter? You need to run to his house and tell him the baby is coming. He needs to come to the pier at once. Scoot!'

Aisling started to cry but Sinead shook her little sister's hands, and said, 'Come on, Ais, this is God's work we're doing.' And their four legs ran as fast as they could up the hill, their cloaks flashing red behind them like flags in the breeze. By the time Dónal had helped Maeve into the bottom deck of the *Brigidín*, a small group of islanders had gathered to witness the excitement. 'Where's Murtagh?' Maeve shouted. 'I'm not going without him.' One of the island women wrapped a shawl around her and covered her legs with blankets that the captain thrust at them. For a seafaring man, he had never looked so unsteady on his feet. 'Don't worry,' he said. 'We'll wait for him.' And then Maeve heard Murtagh's footsteps on the stairs, him calling out to her, and the panic in his voice quietened her own. He rushed towards her, the laces of his shoes traipsing behind him, coat incorrectly buttoned and with cream in his beard. He had barely wrapped his arms around her before the ferry was heading in the direction of Galway Maternity Hospital.

After eighteen hours of labour, Nollaig June Moone was born, at five minutes past five in the morning. Murtagh sobbed when he saw her, gently touching the soft fuzz of golden blonde that covered her little pink head. 'You're a miracle worker, Maeve,' he said. 'You did it.' And his wife felt his salty tears mingling with her own.

Maeve never found the letter she'd written to Nollaig, but it didn't matter. She needed no words to tell this little baby how she felt; Maeve knew she understood it in her bones. She had passed on the knowledge in their secret communion at dawn, when from a mother, a daughter was born.

Inis Óg: 1985

Murtagh was touched that the islanders wore their Sunday best for Maeve's premiere performance of *The Playboy of the Western World*. They sat in their usual seats in Tigh Ned's but adopted airs of formality as they whispered to each other about what to expect. There was no stage, little to set that night apart from any other except that the television behind the bar was not only turned off but covered in a black sheet, and that Ned had stopped serving.

When the chapel bell rang eight times, Murtagh, in his role as stage manager, turned off all the lights in the pub, leaving just the flicker of tealights in jam jars. The audience emitted a few nervous yelps and spluttered laughs before Murtagh switched on the light behind the bar, exposing Ned himself, his auburn hair greased back, dressed in a collarless white shirt, with braces holding up grey tweed trousers from the turn of the century. A lit pipe hung from his lip. Maeve popped up beside him, Pegeen now, her blue-black hair hanging in two tight braids over her shoulders. She wore a full-length dark green bustled skirt, high-collared ivory blouse, and a grey apron that she used to polish a glass. In the moment of her arrival, Tigh Ned's had become Flaherty's Tavern and a hushed awe blanketed the pub. When Sean Lally burst in, transformed as Christy, roaring that he had killed his father, no one laughed, and

Maeve was relieved. The magic of the theatre had worked its spell, curling around the imaginations of the audience as the smoke from the turf fire thickened the air.

By the end of the play, when Pegeen crumples into a heap against the bar, lamenting that she has lost the only playboy of the western world, the islanders were clutching each other's arms, shocked at what they had seen: the sex, the violence, the comedy. It felt as real to them as their own lives.

Maeve waited a beat, her shoulders heaving with each deep breath she drew, and then snapped around, Pegeen no more. She grinned at them as she shook herself back into reality. The rest of the cast gathered beside her and, arms entwined, they bowed while the audience clapped, stamped their feet and hollered. Just one performance, and yet, it would be spoken of for months.

Did you see the way he pretended to be riding that donkey? I felt I was at the race, true as God.

Do you think that they were really up to mischief behind the bar? Father Dónal says they were only coddin', but it sounded fairly real to me.

I always knew there was something special about Maeve Moone, sure she was like a film star in that.

As Tigh Ned's hadn't been able to serve during the performance a collective decision was made that opening hours could extend beyond official closing time. Father Dónal gave his blessing, and Jerome Brennan, the only policeman on the island, confirmed it could be approved on a technicality. He was parched himself after all the excitement, he said. Murtagh was collecting up the props when he heard Nollaig starting to wail from where she lay in her pram in the porch. He saw Maeve's head whip towards the sound, but before he could intercept her she had broken away from the clutch of neighbours surrounding her so she could pluck her baby from the pram, her outlandish skirt impeding her exit as she manoeuvred through the crowd. Murtagh followed a few minutes later; a bottle of milk warmed in the kitchen in one hand; a cup of hot chocolate for Maeve in the other; she had never liked to drink alcohol after a performance, wanted to keep the whole night crisply clear in her mind's eye. He found Maeve perched on the cobblestone wall, Nollaig on her lap, sucking on her little finger. They rocked together back and forth and Murtagh caught the tail end of a tune Maeve was humming as he approached. She turned her face to him; the flush from the heat of the pub faded from her cheeks, eyes glassy, just the rim of her scarlet lipstick left, as if she had drawn around her mouth with a pencil and forgotten to fill in the rest.

'Maeve, my love, let me take her.' He held out his arms. 'Go and enjoy the party. You blew them away!'

She shook her head. 'I'm happier here. Will you sit with me for a bit?'

He placed the bottle and mug of hot chocolate on the wall beside her, threw one leg over and sat sideways, watching her in profile, his hand stroking the small of her back.

'My darkling, you were so wonderful. It almost hurt to see it.'

She smiled at him. 'It almost hurt to do it. Darkling? You haven't called me that in a long time.'

'Haven't I?'

She repositioned Nollaig in her lap and reached for the hot chocolate. 'I wouldn't mind a drop of whiskey in this,' she said, after tasting it.

'They're already asking when the next one will be. Have you thought about it at all?'

She shook her head.

'I'm not sure if I will be doing another one. Maybe. We'll see.'

He brushed her fringe from her forehead, where curls had sprung lose from the braids.

'Did you not enjoy it? I know it was a lot of work, and not a fancy theatre or anything, but you'd struggle to get that reaction in the Abbey. Would you –'

'No. It's harder to have a taste and then go hungry. If you never had a bite, you wouldn't know what you were missing.'

She refused to look at him, her eyes focused on the beacon of the lighthouse in the distance.

'But Maeve, you don't have to –'

'Will you get me my coat, love? We should get her out of this damp night.'

She stood up abruptly and started walking, Nollaig in her arms, though she was too heavy now to be carried such a distance.

The pram stood abandoned in the porch of Tigh Ned's.

Murtagh stood abandoned at the wall outside.

He knew he should chase after her, say something to make this right, but he didn't trust himself not to make things worse. Maeve would never tell him what he wanted to hear; that she was happy, that she would consider another play, that all this was enough for her. How many times before had he desperately needed her reassurance that everything would be okay in the end? But she would never make promises she wasn't certain she could keep. Could never say what he wanted to hear unless it was the truth. And he wasn't prepared to ask questions tonight that might draw from her answers too brutal to bear. Her conviction to the truth was her great strength; his inability to hear it his great weakness.

Instead he watched quietly over the next few days as Maeve ate as little as she could; enough to keep his interventions at bay. As she lay in the bath three nights later, her hair wrapped in an orange towel like a turban, he sat on its edge and squeezed suds along her legs with a sea sponge. 'Don't, Murt.' She hesitated, closed her eyes, and leaned her head back against the silver taps. 'I have it under control.'

Murtagh held the sponge to his face, suds cascading down his arm to where his sleeve was rolled at the elbow, then he dropped to his knees on the floor and took her wet, bird-like body in his arms. He held her there, the ends of her orange turban submerged now in water, until the sound of Nollaig crying penetrated the closed door. She peeled him away, stepped out of the bath and went to her daughter. Murtagh stayed kneeling on their pink bathroom mat, facing the wall, his forehead resting on the edge of the bath. Maeve turned off the light as she left the room, leaving just spears of streetlight to pierce the dusk through the venetian blinds. He waited there until the house fell silent and then plunged his hand in the cold water to drain the tub, but he couldn't get up off the floor.

Not until Maeve came to fetch him and lead him away by the hand to the kitchen.

There they sat at the table, where Murtagh dried his arms with her damp orange towel.

Maeve ate a rice pudding and, in doing so, gave them permission to go silently to bed.

Inis Óg: 1986

Murtagh stepped off the ferry with gripe water for the colicky twins and lavender essential oil for Maeve. Tomás and Dillon hadn't stopped crying since they'd slid into the world eleven days before. Dillon had arrived first, purple and screaming, Tomás reluctantly seven minutes later, with the help of the midwife's impatient forceps, pale and whimpering. Murtagh began to question the moral integrity of his sons, becoming convinced they were conniving in a cruel tag-team manipulation. As soon as one fell asleep, the other would wail, waking his brother up and continuing the vicious cycle. Nollaig, only two years old herself, was all but abandoned; a veritable grown-up in the wake of these two helpless monsters. Maeve was trying to feed them herself, but that couldn't go on much longer. Determined to try for as long as she could, she found the twins refused to feed at the same time and so she was awake constantly as they took it in turns to latch, with various degrees of success. She had begun to hallucinate with exhaustion, advising Murtagh that he himself was downstairs if he needed him. Something would have to give.

Murtagh's head was bent against the sheets of rain that were crashing down on the island. It hadn't stopped pouring since the babies were born, which didn't help. It was never a good idea to keep Maeve confined to the house for long – shackles to her were a dare. So, it wasn't much of a surprise to look up and see her sitting on the low stone wall at the corner where their lane met the main road of the island. Her clothes were drenched, and she sat completely still, looking past him as he rushed towards her, his plastic bag of shopping banging against his leg as he ran.

'Maeve, who's minding the children? Are you all right?'

'I don't know,' she answered. 'I thought you were there.'

'What? You knew I went into Galway! Don't tell me you left them on their own. Jesus, Maeve, anything might have happened.'

She looked at him, grey pools of emptiness where her eyes should be, unmoved by the panic in his voice.

'You'd better go check on them, then.'

He grabbed her by the arm and pulled her to her feet. 'Come on, that's enough, Maeve. Those babies are depending on us. You can't wander off. Things are different now. Are you trying to catch your death of cold?'

Father Dónal stopped at the corner to see what the matter was. His wet black gabardine gave him the look of a seal walking on his hind legs. 'Everything okay here, my Moones?' he asked.

'We're fine, Dónal. Maeve just came to meet me off the boat.'

'I see. Well, while I have you, have you given any more thought to the date for the blessing? I could –' A desperate look from Murtagh silenced him. 'Right, well, another time then. Maeve? If there's ever anything –'

Murtagh cut him off.

'Everything's fine, Dónal. We'd better get home out of this rain.'

Murtagh broke into a run as soon as Dónal's back was turned, leaving Maeve strolling along behind, dangling the plastic bag he'd thrust at her.

When he reached their cottage, the front door was swinging wide open. A terrible chorus of two infants and one toddler screaming assaulted him at the gate.

Nollaig sat in the hallway, her hair plastered to her scalp with sweat, her chubby arms pink with the effort of the tight little fists she was making. Fat tears hung on her long eyelashes like baubles on a Christmas tree. A dirty nappy hung low in her stars-and-stripes pyjama bottoms that Grandma June had sent. Maeve arrived at the doorstep but did not cross the threshold. 'God almighty, Maeve, would you look at the state of the poor creature?' He picked Nollaig up and she clung to his neck with her hot fingers, wiping her dripping nose in his beard as he ran up the stairs to the twins. 'There now, a leanbh, there now,' he whispered, rubbing small circles in her back.

Tomás and Dillon lay side by side in their double crib.

Swaddled each in linen, one trimmed with a green silk ribbon, one with blue, they competed to discover who could scream the loudest.

'Maeve! Maeve! Get up here, I need you.'

There was no answer from his wife, but Áine O'Shea appeared like a vision at the door in a pristine yellow apron.

'I'm sorry to burst in, Murtagh, but I've been listening to those children crying for the past hour and my nerves were gone worrying something had happened. Is Maeve okay? She doesn't seem herself.'

'Áine, I've never been so glad to see someone in my life.

In the cabinet over the stove, there's formula. Would you make me two bottles, please, if you can?'

'Of course, Murt. God love 'em. I won't be a minute.'

Murtagh gave Nollaig a rusk from a packet open on the changing table and she quietened for a moment as she gnawed it. It gave him a chance to pick up his sons and cradle one in each arm. He stood swaying from side to side, singing, for reasons unknown, 'Wooden Heart' by Elvis Presley. When Áine reappeared, he sat in the white wicker rocking chair under the window and she helped him position the babies so he could give them both a bottle simultaneously. She picked up Nollaig and changed her nappy, wiping down her body with a cool flannel and changing her pyjamas. Downstairs, she fed her a mashed-up banana and gave her a bottle of warm milk. In minutes, Nollaig was cooing in her arms and Áine tucked her under the soft lemon blankets in the little bed that Murtagh had built to look like a boat.

Before Áine left, she glanced around the living-room door. Maeve was sitting in her wet coat in front of the empty grate where the fire had gone out. She called her name, but there was no reply, so she slipped away after whispering to Murtagh to fetch her any time.

For once, Tomás and Dillon fell asleep within moments of each other, a spoon of gripe water in their bellies, and Murtagh gently lay them down.

Shaking his arms to relieve the pins and needles that had settled in from holding them, he came downstairs and stood in the doorway, watching his wife.

'Why don't you spend a night at the hotel, Maeve? Have a bath and get some sleep.'

She turned her head to look at him.

'Are you throwing me out, Murtagh? The bad mother?'

He knew he should go to her, but he could not. The shock of what he had come home to still held him in its force field.

'Of course not. But you need a proper rest. Come home in the morning for breakfast.' He hovered at the door, nudging it back and forth with the toe of his shoe.

'The whole village will be talking,' she said, watching him from the corner of her eye.

'There's worse things they could be saying. I'll ring ahead to Michael to let him know you're coming. Why don't you pack some things?'

Her glee to be fleeing the house was undeniable and crushing. As she stood in the hallway, holding his small brown leather suitcase, it crossed Murtagh's mind that maybe she would run for good. As if she could read his thoughts, she stood on her tiptoes and kissed him on the forehead. It was like a crack of light breaking through the fog. 'I'll see you first thing. I promise.' And he was calmer.

The next morning, Maeve slipped back into the house as dawn was breaking. She left her shoes in the hallway and crept up the stairs in her stockings. Murtagh sat in her rocking chair, a son in each arm, snoring softly, baby formula dried on to his forehead. Nollaig was standing up in their crib, holding on to the bars, wide awake but totally silent. As if she was watching over her daddy while he slept. Maeve walked closer to pick her up, but the strength was missing from her arms. Nollaig lay back down and turned to face the wall while Maeve gripped the side of the crib. She knew how she should feel, but could not. When the crow came to sit on her shoulder, she became an orphan, an unmarried woman, childless, friendless, an island lost at sea; the soles of her feet barely touching the earth. She was untethered, ready to take flight, the threads connecting her to the life she loved fraying.

Four days later her mother arrived on a flight from JFK. Maeve was silent for the duration of the drive from the airport but felt safer to have her close.

To not be the mother.

There would be no more walking out in the rain or dirty nappies unchanged, she was told.

As if she'd ever wanted, or chosen, those things.

But she was thankful.

Thankful to be held and thankful to hold.

As Grandma June pushed the twins through the village in their double pram, Maeve sat in the garden, pressing Nollaig's skin against her own.

Impressing a mother's love upon her daughter in the early-morning light.

The touch of love as an act of hope.

Inis Óg: January, 1990

Dear Diary,

I slipped out of bed last night while Murtagh was sleeping.

I waited for that wheezy noise he makes through his left nostril that heralds his deep sleep; the signal that it's safe for me to escape.

Like a biological school bell.

The neon-green numbers on his alarm clock blinked eleven minutes past one as I stood over him, his eyes restless under the lids. I wished I could crawl inside his ear and watch the film projected in his mind . . . but what if I appeared as a monster? Something tentacled and evil from the sea, or winged and manic from the sky?

What if, in the deepest mind of his, there is a knowledge of me that wants him to hate me? What if they try to tell him in his dreams?

Murtagh is so loyal, he would never leave me. He would endure the challenge of living with me and my moods and my difficulties until the end of time if I let him. He only wants to see what's good in me but sometimes I think it might be easier if we named problems, instead of just enduring them.

Shouldn't I be protecting him, and the children, from anything that makes them suffer? Shouldn't I save them from myself if they cannot rescue themselves?

These thoughts run relay races in my mind as I stick plasters on grazed knees, make their favourites for dinner, fill their baths and test the temperature with my elbow. I try to hide behind my love but worry the toxicity will leak from my pores. I went to see Dr Lynch on the mainland, but all he could suggest was trying the pills again, and keeping busy. I could tell he didn't take me seriously, but I'd rather vanish whole than become the walking ghost those tablets turned me into. I know they work for others, but whenever I let one of those little tablets crawl down my throat I feel it expanding through my veins like rivers of ice, freezing every inch of me so that I become a statue. As the effect wears off, I thaw a little, but the next pill compounds the frost, so I am in a constant state of chilling numbness, tentative hope, then numbness again. So, it's back to my own methods – the walking cure, the writing cure, the sleeping through it cure, the drowning in music cure.

But this spell feels very prolonged.

The weeks are counted in new silver hairs on Murtagh's head.

I fear that Sive stole my last anchor when she left my body, so impatient and cross.

When I escaped last night, I was surprised by how mild it was. It didn't feel right to be strolling along with my coat flapping open behind me, no scarf around my throat. I climbed to the lighthouse and leaned my back against the damp white paint, the heels of my Doc Martens pressed firm against the winter heliotrope growing at its foot.

I thought I heard a cuckoo call in the distance – had one lost fellow forgotten to flee for the winter?

I remembered Murtagh laughing at me the first time we heard one here and I confessed that I hadn't thought they really existed but were a made-up bird from fairy tales. They don't have any cuckoos in Brooklyn, as far as I know. I must remember to ask Papa. I echoed the call, but it sounded artificial in my ears, amplified in the silence, and the bird didn't fall for it.

I walked to the edge of the cliffs, precariously navigating the rough rocks that guard the perimeter in the darkness. It was as if, although I wanted to annihilate myself, I still couldn't bear the thoughts of tripping, of scraping my hands and knees on the gravel.

As I drew closer to the edge I tested the ground in front of me with my right toe before I stepped forward, until eventually I felt just the air beneath my foot.

And then I paused.

One more tiny step and it would have seemed that a terrible accident had happened.

With no note left behind, surely there could be no doubt about how I met my fate.

I closed my eyes and pictured the faces of each of my children, the face of Murtagh.

I knew they wanted to call me home, but that they should not, for their own sake.

Hovering with one foot held out in front of me, my arms outstretched, I paused, as if hoping something would happen without my needing to propel myself forward.

I couldn't shake the Christmas number-one song from my ears, Bono's pleading on the Band Aid song, repeating over and over again. Where were all the musical loves of my life when I needed them most?

I wondered if Murtagh would remember to return the new raincoats we'd ordered from Germany and decided were too fluorescent.

I pictured the shelves of the refrigerator, tried to conjure up how much food there was at home before more shopping would be needed.

And finally, I thought of the little watercolour painting that Murtagh had received from Jeremy; a black-winged butterfly just four inches wide. I'd pressed it between the pages of Maeve Brennan's *In and Out of Never-Never Land* to keep it safe until I found a frame and now it struck me that Murtagh would never know where to find it. It seemed an unnecessary cruelty to do that to him.

So, I stepped back.

In truth, it gave me permission to come home because I was afraid to follow through.

I am a coward.

Too scared of what happens next to mothers who abandon their children – even if it's for their own good.

Worried about surviving but being horribly injured and having to account for myself.

Terrified that I would change my mind at the crucial moment.

Or that I wouldn't.

So, I climbed back down the craggy lighthouse path, passing the pier as the first fishermen were preparing their boats. If anyone was surprised to see me out so early, it wasn't reflected in their hat-tips and nods. I stopped at the shop for milk we didn't need and bought hot fresh scones from Síle. She wrapped them in a tea towel to keep them warm for me; it has a picture of St Brigid on it, tending to a lamb with her prayer embroidered underneath.

Brigid is eyeing me cautiously now while I write at the kitchen table and wait for sounds of stirring upstairs.

She would have had the courage, I'm sure.

I spread my fingers over the towel and whispered her words out loud.

> 'You brought light to the darkness,
> You brought hope to the downcast.
> Strengthen what is weak within us.'

If only it were that easy, to have faith, but I don't believe anyone is listening. I wish I did.

So now I will carry on, and try not to imagine how different it might have been.

Instead, I will get that watercolour framed.

And send back the raincoats.

Later that morning, with Nollaig happily settled at school, the rest of the Moone family strolled down to the beach; the boys on either side of their mother, slapping their wellington boots along the pebbly lane, while Murtagh carried Sive in a sling. When they reached the end of the shore they paused to sit awhile on a flat boulder the tide had polished smooth. Murtagh focused a camera on Maeve, her skirt gathered in her hands, laughing as her two sons splashed her, as they teetered at the water's edge. In the foreground of the shot he could see Sive crawling towards them in her striped romper suit.

Murtagh laid the camera on the sand and watched Maeve stand her ground as the beating heart of their family. He loved to see her like this, how a stranger might bear witness to her. Her concentration was always pure, her commitment total. As she held the boys' hands, he knew there was nowhere else she would rather be, that for those moments the universe was exactly as it should be. Any dark stretch of Maeve at her worst was worth these moments of Maeve at her best. He squeezed fistfuls of sand in his hands and tried to stop it slipping through his fingers. Dug deeper into the damp grains. The muscles in his arms tightened and he anchored himself to the ground with his heels. He tried again and again, but the natural order would not be controlled. Eventually he let go, and the sand scattered in the breeze.

That afternoon, while Maeve was working in Makes of Moone, old newspapers were spread across the kitchen table at home so the children could paint without worrying about making a mess. Empty egg boxes held the paints; the brothers shared one carton, but Nollaig had her own – she couldn't cope when the boys forgot to rinse their paintbrushes in the jam jars of water before changing colours. She concentrated on carefully painting a house, like she always did, with blobs denoting the family who lived there. Mossy held the paintbrush in his fist and hit the paper more than he painted, and Dillon, well, he loved to smear the paint all over the newspapers with his hands. Murtagh sat on the kitchen counter above them, calmly reading aloud the arts section of the *Irish Times* over the din.

He looked up when he heard Maeve's arrival in the hall-way. For him, the sound of love was always Maeve's key turning in the lock; she brought home home with her every time. His forever shy smile was waiting when she slipped through the kitchen door and closed it quickly behind her.

'My darlings!' she shouted. 'There is someone special I'd like you to meet.'

Nollaig ran over and held up her painting in front of her face. 'Look, Mama, I did you.'

Maeve crouched down, 'Well, you clearly inherited your father's artistic abilities, dear, because that is marvellous. Definitely fridge-worthy.'

Murtagh started wiping Mossy's hands with a kitchen towel and gathering up the newspaper while Dillon stretched his arms out to Maeve and pawed green paint on to her blouse. She kissed him on the forehead and lifted him down from his chair.

'Who's here?' Murtagh asked her. 'Were we expecting someone?'

Maeve wrinkled her nose at him. 'Not exactly *someone*.'

He froze, his arms full of crumpled newspapers, 'Please tell me you didn't –'

'I did,' she sang, and flung the hall door open.

A tiny black Labrador puppy padded in, yelping in a high pitch, and skidded on the kitchen tiles. Mossy immediately started crying while Dillon tried to run towards him and slipped on his bottom. Nollaig gushed, 'Oh, Mama, Mama, is he ours?', as she tried to pick up his wriggling body.

Maeve kneeled on the floor and pulled the puppy into her

lap while Murtagh comforted Mossy. 'We have to be gentle with him,' she said. 'He's only little and we don't want to scare him. You have to stroke his fur carefully, like this.'

She picked up Nollaig's hand and guided her to smooth his hair in the right direction and the puppy licked her fingers.

'Maeve, where did you get him? I can't believe you didn't tell me about this,' Murtagh said, while Mossy peeked out from behind him, still sniffling. Dillon crawled over and immediately tried to grab the puppy's tail, but Maeve was quicker and caught his hand in her own and frowned at him.

She smiled gingerly at Murtagh. 'I know,' she said, 'I'm sorry, but Dónal intercepted me at the ferry. One of the tourists abandoned him on the beach. Can you believe it? I couldn't say no.'

Murtagh sighed, picking up the dog and looking into his eyes. 'That Dónal knows a soft touch when he sees one, doesn't he? I suppose we're stuck with him now!'

Maeve clapped her hands and gave Nollaig a squeeze. 'So, what are we going to name him? Any ideas, Noll? Maybe you can name him after someone special?'

Nollaig chewed on her lip for a minute and then shouted out, 'Let's name him Granny Teresa.'

Laughter exploded from Maeve and Murtagh and Nollaig's face fell.

'What?' she shouted. 'I love Granny Teresa!'

Maeve pulled herself together and said, 'I know you do, darling, but I'm not sure she'd like having a dog named after her. What about your favourite redheaded friend on the telly?'

'Oh no,' Murtagh groaned. 'Not that screeching puppet!!'

'BOSCO!' Nollaig shouted, and the twins chimed in, 'BOSCO! BOSCO!'

In years to come, Dillon and Mossy would swear they could remember the day Bosco came to live with them, even though it was unlikely their developing memories could have captured it. Maeve never forgot it, though, for he seemed to bring with him the start of a golden era in their family. It was the period when Murtagh received an unexpected commission from Japan for a new series of miniature teapots; that her mother visited for three whole weeks; when Nollaig learned to ride a bike and Maeve finally started surfing. Bosco was a talisman for familial harmony, equally loved by all of the Moones, and almost as perceptive about Maeve's moods as Murtagh was. Often, she would doze in the afternoon, and he would lie, wide awake beside her on the sofa.

Her guardian.

Later that week Maeve hung the photograph taken at the beach in the hallway right beside the front door. She could remember that day now as a happy one, with the benefit of a hindsight that confirmed she was right to be optimistic – the memory alone could conjure how it felt to be imbued with a silver light as the tingle from the cold seawater sent electric shocks of life through her body. A life force that spirited her along for days, then weeks, then months. It brought with it a sense of relief that she had stepped away from the cliff edge on that morning.

It was often so difficult to be happy in the present; who knew how long the peace would last?

Happiness of the past you could luxuriate in, relaxing in

the knowledge that nothing bad had come along to spoil that memory.

Looking back and seeing happiness gave her hope.

For Maeve had learned they were often synonymous with each other in her life.

Hope was the light she could follow home.

Inis Óg: May, 1990

Murtagh sat on the edge of the pier, his grey corduroy trousers rolled up to the knee, his feet dangling in the salty stew of the Atlantic. He transferred strands of seaweed from one foot to the other with his toes, willing its magic to alleviate some of the discomfort of the scabbed wounds on his heels. For his last birthday, Maeve had bought him new runners in an effort to get him jogging to halt the advancing spread of softness across his middle. His spirit was willing but his body was weak, and the acrylic material the shoes were made from grated away the skin on his heels. He had worn the wrong socks but would try again, keen as he was to feel strong and fit again. The boys loved his new regime, too, running along beside him, one on each side, pink faces and fists pumping. He could still beat them in a race. Just about.

He watched them now, sprinting up and down the pier, Dillon the easy winner, Mossy uninterested in running but very interested in the acceptance his brother discriminately offered. Murtagh often felt the urge to tell him to stand on his own two feet, but resisted, remembering how much his own father's demands on his wilting personality caused him to shrivel even more. He craved a Fat Frog ice-pop, the sickly lime-green sweetness on a stick that he'd grown so partial to. *Maybe they could stop at Siopa Síle on the way home. Pick up one of those apple slices for Maeve that she loves.* He smiled, remembering the chaos that morning as she taught the kids how to twist in the kitchen, Chubby Checker blaring from the record player on repeat. He had spun Nollaig and Sive under each arm while Maeve danced with the twins, and then they had jived together while their children cheered with surprise at their moves. Maeve had declared the 'Kitchen Disco' was to become a regular thing and set Nollaig the task of making a poster advertising the next event, for which she promised to acquire a real disco ball.

These May evenings were his favourite time of year; the final dusting off and polishing up of the island before the students arrived from all across the country for Irish college. For three weeks at a time, during June, July and August, they were invaded by a hundred or so secondary-school students who came to be immersed in the language and the culture and, more often than not, engage in ill-advised adolescent romances. For some, it was a banishment, a forced intensive learning before the state examinations; for others, freedom. Inevitably, though, by the end of the three weeks, few wanted to go home. He wrote to tell his mother that the scenes on departure day were akin to what the country last witnessed when their ancestors emigrated, with tears and tantrums and false promises to stay in touch. He couldn't blame them. The intensity of their time there accelerated the intimacy and connections they felt. A summer on that island was all it took to fall in the sort of heady love that would be remembered for a lifetime. The boys stayed on the west of the island, the girls on the east, with the ruins of the castle dividing them. Every night after the céilí dance, they formed forlorn little armies marching away from each other, looking over their shoulders to watch and wave as the new inhabitant of their heart disappeared into the darkness in the opposite direction. Before they'd arrived, they could never have anticipated the hormonal explosions the minimal touching in a traditional set dance could evoke. Every May the bean-an-tis, the women who predominantly looked after the teenagers in their homes, rolled their eyes at each other, offering up lamentations of 'God help us and save us, here we go again' and 'Let's hope we'll have none of the messing of last year,' but in truth the college invigorated the island with income and energy, and they missed the teenagers when they were gone.

Murtagh leaned back on the hot tarmac and tilted his head towards the last of the sun, enjoying the heat on his eyelids, though his legs grew chilly. A shadow fell across him and he stirred, expecting one of the boys, but as he squinted up it was the outline of a man that towered over him. He could not make out his face against the glare of the sun, but a crown of dreadlocks circled his head, held in place by a purple bandana. Murtagh dragged his legs from the water and splashed him as he tried to stand up with some grace. His eyes travelled up from the stranger's dark brown feet, the little black hairs sitting in tufts on his toes, comfortably settled into well-worn Birkenstocks. A thin plait of red leather was wound around his left ankle. He wore green denim shorts, slim to the knee, and a short-sleeved white cotton shirt with most of the buttons opened.

'Sorry to disturb you,' the man said as he shook the speckles of water from his legs, 'but could you point me in the direction of Pól Quilty's house?'

Murtagh couldn't place his English accent but was

overwhelmed by a sense of familiarity, although he could not fathom where they may have met before. Something about the dark pools of his eyes – where had he seen them before?

Dillon and Mossy crashed into their father's legs and diverted his attention for a second as he gathered his thoughts. Dillon spoke first. 'Who are you, then?' he asked, staring up from under his red baseball hat while Bosco licked the stranger's toes.

Murtagh shushed him, pulling the dog away. 'Have some manners, Son Night. You, too, Bosco.'

'That's okay.' The newcomer crouched down to shake Dillon's hand and stroked Bosco's fur. 'I'm Fionn and I'm here to teach for the summer.'

'You don't sound Irish,' Dillon answered, and Murtagh clasped his hand over his mouth as Fionn laughed. 'I'm sorry,' Murtagh offered, 'I think Dillon is suffering from heatstroke and has forgotten himself. I'm Murtagh, Murtagh Moone, and I'll happily show you where Pól lives if you can bear these two coming along.'

'That would be lovely,' Fionn said, pointing at each of them in turn. 'So Murtagh and Dillon – that leaves . . . ?' he asked, wriggling his finger at Mossy, who stared at the ground, rummaging in his pockets for something unknown.

Murtagh gave him a little nudge. 'And this is Tomás – we call him Mossy.'

'Good to meet you, Mossy. And you're right, Dillon, I don't sound Irish, do I? But I'm fifty per cent of the way anyway. My mother is from Kells, but my father was from the Caribbean. I grew up in Birmingham. Do you know where that is?'

Mossy shook his head. 'So, can you speak Irish, then?'

Fionn nodded his head, 'I try. Birmingham's in England, but my mum sent me to Irish lessons all through school. I can even do a jig if you ask me nicely.'

Murtagh laughed as he rolled down his trouser legs. 'Is that what you're here for? The dancing?'

'Well, not exclusively. I'm doing my PhD in Irish Studies at UCD, so I'm on teaching placement here for the summer.'

Fionn was weighed down by a bulging orange rucksack with a ukulele strapped to the front in a woollen tartan case; his back called to Murtagh's mind the crescent moon of the currach boats on the strand.

'Are you okay to carry that? We're a good ten minutes from Pól's,' said Murtagh, unsure if he could take the weight himself, but Fionn waved him away. 'We've walked further, this bag and me, and in much less friendly company.'

They set off together, Mossy falling into step beside Fionn as they headed towards the village. 'Is that a kid's guitar?' Dillon asked, miming air guitar as he ran along the top of Siopa Síle's front wall. Fionn turned and bent over so Dillon could take a closer look. '*That*, my friend,' he said, 'is no kid's guitar. *That* is a ukulele, the king of all instruments, although I have known a few kids to play it in my time.'

'A ulikayle? Can you teach me?'

Murtagh held out his hand so Dillon could jump from the wall.

'Son, it's UK-U-LE-LE, but please don't terrorise the poor man. He's only just arrived and will be doing enough teaching this summer.'

Fionn laughed. 'It would be no bother. Maybe you can show me some of the good surfing spots in return.'

Dillon's face fell. 'I don't know how to surf either, but my mam does. I've been asking her can I go for aaaaaaaages, but I'm not a good enough swimmer yet.'

Murtagh raised his eyebrows at him. 'Gosh, it's hard to be Dillon sometimes, isn't it? It's not a ukulele you want, son, but the world's tiniest violin.'

When they reached Pól Quilty's house, Murtagh paused outside and shook Fionn's hand.

'Welcome to the island, Fionn.'

'Thanks for walking with me. I'll see you around, no doubt.'

'Nowhere to hide, I'm afraid.' Fionn frowned, and Murtagh held up a hand in protest. 'Not that I'd want to hide, I just meant –'

'Don't worry, I get it,' Fionn said, smiling as he adjusted the weight of the bag on his back.

He turned to walk up the footpath to Pól's door while Murtagh balanced himself against their stone wall to slip his sandals on his now-dry feet.

He stared at them for a moment, noticing, for the first time, the fuzzy blond hairs that grew in tufts across his own toes. *How strange to have never noticed that before.*

When he looked up again Fionn had been swallowed into the hallway of Quilty's.

Less than a week later, Fionn was eating breakfast in the Moone home. He turned his nose towards the sky like a werewolf and filled his lungs with deep breaths.

'That aroma,' he said. 'It smells like coming home, only to no home I've ever known.'

Maeve cut a slab of spelt loaf, slathered runny butter on top and held it out to him. He stole a bite straight from her hand, before taking it from her, and she started in surprise.

Fionn licked his fingers and brushed a scattering of crumbs from his new Aran jumper into the sink. He looked like an advertisement for Bord Fáilte, the Irish tourist board: handsome, healthy and fully embracing the island's culture.

'That's Murtagh's bread. It's his morning ritual: first he bakes, then he pots.'

Murtagh paused midway through pulling on the blue mechanic's boiler suit that he wore to work over his civilian clothes, what he called his *civvies*.

'The principles are similar,' he said, miming kneading the dough with his hands on the table.

Fionn held the arms of the boiler suit out straight so Murtagh could stretch into it while Maeve rinsed crumbs down the sink, wiping it half-heartedly with a green sponge squelchy with washing-up liquid.

'I've always liked the thought of pottery,' Fionn said, 'but I've never tried it. Never tried baking bread either, come to think of it.'

'You'll master the bread quicker, but you're welcome to visit the studio some time if you'd like to give it a go.'

Murtagh zipped up the front of his overalls and yanked down the sleeves of his jumper from where they were caught at the elbows.

'I don't suppose you have time now, do you?'

Murtagh hesitated and Fionn backed towards the hall

door. 'I'm sorry, I didn't mean to put you on the spot. I know you have your work to do.'

'No, no, it's fine. I was just gathering my thoughts about what the day held. Come on over for an hour anyway and see how it goes.'

This time, Fionn was the one to hesitate. 'Are you sure? I feel like maybe I've pushed you into it now and I don't want to be a nuisance.'

Maeve rolled her eyes at him. 'He wouldn't say it if he didn't mean it, but what about your new jumper?'

Fionn's eyes darted from one to the other as he tugged on his right ear. 'I'm not wearing anything underneath it, I could go home and –'

Maeve laughed at him, shaking her head. 'That scratchy wool must be eating you alive.'

'I'm ashamed to say I've run out of clean clothes,' he admitted, grinning.

Maeve rustled in the airing cupboard in the kitchen and threw a grey-and-white pinstripe shirt towards him, the sleeves splattered in what looked like yellow paint.

'Murtagh already wrecked this one, so you might as well give it a spin.' She laughed again. 'Give it a spin, get it?' The two men looked at her and she threw her hands in the air. 'I'm wasted on you.'

Fionn turned towards the corner and pulled the sweater over his head, bending over as if to hide as much of his exposed back as possible. Maeve noticed a scar to the right of his spine and glanced at Murtagh to see if he'd noticed, too, but he was staring at his feet, steadfastly rubbing at a stain on his boot. Fionn turned around, rolling up the sleeves, which were too long, and tucking the tails of the shirt into his jeans. It smelled of lemony soap, but an earthy undertone broke through. Maybe it was the smell of clay. When Maeve caught him burying his nose in the fabric, he straightened up and returned the small smile she gave him.

Fionn followed Murtagh out of the back door and turned into the lane that would lead them along the pier road to the studio. He looked over his shoulder and saw Maeve watching them from an upstairs window, but she slipped behind the curtain before he could wave.

Fionn had never been inside a potter's studio before and his eyes skipped from one mysterious object to another when Murtagh flicked on the light switch. He gazed at the rolling pins, rulers, the Kilner jars filled with tools, and the ephemera Murtagh used to make impressions in his work: pine cones, shells, buttons, a cheese grater, cookie cutters, pineapple skin, dried seaweed, string. Bags of clay sat beneath a ceramic sink, with a black plastic trash can for the reusable wet clay.

Murtagh led him into a windowless anteroom. 'In this annexe, the magical art of glazing happens.' It looked to Fionn like an apothecary's: to the right, shelves displaying pots retrieved from the kiln ready to glaze; to the left, finished pieces waiting to be packaged; and all across one long, low bench sat the glazed work ready to fire.

Fionn crouched before a row of aluminium buckets and read out their names from the yellow labels on their lids: 'Chrome Red, Yellow Iron, Celadon-Green, Cobalt Blue, Earthen Moss, Black Sapphire, Lugano Blue, South Pacific, Symphony Blue, Sapphire Black and Brilliant White.'

He was shocked to see how pristine everything was, not a speck of dropped clay anywhere. 'That's part of the ritual,' Murtagh explained. 'Every evening, you clean the studio of the day's work so you have a new canvas the next day. You're not polluted by the energy, or the clay, of the day before.'

Fionn returned to the main room and tentatively sat on the potter's stool. He tapped the pedal with his right foot, watching it spin faster and faster. Murtagh rested a hand on his shoulder. 'Hold your horses, young Padawan. You're not going anywhere near the wheel today. First, you need to make friends with the clay.'

Murtagh lifted the lid on a white barrel and withdrew a cylinder of clay. He tore away a handful and began to press and fold it in his hands, softening away its corners. He rolled it across the table towards Fionn. 'Play with it for a bit, see what you can make.'

Fionn stared at the lump of clay in front of him: 'But I don't know what to do.'

'That's because you haven't tried yet. Consider this – when you ask a child to draw you a picture, or tell you a story, they never refuse because they "aren't creative". We just learn as we get older whether we're allowed to call ourselves that any more because we're trained only to invest time in what we are "good at". And it's a tragedy – when we can't create purely for the joy it brings us. Don't be afraid to play, Fionn. It's good for the soul!'

Murtagh left him alone with the clay and retreated to the glazing room, where Fionn could hear him mooching about, lifting the lids on glazes and stirring them, running water in the sink. Reluctantly he took the ball of clay in his hands and squeezed it. Rolled it into a banana shape then squashed it back together. He picked up a rolling pin and spread the clay flat on the table before cutting out an oval. A picture began to form; he worked up two small lumps and found a pair of eyes appearing before a nose, then a mouth and two eyebrows. He rolled long strings in his hands and curled them about the forehead, drew lines on the face with the end of a pencil, made the character smile. When he sat back, he was surprised to see some life there. It unnerved him a little.

He jumped when Murtagh's voice spoke in his ear. 'Excellent work. Now you are ready to enter the wonderful world of pinch pots.' Fionn smiled at him, conscious of his creation coming alive in the room.

'The thing about clay,' Murtagh said as he cleaned the surface with a muslin cloth, 'is its capacity to allow the obsessions of the interior world to become manifest.' And with that, he slapped a mound of fresh clay before Fionn and left him to it.

Over the following weeks, Fionn proved popular with the islanders and students alike; he strummed along on his uke to all the traditional Irish songs they played but could also play ukulele versions of most of the songs in the charts. The older girls at the college translated the lyrics of 'Nothing Compares 2 U' by Sinéad O'Connor into Irish and he accompanied them when they performed it at the weekly Saturday-night concerts they held in the hall. Maeve smiled indulgently as Nollaig gazed up at Fionn on the stage; how many hearts would he be leaving with that summer, she wondered, but she admired him – how he managed to deflect all the crushes without anyone ever feeling crushed. That wasn't easy, she knew, and she was pleased to see his influence on Murtagh. The pottery lessons continued, and their friendship grew, so now the pair often went on walks in the evenings together, covering miles of the island's byways. Sometimes she joined them, but she preferred to do her walking alone. When she asked Murtagh what they talked about he seemed mystified. 'You know, nothing. The usual!' replying, as if he'd never properly considered before how they spent their time at all. But he was moved by the easy camaraderie of their friendship; not since Jeremy had he found another man he could connect with like that, able to discuss life's minutiae in a way that felt so profound. He felt unafraid to be vulnerable with him; to share some of Maeve's struggles, and see how Fionn embraced her as a whole person. It was an unmitigated joy to see how Maeve and Fionn enjoyed each other's company; all of them outsiders on the island finding common ground on their little patch together.

One evening while Murtagh made hot whiskies, Maeve and Fionn sat in two dilapidated wicker chairs in the garden.

'Have you someone back in Birmingham missing you terribly, Fionn?' Maeve asked.

He hesitated before answering, gazing out across the fields that stretched for miles behind the cottage. 'I do, but . . .'

Maeve stood up and stretched into a yoga warrior pose. 'I don't mean to pry. Ignore me.'

He twisted the turquoise fabric bracelet on his left wrist while Maeve waited for him to speak again.

'It's just that I wish they weren't.'

She turned her head slightly to watch him in her peripheral vision.

'Weren't?'

'Weren't missing me.'

She spun her arms in slow circles, clockwise first, then anticlockwise.

'Ah, I see. Well, maybe the distance will have helped.'

He cringed, folding his arms across his chest, and held her gaze. 'You'd think so, wouldn't you?'

Murtagh crunched up the gravelly path to where they sat, three different glass tumblers perched precariously on a tin tray and a packet of chocolate digestives wedged under his arm. Maeve released them from him and tutted. 'That's not the best combination, Murt dear, could you not find anything better?'

'What's better than a chocolate digestive, eh? Delicious any time, anywhere, with any drink.'

She laughed. 'You're getting tipsy.'

He placed the tray unsteadily on the grass between them, spilling some of the whiskey.

'I know,' he said. 'And on a Tuesday night. Isn't life wonderful?'

Fionn stood up and put his chair back against the turf shed wall, where it usually rested.

'You're not off already, are you?' Murtagh asked, his eyebrows arched.

Maeve watched Fionn in silence.

'I just remembered some marking I've to do for the morning. It was when you said Tuesday, it hit me.'

'Will you not finish your drink at least?' Murtagh tried in vain to stand up again.

'No, I'm grand. Stay where you are. I'll see myself out.'

Maeve followed him through the house to the front door and handed him his raincoat from the hook. 'It wasn't something I said, was it?'

He leaned in and kissed her on the cheek. 'Of course not. Thanks, Maeve. I'll see you tomorrow.'

She touched her face where he'd kissed her.

He'd never done that before.

Maeve studied her reflection in the mirror for a moment, licked her middle finger and wiped away a smudge of mascara from under her eyes.

She looked exactly the same but suddenly everything felt utterly different.

Inis Óg: 1 July, 1990

Five hundred thousand people gathered outside the Mansion House in Dublin to welcome home the Irish football team who had, against all odds, reached the World Cup Quarter Finals in Italy. In a joint celebration that electrified the nation, Nelson Mandela would also be accepting the Freedom of the City of Dublin at the same time.

On the previous evening, Maeve prepared packed lunches and coaxed Dillon and Mossy out of their green jerseys for long enough to have them freshly laundered in anticipation.

Nollaig's green-and-orange markers ran out of ink as she feverishly coloured in banners for them to wave while Murtagh marched around the table with the boys chanting, 'Ooh ahh, Paul McGrath'.

A mass exodus was expected from the island on the first ferry and Father Dónal had arranged a coach to bus them from Galway to Dublin and return home that evening. It would be the boys' first time visiting the city and Nollaig delighted in teasing them about her own past experiences:

'When Jeremy visited, we went to the zoo in Dublin, but we won't have time tomorrow, Daddy says, so you won't see the animals, like I did.

'The buildings are so huge you can't even see the sky.

'You have to hold a grown-up's hand all of the time because of the traffic and the kidnappers.'

Mossy's eyes were round as full moons listening to his big sister, but Dillon remained unimpressed. 'They can't kidnap me because I know *karate*!' he shouted, jumping off the sofa with a kick in the air that narrowly missed Bosco.

'Thank you, darling,' Maeve said, pulling Bosco into her lap, 'but no one has to worry about kidnappers. Tomorrow is a day of celebration and the potential kidnappers will be too busy enjoying themselves to be on duty, understood?'

Nollaig sat on the floor in front of her mother so she could plait her hair to keep it under control during the night.

'Now, off to the Land of Nod,' Maeve said, 'or you'll be too sleepy in the morning to get up and we'll miss everything.'

Mossy and Dillon begrudgingly stomped out to brush their teeth while Murtagh carried Sive upstairs in his arms and tucked her in. It took longer than usual for the blanket of silence to smother the house that evening. 'It feels like Christmas Eve,' Murtagh said, pouring himself and Maeve a thimble of brandy. 'I'm excited myself.'

'I'm going to draw a bath,' she said, and ruffled his hair as she passed him. 'You head up to bed, too, and I'll be along soon.'

Murtagh watched his wife leaving the room, noticed the tremble in her fingers as she missed the door handle on her first attempt. He stood up to help but she waved him away with that impatient flick of the wrist that was so familiar. Listening to the pipes cranking into life and his wife's tread on the floorboards overhead, his stomach began to double.

Not tonight. Please, Maeve. Not this time.

When he passed the bathroom door on the way to bed there was but a tiny orange glow creeping under the crack of the door. He pictured the row of tealights staggered along the windowsill, breathed in the lavender essence that curled into the hallway.

Despite his worry about Maeve, the brandy and the comforting embrace of their duck-down duvet lulled him and he fell asleep with his glasses still perched on his nose and A. S. Byatt's new novel, *Possession*, dangling from his grip. He jumped when Nollaig tugged his hand and leaned in close to whisper in his ear, 'What's wrong with Mammy?'

He swung his legs out of the bed and put his arm around her: 'I'll check on her. Don't worry, love,' he said. 'You run back to bed, there's a good girl, we've a big day tomorrow.'

He found Maeve on the bottom step of the stairs, her hound's-tooth shawl tight around her as she stared out at the silver moon through the small hallway window. She softly tapped the side of her head against the bannister, keeping a steady rhythm, as from somewhere deep inside her a low groan dragged across the silent space between them.

Murtagh knelt before her, holding her face in his hands.

'Maeve, are you okay? Will you come to bed with me, my darkling?'

She twisted her neck away. Curled up so her face lay against the carpet on the stairs with her eyes closed.

'It's coming,' she whispered. 'I can feel it settling on my skin like a fog.'

She shivered and Murtagh wrapped his body around hers.

'It will be all right,' he said. 'I promise. Come and get some sleep, maybe you'll feel better in the morning.'

Murtagh picked her up in his arms, just as he had carried their youngest daughter only a few hours before, and slowly climbed the stairs. Her fingers gripped his back, her breath hot on his neck.

He grimaced to see Nollaig watching them from her bedroom doorway, gestured with his head for her to go back to bed, but she ignored him. Instead she stood silently watching them, sucking her thumb, as if they were a float in a parade.

The next morning, Maeve could not drag herself from bed.

Nor bear to have the curtains drawn.

Refused to touch the tea and toast he brought.

The room was dark, stuffy and felt a foreign land to him once again as he manoeuvred through the enforced night time as he tried to retrieve his belongings.

When Fionn rang the doorbell to join their pilgrimage to the ferry it was Nollaig who answered the door, still in her nightdress. 'We're not going,' she said, holding the door open wide for him. 'Daddy's in the kitchen.'

Mossy and Dillon were as stunned by the news of the cancelled trip as Nollaig was not. Dillon threw his glass of juice on the floor then bawled with the shock of the smash. Mossy was even paler than usual as he tugged on the label of the Irish jersey he had put on himself backwards. Murtagh looked up and saw Fionn spectating the scene.

'I'm sorry,' Fionn said. 'I didn't mean to interrupt.'

Murtagh tightened the belt on his robe and told the twins to go with their sister and see if there were any cartoons on.

'But we're not allowed to watch telly in the mornings,' Nollaig protested. 'Just because –'

'This once is fine,' her father interrupted. 'And each of you take a banana.'

Nollaig stomped out after the twins with three bananas scooped up in her nightdress. Murtagh closed the door behind her and Fionn asked quietly, 'Is Maeve all right? What's happened?'

Murtagh sighed, resting his head in his hands on the counter before he spoke again. 'She's fine, but she's not well. It's really not her fault.'

'So, no trip to Dublin?'

'No, and you'd better be on your way or you'll miss the ferry yourself.'

They walked down the hallway together, past *The Flintstones* theme tune blaring through the sitting-room door, and paused on the front step. 'I have to say, if Maeve was my wife, I don't think I could allow her to disappoint everyone like this.'

Murtagh took a step back, and answered, 'If Maeve was your wife, you'd have no choice.' And he slammed the door.

He rested his back against it and jumped at the sound of the doorbell.

Fionn held up his hands.

'I'm sorry,' he said. 'I know I shouldn't have said that. I just . . .'

'No, you shouldn't,' Murtagh replied, but kindly.

'I don't suppose I could bring the kids with me?'

Murtagh hesitated. 'You're kind to offer, but I think it

might be best if we stick together today. They can be a handful. And I don't want to leave Maeve.'

'We could bring them together? Could you ask her? We both know she wouldn't want them to miss it if we could manage it.'

'Please, Daddy.' Murtagh felt Nollaig's small hand in his own.

Fionn gave Murtagh's shoulder a gentle nudge and he reluctantly climbed the stairs. Before he could say a word, Maeve turned her head towards him and told him to go. It was a relief, she said. The right thing.

That evening, Fionn came home with the Moones for a midnight feast of fish and chips. He was sunburnt on his nose, with the faintest whiff of alcohol on his breath, as he doused his food in vinegar. Maeve was nowhere to be seen.

From his rucksack he produced a huge toy koala bear with a green, white and gold scarf tied around his neck. 'I made a new friend today,' he said. 'This is Packie.'

'Like Packie Bonner!' Dillon shouted.

'Exactly,' Fionn said. 'I was wondering if you might be able to look after him for me. He gets bored of adults quickly.'

'He's so cuddly,' Nollaig said, burying her nose in his fur before she passed him to Mossy.

'Can I go show Mammy?' he asked.

'Let's wait until the morning, son.'

Packie soon became a fully-fledged member of the Moone family; his narrative evolved in almost as much detail as the children's did. Murtagh loved to position him in action poses throughout the house while they were at school. They would come home to find Packie reading the newspaper in the living room, or just finished a glass of milk at the kitchen table, listening to classical music as he dozed on the sofa, or polishing the kitchen counter.

And so Fionn had saved the day.

In the memories of the Moone children, the first of July 1990 didn't remain fixed in time as the day they missed the Ireland team homecoming because their mother was sick; instead it became remembered as the day Fionn brought them to Dublin and brought Packie home. And it was the day Fionn unlocked the secret to the Moone family dynamic and became more than a temporary resident on the island; he had a permanent place in their hearts now that would extend beyond the end of summer. Beyond walks, and talks, and hugs. Beyond the three months he spent thinking and dreaming all over the island, and in the most private parts of their home.

Inis Óg: August, 1990

On the twenty-third of August, the last of the summer college students departed, riding the usual waves of hysteria. Murtagh stood with the twins and Sive to watch the *Róisín Dubh* ferry bob away with them, thinking how many of his eggcups would appear on kitchen tables across the country in the coming weeks. As the least expensive piece of his work available in the shop, they were popular mementos for the students of their time on the island. So many of Maeve's black-and-white photographs captured the teenagers in their shop; some with eggcups balanced on their head or held over their ears or noses. It struck him that she hadn't taken many photos that summer; the only time he could remember seeing her camera was the day they had all gone swimming with Fionn and discovered the seal pups in the cove near the lighthouse. He remembered how elegant Fionn had been in the water; how he sliced through the tide like a knife. Maeve took his photograph while he lay drying on a rock, water rivulets dripping from his dreadlocks on to the stone, and she demanded to know if he was really a selkie.

'A selkie?' he'd asked, squinting at her in the sunlight.

'Ancient myths tell us of seal folk who become human when they shed their seal skins on land,' she answered, watching him through the lens. 'They are known for their powers of seduction.'

And Nollaig asked, 'Mammy, what's seduction?'

It was difficult to think of Fionn leaving; he had become so important to the children with his energy, his kindness. Murtagh knew they would be upset to wave him off on the last boat that evening, how Nollaig had been busy all morning making him a card with shells from the beach glued on to it.

As they approached their house, Sive on his shoulders, each boy holding one of his hands, he saw Nollaig running up the lane to meet him. She was crying big, wet tears, and shouting, 'Daddy, Daddy!' He broke into a run, dropping on one knee before her. 'What is it, Nollaig? Is Mammy all right?'

'It's Bosco,' she sobbed. 'He's on the road. Covered in blood. There's ants on him, Daddy!'

Murtagh looked past her as the twins ran ahead. They stopped short over Bosco's body while he sprinted to catch up with them, holding tightly on to Sive. Tears made dirty tracks down Mossy's face, but Dillon was completely still and silent. 'Get me a towel, Nollaig, love. Or a sheet. Quick now. Come away from there, lads. Run inside and call your mam.'

The boys looked relieved to be sent away.

Nollaig came as far as the gate and threw a striped blue sheet off the washing line at him. For a moment, Murtagh hesitated when he saw it was one of the good linens but shook it out, nonetheless. He knelt beside Bosco and closed the dog's eyes, cursing whoever had run him over and left him there for his daughter to find. 'It must have been one of the bikers,' he said, remembering the blessing Father Dónal had given the three shiny new Honda motorcycles that had arrived on the ferry the previous week.

He wrapped Bosco in the sheet and carried him through the house to the back garden, where Mossy was waiting for him.

'Mam won't answer the door,' he said. 'I think she's asleep.'

Murtagh looked up at the bedroom window and saw the curtains were drawn as Nollaig tugged at his sleeve. 'Daddy, we need to have a funeral.'

Murtagh nodded and carried Bosco to the end of the garden, where the cabbages grew. He found a shovel in the shed and started digging, Mossy and Dillon helped with the plastic spades that were normally reserved for sandcastles. Nollaig wrote her mother a note and pushed it under her bedroom door, her ear pressed against the wood to see if she could hear her moving, but there was only silence.

It was the first time Murtagh could remember when all his four children went to bed with no complaints. As if they, too, were glad to see the day's end. Later he caught himself in the act of pouring Bosco's dog food into his bowl as if nothing had happened, then forced himself to gather the dog's belongings and carry them out to the shed. As he walked back across the lawn, undeterred by the damp settling into his socks, he heard the low moan of the last departing ferry on the wind. It struck him that Fionn was gone, and no one had been there to say goodbye. He crouched before Bosco's grave and flattened the clay with the palm of his hand, wondering how he could ever have fallen so much in love with a dog. It was the first time the children had been exposed to a death and it felt much too soon.

Murtagh stood under a scalding shower and wept.

He wept until the water ran cold.

And then wept while he stood there shivering.

Wept as Maeve opened the door of the bathroom and stood watching him for a moment, her face pale, hair matted, Nollaig's note in her hand.

Wept while she held up a towel for him to walk into.

As she sat beside him on the bathroom floor, her arm around him, rubbing his back in small circles.

And then, without a word, they went to bed.

Inis Óg: August, 1994

'I thought when you said we were going camping we'd be going a bit further than our own back garden,' Nollaig protested with a pout, a pillow shoved under one arm, a six-pack of Tayto under the other.

Maeve rolled her eyes at her daughter as she spread her own tattered yellow sleeping bag on the grass beside their tent. 'Camping isn't about where you go, darling,' she said. 'It's about the adventure of sleeping outdoors, under the stars, breathing the night air in our lungs. And besides, this way, we can still use a proper loo.'

Murtagh opened the back door, balancing a tray with mugs of hot chocolate and a basket of cocktail sausages dribbled in mustard and ketchup. The twins burst past, almost toppling him over, carrying a *Thomas the Tank Engine* duvet between them. 'We're eight now!' Dillon shouted. 'So we can stay up as late as we want, can't we, Mammy?'

He was wearing mismatching pyjamas and red slippers on the wrong feet. Maeve pulled him into her lap and swapped the slippers over. 'Tonight, you certainly can. Have you brushed your fiacla?' He bared his teeth and pushed his face close to hers. 'Gleaming,' she said, and kissed him on the nose.

'Mammy, Mammy, check mine.' Sive opened her mouth

wide and Maeve shone a torch inside to give a thorough inspection. 'Excellent work.'

Maeve stood up, clapping her hands. 'Now it's time for the performances.'

She stepped on to the wooden pallet Murtagh had positioned in the garden; four tall ivory candles perched on saucers in each corner to denote the stage.

'For tonight's concert, each child will take to the stage in alphabetical order.' She looked across the grass at her children. 'So, who does that mean goes first?'

'*Dillon!*' Mossy shouted, 'D for Dillon!' Murtagh high-fived him and he beamed, while Dillon reluctantly stood up on the pallet.

'I'm going to tell some jokes,' he said, shyly at first. 'But if you've heard them before, you have to laugh anyway. Them's the rules.' When he was nervous, he developed a slight lisp.

'Ladies and gentlemen,' Maeve announced, 'I bring you the comedy stylings of Dillon Moone.' Murtagh wolf-whistled and flashed his torch on and off at the stage.

Dillon started his routine, barely pausing before each punchline and the next joke. It was hard to follow, but he laughed so hard himself it became infectious.

What's brown and sticky? A stick.

What did one snowman say to the other? Can you smell carrot?

What do you call a dinosaur that's sleeping? A dino-SNORE.

What is fast, loud and crunchy? A rocket CHIP.

Why was 6 afraid of 7? Because 7 8 9.

Why did the cookie go to the doctor? Because he felt crumby.

How do we know the sea is friendly? It waves.

What do you call a funny mountain? HILL-arious.

Sive didn't understand all the jokes, but she laughed the loudest, running forward to plant a sloppy kiss on Dillon's face as he gave a big bow and stepped off the pallet stage. She idolised him, even though it was Mossy who took the best care of her. She was only the first of many who would love Dillon unconditionally in his life, spoil him with her love, and prevent him from ever truly learning from his mistakes, but it would have been impossible to predict then how his heart would one day harden as he returned his little sister's embrace.

Nollaig was already standing up, waiting for her father to introduce her.

'Now, for something a little different, Nollaig June Moone will read to us her prize-winning essay on the hole in the ozone layer, "CFC-U-Later"'.

'Not again,' Dillon moaned, his mouth stuffed with cock-tail sausages. 'I'm sick of CFCs.'

'Now, now, son,' Murtagh interrupted. 'You appreciated an attentive audience for your comedy repertoire, so please show your sister the same courtesy. I, for one, can't get enough of the CFC chat.' Nollaig stepped up on to the pallet, pushed her glasses further up her nose, and began.

'CFC is an acronym for chlorofluorocarbon. These are hydrocarbons that contain carbon, chlorine and fluorine. CFCs are often found in fridges and spray cans such as deodorants or air fresheners. They are —'

Dillon started to make loud snoring noises and Mossy and Sive buried their faces in the pillows to smother their laughter while Nollaig continued obliviously. Maeve poked

Dillon with her foot until he stopped. While Nollaig persevered through seven pages of her copybook, Maeve reclined
against Murtagh's knees and he rubbed her shoulders. He
whispered in her ear, 'You weren't having an affair with a
scientist before Nollaig was born, by any chance?' She
slapped his knee and whispered back, 'That's all you, darling, I'm afraid.'

'And that is why' – Nollaig paused for dramatic effect,
putting the copybook down and clasping her hands together
before she continued – 'we must all unite and shout, "CFC-
U-Later".' She waited a moment for her applause, but her
parents chimed in a beat too late and she stomped off the
pallet and plonked down on her sleeping bag with a disappointed sigh. It's not easy saving the planet when you're
nine.

'Excellent work, darling!' Maeve called out as she crawled
across the grass towards the stage. 'Entertaining and
educational – what more could we ask for?' Nollaig didn't
meet her eye but focused instead on submerging marshmal-
lows in her hot chocolate, enduring the burn on her
fingertips.

'And now for our penultimate performance, we have a
double act extraordinaire. I present to you Tomás, a.k.a.
Mossy, Moone and Sive Moone.'

Mossy gripped his electric-blue ukulele hard in his right
hand and Sive's sweaty palm in his left. They had been practising for days but he still didn't think they were ready. He
sat on the edge of the pallet and plucked each string to check
it was still in tune. Maeve nodded at him reassuringly and
then he began strumming the three chords of 'This Little

Light of Mine'. Sive joined in at the wrong time, forgot which verse she was on and sang in a completely different key but performed with total conviction. It was ridiculous and sensational, and the family cheered madly at the end. Sive hid in the folds of her mother's nightdress while Mossy carefully packed away his ukulele in the tartan case, the one he'd requested to be just like Fionn's, and brought it back indoors for safety.

'Is it your turn, Mammy?' Sive looked up at her mother. 'Will you sing us a song?'

Maeve looked over at Murtagh, who gave her a big thumbs-up, so, with feigned shyness, she stood barefoot on the pallet and began to sing about all of her favourite things in a perfect imitation of Julie Andrews. As she reached the final chorus, Murtagh handed her a pillow case and she moved through the children, producing for each of them a present wrapped in brown paper and tied with string. For Nollaig, a red-and-black checked notebook with a yellow pen tucked into the spine; for Dillon, a slinky that he immediately started chasing around the garden; for Mossy, a cassette of play-along ukulele classics; for Sive, a fluffy-cloud teddy with a smiling face and long, fluttering eyelashes. All to become new favourites.

When they eventually settled down, no one wanted to sleep inside the big blue tent, so they arranged their sleeping bags on the grass in a circle with their heads almost touching in the centre. Maeve listened to her children wriggling and burrowing down, and when a calm fell, she said, 'Let's all take it in turns to say one thing we like and one thing we don't like.' She paused. 'You know, that's sometimes all you have to go on in the world, trusting your own instincts, my loves. I'll go first. I like sleeping outside with my family, when the stars are shining like light bulbs in the sky. I don't like when some of those same people get toast crumbs in the butter.'

Sive giggled and whispered, 'Sorry, Mammy,' and her mother leaned over to kiss her cheek.

Murtagh was next. 'I like when I have all my pots made for the week and know I have the whole weekend to relax with my mad Moones. I don't like when I get hay fever and can't stop sneezing. Nollaig?'

'I like winning essay competitions. I don't like PE, especially camogie,' she said.

'I'm with you there,' Maeve answered. 'I always hated gym, too. All that unnecessary sweating. Awful.'

Dillon piped up next. 'I like free-wheeling on my bike. I don't like essays about CFCs.'

'Daddy!' Nollaig shouted. 'That's not fair. My essay can't be the thing he doesn't like. I want to change mine. I don't like when Dillon is a pain.'

'Sssssshh, love,' Murtagh said. 'He's only teasing. Dillon, can you think of something else you don't like, please, son?'

'Fine, I don't like cheese.'

'Lovely,' Murtagh said. 'How about you, Mossy?'

'I like learning new songs on the uke. I don't like that Fionn isn't here to teach me any more.'

'Aw, Moss,' Maeve said. 'I'm sure he'll come visit again soon and you'll have loads of new songs to play him. Sive, are you still awake, love?'

'Yes, Mammy. I like singing with Mossy. I don't like when you get sad.'

Murtagh reached out and took Maeve's hand.

'Well,' he said. 'I think we should all close our eyes now and try to get some sleep. The back door is open if you need anything during the night. Goodnight, my dears.'

'Daddy!' Sive called. 'I didn't get a kiss goodnight.'

'Oh, you never miss a trick,' he said. 'I'll come and do the rounds.'

He crawled out of his sleeping bag and planted a strong kiss on each child's forehead.

Sive whispered in her mother's ear, 'Will you carry me inside to the loo, Mammy?'

'Carry you?' Maeve smiled. 'You're a bit big for that now, aren't you, darling?'

'I know,' she said, reaching up her arms. 'But just one last time, then?'

Maeve scooped her daughter up and held her tight as she carried her indoors, her face buried in her hair.

When she returned she lay down on her back with her eyes closed. Murtagh stood over her, watching her diaphragm rise and fall with deep breaths. In the moonlight, she glowed unnaturally bright. He swallowed a sense that her future was written in those blue veins that ran in rivulets under her porcelain skin, like tiny cracks in a vase. Would a weakness in the work eventually cause it to shatter? Or were the fault lines where the strength was?

He crouched down and rubbed her feet through the sleeping bag; Maeve pulled away, but he tugged her foot harder and she sat up on her elbows to see him beckon her with a tip of his head. She sighed but slid out of her bag and followed him around the side of their house to the front wall.

'Do you remember we used to call this our worry wall?' he said. 'No worries allowed past the gate.'

She climbed up and sat with her back to the house, her bare legs grazing the damp cobblestones. 'If my mother could see me, she'd say I'd get a cold in my kidneys sitting here.'

Murtagh stood behind her, rubbing warmth into her arms, and she leaned her head back against his chest. He inhaled her apple smell, and swallowed hard. 'Will you do the nightingale poem for me, love?' he asked, his voice muffled by her hair.

'Seriously? I don't know if I remember – Are you sure? Keats? Now?'

'Do it for me, my darkling, whatever you remember.'

'Maybe just a little bit, then,' she said, and leaned forward, placing both palms down on the mossy wall on either side of her.

'My heart aches,' she began, paused, and started again, her voice more confident now.

> 'My heart aches, and a drowsy numbness pains
> My sense, as though of hemlock I had drunk,
> Or emptied some dull opiate to the drains
> One minute past, and Lethe-wards had sunk:
> 'Tis not through envy of thy happy lot,
> But being too happy in thine happiness –
> That thou, light-wingèd Dryad of the trees,
> In some melodious plot

Of beechen green, and shadows numberless,
Singest of summer in full-throated ease.

Fade far away, dissolve, and quite forget
What thou among the leaves hast never known,
The weariness, the fever, and the fret
Here, where men sit and hear each other groan;
Where palsy shakes a few, sad, last grey hairs,
Where youth grows pale, and spectre-thin, and dies;
Where but to think is to be full of sorrow
And leaden-eyed despairs;
Where Beauty cannot keep her lustrous eyes,
Or new Love pine at them beyond to-morrow.

Darkling I listen; and, for many a time
I have been half in love with easeful Death,
Call'd him soft names in many a musèd rhyme,
To take into the air my quiet breath;
Now more than ever seems it rich to die,
To cease upon the midnight with no pain,
While thou art pouring forth thy soul abroad
In such an ecstasy!
Still wouldst thou sing, and I have ears in vain –
To thy high requiem become a sod.

Forlorn! the very word is like a bell
To toll me back from thee to my sole self!
Adieu! the fancy cannot cheat so well
As she is famed to do, deceiving elf.
Adieu! adieu! thy plaintive anthem fades

Past the near meadows, over the still stream,
Up the hill-side; and now 'tis buried deep
In the next valley-glades:
Was it a vision, or a waking dream?
Fled is that music: – Do I wake or sleep?'

Inis Óg: February, 1996

Dear Diary,

The wind is blowing from the east.

What a torment.

It always brings one of my headaches with it, scattering debris about my feet, unearthing saplings of hope before their roots are secure.

It carries the voices from the schoolyard into my room as if the radio was blaring static in the air between stations.

Murtagh loves to hear it, the life from the schoolyard, but it chills me.

They sound like a flock of seagulls screeching, competing with each other to banish any ounce of silence. I hate to think of my own children amongst them.

Are they being drowned out, or are they the drowners?

I sometimes wonder who they are when we aren't there to witness their behaviour, who they will become after we've gone.

Sometimes they feel like strangers to me.

As if they belong to someone else.

As if I am babysitting and their real mother will come to collect them soon.

Not that I could ever say such a thing aloud, not even to Murtagh, who loves to spot the little bits of me and him in them as they appear.

I hate that game. It frightens me to think what genes I have passed along, genes they may already be hiding.

Of course, I love them.

Of course, I do.

But sometimes I feel I've somehow kept them at arm's length, like I don't want to become too attached to them, or they to me. That's absurd, though, isn't it? And I've never been very good at keeping my distance, despite my best/worst intentions.

I need to know they love me, and sometimes I test them.

Pull away to see if they will chase me.

That's not an easy thing to confess, even to myself, but I do.

Murtagh never seems to have these struggles, he says your heart gets bigger the more you love. That the more energy he gives the children, the more it energises him.

But it's not more heart I need, just some peace, some privacy, some time to myself.

I suppose it must be different for men, they've never felt their child feed on their own body, take their life source from theirs.

I feel Nollaig monitoring me sometimes, so suspicious.

I think she can read my mind. It's ridiculous, but I find it unnerving and it brings out the worst in me. Last night I felt her watching me from the landing as I massaged rose oil into my legs. Why wouldn't she come in instead of lurking about?

In those moments I know I should reach out to her, call her closer, but something holds me back. Instead I stretched my leg out and slammed the door with my foot without ever looking up.

What are all these minor aggressions doing to us?

I don't know, but I'll make it up to her.

I always do.

And we'll forget anything ever happened.

Or at least never mention it, and that's the same thing in the end, isn't it?

I don't know what I would do if I couldn't write these lines into the ether. My mother used to warn me never to write anything down you wouldn't want to see on the front page of the newspaper, but I'm not worried. No one is interested enough in what mothers think for it to make headline news.

As long as nobody starves and the children turn up for school, nobody asks any questions.

It's okay for women to starve, though, a little bit, enough to be as skinny as possible without getting ill. The purpose of the body has nothing to do with their own health or well-being, as long it pleases others and works as an incubator. I try to teach my daughters the opposite, but I am no advertisement, I know.

I must try harder.

What lessons am I teaching them through my very existence?

Eat well but don't get fat, be slim but not too skinny.

Follow your dreams but prioritise your family.

Dress well for your own esteem only, but never leave the house without your make-up on.

Be confident but not aggressive.

Be sociable but not loud.

Celebrate your talents but don't be arrogant.

Don't settle for less than love but don't have unrealistic expectations of love.

I don't know how to advise them to be a woman of the world because what can I honestly tell them? You will never get it right, so please yourself?

I wish someone had told me that once upon a time.

Then maybe I wouldn't be filled with so much white noise.

If I wriggle my toes, I can hear it crackling, running on a power grid throughout my body, accumulating in this screaming inside my head.

Harmonising with that flock of seagulls from the school-yard into a vicious cacophony.

Dancing on that easterly wind, whispering in my ears.

I'll try to sleep, close the curtains, cover my head with the heaviest blankets.

In my dreams, sometimes I am deaf to the noise.

If I am ever so quiet, the wind might blow past me instead of through me.

If I make myself very small.

Inis Óg: October, 2001

After changing out of her school uniform, Nollaig slipped quietly out of the house to avoid an interrogation about where she was going. Just in case, her story was straight: maths grinds at Dervla's; nothing suspicious there, but she'd rather not fib if possible. Lying contravened the high ethical code against which she measured herself at all times. The truth, and resisting the temptation to hide snacks in her room, were the principal pillars of her virtues, although she upheld the former more successfully than the latter; it was hard to binge in front of a mother whose nose twitched when any food packaging crinkled.

Meeting Aindí O'Shea at the back of the boathouse didn't strictly fall in line with her morality guidelines either, but it was okay, she decided, as long as nothing untoward happened. Agreeing to meet him there implied nothing. She would make that perfectly clear and, if need be, he would just have to reconsider his expectations, disappointing though that may be for him.

The handle of her hairbrush protruded at an awkward angle from the pocket of her cardigan and hit her right knee with every step. Maybe bringing it had been a mistake, but she wanted to wrestle her mop into submission once she reached the pier after walking in the wind. Her new white jeans were splashed with mud before she made it to the end of the lane, but she hoped he wouldn't notice. It was hardly her fashion sense he was interested in – that was never her forte – although she struggled to think what it was he did see in her. Before leaving the note in her school locker, he'd never paid her any attention at all, much as she'd tried to attract it. The sporty girls were more his speed. Wasn't that the way it always worked? The GAA football lads with the camogie girls, the muso girls with the grungy boys, and the kids whose parents socialised at the golf club drawn together by the sheer magnetism of their genes. Nollaig wasn't sure where she fitted, but maybe it was her individuality Aindí liked. Maybe. She pulled her shoulders back and walked taller.

Nollaig paused on the pier, brushed her hair vigorously with exactly one hundred strokes, and wiped her clammy hands on her jeans. The sandals were a mistake, too, she thought, too childish, but it would have been a bit much to clamber down here in her mother's high heels. She pulled in her stomach and tried to walk nonchalantly around the cliff edge towards their meeting point. It was difficult to know from how far away he could see her approaching and eager was never a good look. She rubbed her teeth with a hand-kerchief in case they'd been stained by her orange-red lipstick and wished she had thought to bring a little mirror. One more deep breath, and it was time.

When she looked around the edge of the boathouse she was surprised to see that Aindí was still in his school uni-form. A black T-shirt peeked out from the open collar of his school shirt, the grey tie hanging from his pocket. This was taking casual to a whole new level. He was sitting with the

GAA gym holdall the lads all used as a school bag open beside him and frowning in concentration at a yellow copybook. He didn't stand up when he saw her there, but smiled out from under his long brown hair, parted in the middle like a pair of curtains. Disappointingly, the roots were greasy.

'Nollaig! Thanks a million for coming. Sorry if it all seems a bit weird – asking you to meet here like this.'

Nollaig perched on a boulder close to him, conscious of how her top rose up a little over the waistband of her jeans, exposing her lower back and what Dervla called her cute little muffin top.

'It's not weird,' she answered, with a wink. 'Sure, isn't this what all the kids are doing these days?'

He looked a bit bewildered but gave a half-hearted laugh.

'The thing is, Noll –'

He paused as she slid down the side of the rock and inched a little closer.

'The thing is,' he continued, 'I failed maths in the mid-term and Pat says if I don't get at least a C at Christmas he's going to drop me from training. I can't let on at home or my da will fleece me, so I was hoping you might be able to give me a few grinds? Just between ourselves, like? Dervla said you've saved her life.'

Nollaig drew little circles in the sand with her finger then brushed them away.

'Dervla? Are you two friendly?'

'Did she not tell ya we're seeing each other? Don't tell her ma, though, or she'll hit the roof. She has it in for me big time since we had that end-of-summer party at her house.

Terribly sensitive about her *gladioli*, it seems. You were there, weren't you?'

'No, I wasn't.'

With some effort, she stood up, so her shadow fell across him.

'I can do Tuesdays after school – if we meet in the library, we can catch the later ferry home. Okay?'

He punched her in the leg. 'You're a legend, Noll. Thanks a million. And you won't tell anyone, will you?'

She shook her head.

'Are you walking back to the village?' she asked.

'No, go on ahead there. Derv is meeting me here at seven. It must be nearly that now.' He pulled out his mobile and squinted at the screen. 'See ya Tuesday, so.'

Nollaig gave him a little wave, but he was so engrossed in texting that he didn't look up to see it. As soon as she turned from the pier she started to run. The hairbrush fell from her pocket, but she didn't bother picking it up.

She wouldn't cry. No way. Why would she cry over that snake in the grass and that big eejit getting together? It was his loss.

While Nollaig had been beautifying herself for her pseudo-date, Sive had been busy pretending to do her homework at the back of the St Francis's School music room. She was so elated to be in the boys' school that it was difficult for her to concentrate. It smelled different from her own convent school on the other side of the river; after only two months as a first-year there, she still hadn't become indifferent to the new-school odour that assaulted her every time she spun through its blue revolving doors: fresh paint, bleach, the stew of fried onions, cheese and milk that lingered around the home economics kitchens, the chemicals that crept under the door of the science lab, and an underlying scent of dust and damp that she decided was the aroma of nuns. In St Francis's, however, all she could smell was boy: a low hum of body odour, rubber footballs and Lynx deodorant.

She had been to the dentist after school so Mossy and Dillon had reluctantly agreed to her sitting in on their band rehearsal so they could catch the last ferry back to the island together. As long as she 'stayed out of the way' and 'didn't make a show of them'. Babysitting your little sister, Dillon proclaimed, 'was not very rock and roll'. She sat with her back to a freezing-cold radiator and stretched her legs out on her schoolbag. With her French folder open unconvincingly on her lap, she watched her brothers laboriously arrange their gear on the little stage at the top of the classroom. Mossy tuned his Sunburst LA electric guitar while Dillon helped their new drummer, Podge Harrington, set up his kit. 'You know how many times bands have covered "Johnny B. Goode"?' he shouted over at Mossy. 'Like, three hundred or something. Mr McEvoy told me – we should be doing something different.'

Mossy ignored him, nodding at Barry Ramsbottom, who had arrived with his bass guitar wrapped in a black plastic bag.

'No case yet?' Podge asked, and Barry shook his head. 'No, I'm still paying for the new patio window, so I'm broke. Ma said she might get me one for Christmas – *if* there's no more trouble.'

He plugged his bass into the amp and caught Sive's eye. 'Who's this, then? Our first groupie?'

Dillon threw an apple core at him. 'Leave it out, Barry, that's our kid sister – ignore her.'

'I'm not sure I'm ready to play in front of an audience,' he said, plucking each string in turn, each note ringing clean.

Dillon laughed. 'She's not an audience, she's not even listening to us. C'mere, have you thought about any names? I was thinking Slime or Thunk, ya know? Something short that will look big on posters?'

Podge snorted, hitting his snare drum absent-mindedly. 'What posters?'

'For our gigs, stupid. We have to be gigging by the summer, that's the plan.'

'Well, no one's going to go and see a band called Slime, are they?' Barry said. 'I wouldn't want to go and I'm *in* the band.'

'I had an idea,' Mossy said. 'What about Night and Day?'

Dillon sighed, shaking his head. 'You mean like Mam calls us? No way, Moss. Why not just call ourselves The Twins and be done with it?'

Podge jumped in. 'Well, because there's four of us, for a start. I like it, I'm with Mossy. It sounds like a Smashing Pumpkins song. We could do cool artwork with moons and suns and stuff. Barry, you have the deciding vote.'

Barry shrugged, guzzled half a bottle of Lucozade and wiped his mouth on the sleeve of his school jumper. 'It's better than Slime, I suppose.'

Podge high-fived Mossy with more gusto than was returned and scrawled *Night and Day* across the whiteboard behind them in blue marker.

'Sive, will you take a picture? For the archives.' Mossy pulled out a Polaroid camera from his army-surplus school-bag. She walked towards them, pausing halfway to pull up her stockings, then looked at them through the lens of the boxy black camera.

Dillon sat on the front of the stage, legs spread wide in the uniform slacks that his mother had transformed into skinny drainpipes for him. He was still sulking about their name but tilted his head expertly away from the camera so his curls fell across one eye, like she'd seen him practising at home.

Podge pulled his blond ponytail over his shoulder and held his drumsticks in a cross over his head.

Barry posed with his bass balanced on one raised knee, his head of fuzzy ginger thrown back so the acne on his Adam's apple was exposed.

Mossy lurked beside his amp, turning his head at the moment of the click so that his face became a blur of blond hair and black bobble hat.

The photo whirred out of the camera and Sive shook it gently between her fingers while they clumsily launched into 'Johnny B. Goode'. Each band member seemed completely oblivious to what the other three were doing, and Dillon just made up his own words. His performance was predominantly swagger, but what he lacked in talent he more than compensated for with attitude.

Sive sat back down and discreetly twisted little rolls of tissue paper into her ears. She wrote *Night and Day, 25 October, 2001* on the white strip at the bottom of the Polaroid picture with a purple metallic pen and watched them run through the song for the third time.

She wondered how long it would be before they realised that Mossy was the twin who could sing and if she could convince him to give her guitar lessons.

She considered how good she could be by the time she was sixteen if she started practising now, started listing band names in her notebook, and soon Night and Day did lose her attention as she dissolved into her interior world. It seemed there were more interesting things than boys after all. It was a relief.

Just before six, the janitor stuck his head around the door with a five-minute warning and the rehearsal wound down. Sive saw Mossy slide his lunchbox on the floor over to Podge, where he sat packing his drums. Without a word, and without meeting his eye, Podge took out Mossy's leftover sandwiches and a Twix and shoved them in his schoolbag.

On the walk to the pier, Dillon trailed his bag along the street, listening to Fugazi at full volume through his headphones. His siblings ignored him and talked about Sive's art project for her school's upcoming exhibition.

'I'm thinking about selkies,' she said. 'I'm wondering if I can use the photos I took of the seals but try to draw the metamorphoses on the prints themselves. Do you know what I mean?'

Mossy thought about it for a moment. 'It might work if you scratched out the ink on the photos with a needle? And then drew over them? Have you talked to Mam about it? You know she loves those selkie stories. I'd say she'd have some ideas.'

She stopped to tighten the laces of her Doc Marten boots. 'No,' she said, without looking up at him. 'Don't mention anything, will you?'

Dillon tuned into the conversation as a song ended. 'Why don't you want Mam to know?' he asked, giving her shoulder a nudge so she lost her balance.

'It's no big deal,' she said, walking now. 'I just don't know if I can cope with her coming to the school yet, that's all. None of my new friends have even met her.'

The brothers strode along on either side of her, Mossy attempting to catch Dillon's eye to gesture for him to calm down, but he was too slow. Dillon grabbed his sister's arm and turned her towards him. '*Sive!*' he shouted. 'That's so lousy. You sound like you're ashamed of her. I'm so telling her what you said. I bet you'll want Dad there, though, right?'

Mossy pushed him away and walked between them. 'It's okay, Si,' he said. 'I know she can be a bit . . . unpredictable, but she'd want to be there.'

'I know,' she replied, her eyes growing wet. 'But I just don't want to be worrying if she'll make it and then be disappointed when she doesn't show. I'd prefer to not have her involved at all and then I don't have to worry about it.'

Dillon shook his head at his sister then sprinted off down the street, headphones restored to his head, drowning out her voice as she called after him.

Mossy picked up Sive's schoolbag and slung it over his shoulder.

'Don't worry,' he said. 'He won't say anything. You know he hates any chat about Mam. The Unmentionables.'

On the ferry, Dillon stood on his own on the top deck, seemingly oblivious to the bitter wind that blew through him, while Mossy and Sive huddled against a radiator in the cabin.

Dillon's eyes stayed fixed on the mainland; Mossy's searched for the island.

Mossy thought about what he had said; why there was so much silence around the topic of their mother. Her unknowable state of being lingered over every future plan: would they go on holidays this year? Could friends come and stay during the summer? Would Dad finally visit Japan with Jeremy? Their daily lives were consumed by temperature-taking: listening as they came through the door for her voice; catching a whiff of whiskey from her breath as she kissed them goodnight; seeing the curtains drawn in her bedroom. Their father refused to discuss it, but when did children ever need to have what they witnessed explained? Even if they couldn't name the truth, they could feel it in their bones.

He remembered one day as Sive ate fishfingers at the kitchen table how she had asked their father if Mammy was mad. 'That's what the kids say in school,' she said. ' "Psycho Mammy", that's what Kitty Malone said. What's a Psycho Mammy?'

Murtagh had swiped her plate away, snatching a piece of fish from her hand, and pulled her up off her chair. Mossy watched him lean in close to her face and say in a terrible voice he'd never heard before, 'Kitty Malone is a wicked girl. Don't ever let me hear you say such things again. Your mother gets poorly sometimes, all right? Just like we all do.'

Sive started crying. 'Am I in deep trouble, Daddy?'

He gave his daughter a hug. 'Of course not, love, but remember what I said. Okay?'

A few minutes later Mossy followed his father out of the

house and saw him striding off in the direction of the Malones' farm.

He wondered now if that's how adults ended up so insecure; so often children are told not to trust their instincts by parents who think the truth is too blinding. It had happened to the Moones and now they were all committed to a family narrative that could never be unravelled. They could say their mother was embarrassing, exhausted, eccentric even, but never mad. They had learned not to ask where she was at times when she should be there, to pretend not to notice how she drifted into herself sometimes when they were all together, or to be surprised by finding her sitting alone on the stairs, staring into space. And Dillon was the greatest advocate for that story; he wouldn't – he couldn't – see the truth. Could only hold one image of his mother in his mind; as if to accept her troubles was to negate her love.

As the boat carrying her siblings docked at the port, Nollaig was bursting through the front door, where Maeve was hanging up the telephone in the hallway. 'Woah, woah!' she called as her daughter brushed past her and pounded up the stairs. Maeve ran after her and arrived just in time for the bedroom door to slam in her face. She knocked once, twice, and then gently inched the door open. Nollaig was scrubbing off her make-up with facial wipes from a plastic tub she squeezed between her knees.

'Honey, what is it? Did something happen?'

'No, of course not. Nothing ever happens to me.'

Maeve caught her daughter's eye in the mirror and edged closer.

'Do you want to talk about it?' she asked, smoothing the hair back from her daughter's face.

Nollaig shook her head. 'I just want to have a lie down.'

'But it's only seven o'clock.'

'Mam, I'm tired, okay? You get to go to bed whenever you want, so why not me?'

Maeve released her hands from her daughter and stepped back.

'Well, if you change your mind, I'll be downstairs.'

She walked out of the room with all the grace that Nollaig had so desperately aspired to earlier.

'Mammy, I'm sorry!' Nollaig called after her.

Maeve paused then swung the bedroom door back open.

'Darling, I don't know what's happened, but I could hazard a guess,' she said, watching Nollaig in the mirror. 'All I will say to you is this, someone will come along who will never make you feel like this, who will only make you feel stronger, happier, alive in yourself. As soon as a boy makes you doubt yourself, or puts you down, or dismisses you, or does anything to you that makes you feel disrespected, then that is the same moment you walk away and refuse to give him any more of your time. It really is that simple.'

Nollaig turned around on her stool. 'But Mammy, he hasn't done anything to me. That's the problem. He doesn't even see me.' She blew her nose in the wipe in her hand and dropped it on her dressing table.

'Well, thankfully, no one can force anyone else to love them,' Maeve said. 'But the right person will see you, at the right time. And until then, you don't surrender your ability to be happy to anyone. Okay? And if you can make that your philosophy now, you'll save yourself so much pain, darling. I promise you.'

Maeve gave her daughter a hug that wasn't met with the usual resistance.

'It's easier said than done, Mammy,' Nollaig mumbled into her shoulder.

Maeve looked straight into her daughter's eyes.

'Really? Does this feel easier to you?' she asked, handing her a handkerchief. 'Now, I've been busy organising boxes from the attic this afternoon and have some photographs of your father and me that should cheer you up. Come on, I'll show you.'

Maeve led her daughter by the hand down the stairs to where the contents of a battered rucksack were spread across the kitchen table.

Nollaig noticed how straight her mother sat and mirrored her posture.

'Are you sure I'll meet someone, Mammy?' she asked as her mother opened a photo album with a blue velvet cover.

She rested her hand on Nollaig's. 'Honestly, no, I'm not,' she said. 'How could anyone know such a thing?'

Nollaig slumped on her stool, but Maeve lifted up her chin and ignored her squirming.

'You know what I am sure of, though?' she asked. Nollaig shook her head, still in her mother's grip.

'I know that you won't settle for anyone. And even if you did end up on your own, you would be completely fine. You are worth more than being defined by a relationship. Got it?'

Nollaig nodded. She was Maeve Moone's daughter, after all, and she decided that counted for something.

Dillon stormed into the kitchen first, with Sive and Mossy trailing behind. Their row was temporarily forgotten as the album drew them like a magnet towards photos of the life their parents had lived before they were born:

- Maeve drinking cider on a bench at the Dandelion Market in flares and a frilly blouse.
- Maeve and Murtagh at a bonfire on Dollymount Strand where people sat playing guitars in the dunes.
- Maeve with Edna O'Brien at a book signing in Foyles on Charing Cross Road in London.
- A Polaroid of them either side of Bob Geldof in Temple Bar.
- Maeve with her theatre group at Trinity College, all dressed in red polo necks and black dungarees.

Photos of when they were just lovers; before they were parents.

They looked like people their children would want to be friends with.

As beautiful as only strangers can be.

Sive slipped away to her bedroom and returned with a manila envelope of her own photographs. Laying them out side by side on the kitchen counter, Maeve stood beside her daughter and absorbed the images of the seals. 'Tell me their story,' she said, and Sive began to explain her vision for the project: how people change to survive their environments, how love can trap you in a prison of your own making. And

Maeve wondered where her daughter had learned these human truths.

It was after midnight when the mother and daughter followed the rest of the family to bed.

Sive was full of inspiration, with the new confidence in her work that Maeve had awarded her.

Maeve was acutely proud of her daughter's ambition.

And when, two weeks later, they stood before Sive's exhibition at the secondary school, it felt as if Sive had taken her first steps into the world as an artist.

With a little nudge from her mother, she saw what her purpose should be and she realised, with a deep sense of shame, how much Maeve had prepared her for this.

At last she saw Maeve as an inspiration, a creative woman with something to say, whose genius was so often hidden. She no longer saw her as just the mother who she'd longed to behave like all her friends' mammies. She realised that whatever she had felt was missing in Maeve was made up for in ways that were much more important.

Instead of a burden, Maeve became a blessing. And though some days would come again when she found that hard to remember, she would never now unlearn that truth.

From a woman, a woman was born.

Inis Óg: December, 2004

Maeve waited alone for her family to return. Sitting on the damp back doorstep, her bare legs trembled beneath her white linen dress as she sipped whiskey from a mug Murtagh had made. In the distance she could hear Áine O'Connor's family cheering as they turned on Christmas lights, but Maeve's own house was silent.

Her mind raged, spiralling to the edge of her sanity, before collapsing in upon itself once more. She stumbled back inside the house and recovered her balance against the kitchen sink.

Before her plan became cognisant Maeve's hand found the last-remaining sea-green vase of those Seamus O'Farrell had left them all those years before, and she threw it with all her strength at the wall. It smashed into smithereens on the floor tiles. She wrapped a shawl around her and fled back into the night, walking over the broken pieces of vase in bare feet.

There was no moon in the sky as Maeve wound along the lane to the chapel on the hill.

Inside, she stood before the votive candles with their patient wicks, her hands shaking as she searched in vain for some matches to light one.

In the shadow of the crypt she lay on the marble tiles and stared at a statue of the Virgin Mary that blurred before her

eyes. The mother against which all Irish mothers were measured, and condemned if found lacking.

It was there that Murtagh found her, her feet blue and
eyes red, curled up into a tight little ball.

He shook her gently, and she quietly followed him, his
hand holding hers inside the pocket of his duffel coat.

But they didn't speak.

There were no new words to discuss old ways.

The silence lengthened between them.

At home, she crawled into bed in the same clothes, and
Murtagh left her alone to prepare a bed for himself in the
living room.

All evidence of this was gone by morning; the smell of
baking bread wafted through the house, as usual.

Maeve didn't come down for breakfast, and no one asked
where she had been the evening before, as Gerry Ryan's
voice boomed out from the radio to fill the silence.

Sive stared at her father as he buttered a stack of digestive
biscuits to take to the studio with him for lunch.

She thought he looked older but convinced herself she
was imagining it.

There was a loud bang from overhead, and it sent a charge
through the kitchen.

When after a moment there was no further noise they
continued mechanically eating the soggy scrambled eggs that
normally provoked their derision.

A strange heightened feeling had settled amongst them,
like an unwanted stray.

A new vase was sitting in the middle of the table.

Inis Óg: September, 2005

'I'll be home on the last ferry this evening, if not before, love,' Murtagh said.

Maeve was stretched across the living-room sofa surrounded by the weekend papers, two half-drunk cups of coffee on the carpet beside her, a bowl of red grapes resting on her belly.

She peered at Murtagh over the top of his own reading glasses and smiled to see he was wearing his old brown corduroy blazer; these days, it had been mostly usurped by Sive for its authentic seventies credibility, but he could still squeeze into it. Just about.

'Are you sure you don't mind me staying here?' she asked. 'I bet Áine could find someone else to sit with her girls.'

Murtagh sat on the coffee table while he tied his shoelaces. 'No, it's okay,' he answered. 'He says he only has a few hours, so it's not worth causing her stress over it. I must say, though, I wish he'd given us a bit more notice.'

He shuffled together the newspapers and gave the armchair cushions a half-hearted plump, opened the window and shook the curtains, then collected up the cups to return them to the kitchen.

'Still, it will be lovely, though, won't it?' she called after him. 'I'm so curious to hear how much he's changed. I can't imagine Fionn looking older. How old is he now? Thirty-eight? Thirty-nine?'

'Something like that,' Murtagh shouted back as he performed a quick blitz on the kitchen, closing the lid on the bread bin and rinsing an empty milk bottle, spritzing the windowsill succulents and straightening the kitchen chairs. He draped Sive's leather jacket and Maeve's red silk scarf over his arm and hung them up before leaning over Maeve to kiss her goodbye on both cheeks.

'Bring me home something nice,' she said. 'A surprise. And don't forget to post the letters.'

He collected the pile of powder-blue envelopes from the mantelpiece and glanced at the addresses; she had written to Jeremy and her mother.

'What are you sending to Jer?' he asked.

'Some Rothko postcards I picked up that I thought he'd like. I said you sent your love.'

'These days, you seem to talk to him more than I do.'

He rested the envelopes on the ledge beneath the mirror in the hallway while he combed his beard and then immediately left without them.

On the walk to the ferry, Murtagh felt moisture in the air and scanned the sky overhead for the cumuliform clouds that signalled impending bad weather, but the glint of the light made it difficult to discern, and he shoved his hands deeper into his pockets and hurried on. The last man to board the boat, he was relieved to find himself alone on the upper deck. It was so hard to be an introvert on the island; the anonymity of the city was the only thing he'd truly missed from their life in Dublin. After all of this time, and no matter how much the island had become home, he still felt overexposed there when everyone he met knew his name and felt completely entitled to enquire about his business. As they tipped and bounced towards Galway he felt his spirits lifting; the thought of browsing in Charlie Byrne's bookshop, weaving amongst the market stalls on Shop Street with an eye out for something for Maeve, perhaps discovering a new green cardigan in Anthony Ryan's drapers to replace the one that Mossy had shrunk in the washing machine, rejuvenated him. And then he had Fionn to look forward to.

Fionn had telephoned the night before while he and Maeve were immersed in preserving the last of their tomatoes in the Kilner jars that they never seemed to have enough of. Fionn was in Dublin for a wedding, he'd said, and had been struck with the idea of coming to Galway for the afternoon before he flew back to London. It was strange to hear his voice on the telephone. In the time since he'd left the island, throughout his travels, the three had exchanged dozens of letters and postcards, but Fionn had never been much of a telephone or email person, preferring the art of letter-writing to maintain his connection with the Moone family, and Maeve and Murtagh in particular.

Through the stories he told, the anecdotes from his travels, the words he used to express himself, he shared his whole life with them in beautiful, imperfect handwriting. The sort that writes its way on to your heart.

Was the Fionn they knew from his letters the most authentic representation of him?

Or a carefully curated persona?

It made Murtagh sad to think of how the internet had robbed his children of the joy of a letter landing on the mat with your name written by the hand of someone who loves you. There and then he decided that he would try writing to them all one day, when he was ready to share some memories, maybe when the physical distance between them grew.

It was strange now to accept that so much time had passed since he had last seen Fionn; it was never meant to be that way. There had been so many attempts over the years to reunite, but one thing or another had always prevented it. And yet it did not feel so long since they had last all sat together. Maybe that was the power of letters. The power of that summer.

It was starting to rain as he strode up from the pier so he called into Connell's cheesemongers to borrow an umbrella from Cathal there; he left with a chunk of Camembert wrapped in wax paper for Maeve and a branded umbrella declaring Connell's to be Purveyors of Award-Winning Cheese and Charcuterie. Along Shop Street he strolled, untroubled by the puddles that formed quickly in the streets. It was autumn, his most beloved season, with the new beginnings of 'Back to School' fever, always contagious, making it feel like a new year.

In Eyre Square he manoeuvred around the construction work to stand before the Galway Hookers Fountain; it was his favourite installation of public art and he admired once again the way the stylised steel sails seemed so perfectly to capture the spirit of the boat they were modelled upon. While the silver rain mingled with the spray from the water jets, he was mesmerised as his thoughts wandered to the conversation he would soon have with Fionn.

It would be easy to speak of the children, his work, the

islanders Fionn had known, but what of Maeve? How much did she tell him in her letters?

How could he ever explain in a single afternoon how complex their lives were whilst appearing so simple?

How the previous year had been her worst yet.

All that he had avoided writing down – was Fionn able to read between the lines?

How the menopause seemed to have rattled her even more.

How the GP in Galway had prescribed Valium and vigorous exercise and shown her the door.

How she had refused to allow her parents to come for Christmas, and once again in spring.

How, that time, when she finally seemed to resurface, she was different. That a horrible resignation had settled upon her and her spark was barely reignited.

How it hurt him to see how much it hurt her to do things that once were so easy.

How slowly she had decluttered her life and responsibilities so the day's expectations were easier to manage.

How she had promised him that things would never get so bad again as that past year.

And he wanted to believe her because she never made promises she couldn't keep.

But it frightened him.

What deal had she struck that ensured she could keep that promise?

How could he confess to Fionn that he saw all of those things but pretended not to?

That he relied on the sheer force of his will to help her get better?

He became aware of a new silence in his ears and realised that the persistent beating of rain on his umbrella had stopped; he shook it, closed it with its little pink button, and it became a walking stick that beat out a steady rhythm on the flagstones as he made his way to the new Eyre Square Hotel, only a few weeks open. They had agreed to meet in the lobby bar and as Murtagh crossed the square he could almost taste the hot whiskey he longed to order.

Back on the island, Maeve sat cross-legged on her bedroom floor. She dragged an old suitcase out from under the bed and removed five moleskin journals; one for each of the previous years. Inside the cover of each she had drawn a little table: in the column on the left, a blue star and black circle: on the right, corresponding numbers.

2000: 273 blue stars / 92 black circles

2001: 219 blue stars / 146 black circles

2002: 248 blue stars / 17 black circles

2003: 288 blue stars / 77 black circles

2004: 189 blue stars / 176 black circles

Blue stars for the days she felt well; black circles for the days of crow.

She opened her diary for the current year and slowly turned the pages, counting the stars and circles for each week and jotting them down on a sheet of Sive's graph paper. 257 days had passed. 180 were black circles.

Folding the sheet inside her journal, Maeve tidied the suitcase and its contents back under the bed.

Downstairs, she shrugged on Murtagh's duffel coat, pulled the hood over her head and breathed in the smell of him. Just like the sea, but better.

As she followed her well-worn path to the lighthouse she paused at the foot of the castle when a perfect white stone, oval like an egg, caught her eye; she slipped it into her pocket.

In the Eyre Square Hotel, Murtagh eased his damp shoes off, glanced around the room to check he was still alone and warmed his socks in front of the open fire. With one eye on the doorway for the waiter with his whiskey, he nestled further into his armchair, surprised by how relaxed he felt, relieved that the anxiety that had gripped him at the fountain seemed to have loosened its hold. And then, from his breast pocket, a shrill tone startled him. How he hated that noise, and how mobile phones had invaded all pleasant moments such as this. With irritation he squinted at the unknown number that floated on the screen. He pressed the button to release its message and sighed. Fionn had missed his train; he wouldn't be able to make it after all.

The waiter presented his drink on a sterling-silver tray, but the aroma of lemons and alcohol seemed unpleasant to him now, tinged as it was with the disappointment he could taste in his mouth.

Instead of drinking it, he left behind enough euros to cover the bill and left.

It had started to rain again, and the sky turned thunderous as he rushed to catch the earlier ferry. The crossing was turbulent, the wind seeking vengeance on the boat for some unknown hurt, and Murtagh's stomach rolled with the waves in uncharacteristic upset. When he finally reached home he was relieved to find Maeve waiting, and a spicy soup steaming on the range. She placed her cool hand on his hot forehead and worried he might have a fever. 'Probably for the best he couldn't come,' she said. 'The last ferry mightn't sail.'

Murtagh nodded in agreement, but when Maeve comforted him, it brought him little comfort.

That evening she drew a perfect blue star by the day's date but knew in her heart that she would never have enough stars now to outweigh the black circles. And that she would not – could not – allow herself to break her own promise; for her to remain here as a wife, a mother, a friend, she must give them more days of blue stars than black circles.

There weren't enough blue stars left in the skies.

And so, she must now begin to make them all ready.

To help them to understand that truths believed universal are not always personal truths – and that when you allow yourself to understand this, you may find unexpected peace.

To allow herself to become strong enough to set them free.

Inis Óg: Christmas Eve, 2005

Maeve kneeled on the red Persian rug in front of the fireplace and warmed her hands. The pattern of the weave made impressions on her skin as she watched the flames lick the darkness.

She heard Murtagh's tread on the landing upstairs, the creaky floorboard, the whirr of the bathroom fan for a moment. Closing her eyes, she imagined him blinking in half-sleep as he shuffled in his slippers, striped pyjamas creased, hair tousled.

She whispered his name.

Once.

A second time, louder, and then clasped her hand over her mouth, swallowing hard.

Listening to his retreat, her heart pounded until the bedroom door clicked closed. She turned to sit on the floor with her back against his leather armchair, cool through the delicate silk of her beloved peacock-blue dressing gown.

Around her were the scattered remnants of the gold ribbon and silver wrapping paper that she had used for the presents. She plucked a piece of Sellotape from the rug, rolled it into a ball between her finger and thumb and tossed it into the coal bucket.

The gifts under the tree were perfect.

A Crosley vinyl record player in a deep-purple suitcase for Sive.

The Letters of John Keats in hardback for Mossy.

An oxblood slim leather jacket for Dillon that Jeremy had hunted down in Soho on her behalf.

A fleur-de-lis silver and turquoise nurse's watch fob for Nollaig.

But she had no present for Murtagh this year.

All she would leave him was the letter.

Maeve tidied the living room, remembered to return the scissors to their correct place in the sideboard drawer for perhaps the very first time.

From behind the sofa, she pulled out a London Underground tote bag Sive had bought in Camden Market. It contained the midnight-blue velvet dress she'd worn at Murtagh's last birthday party, black woollen tights, underwear, the yellow torch from under the stairs. It struck her that someone would eventually have the job of removing these clothes from her body and, wondering if they would judge her for wearing mismatching underwear, she rummaged in the laundry basket for a different set.

She dressed in darkness.

Stood before the mirror in the hallway brushing her hair, pulling the sides back with two slim tortoiseshell combs, smoothing a little concealer on the dark circles under her eyes.

She slipped her arms into her coat, her feet into Doc Marten boots; she pulled the laces tight.

With every crinkle of fabric or brush against the furniture, she froze, ear cocked towards the stairs for sounds of movement.

She was so close now.

To be interrupted would destroy her.

Maeve paused in the hallway, turned off the light and stepped through the front door, closing it softly.

Outside, she stood and rested her head against the brass knocker.

In her mind she walked through the bedrooms of the house, kissing each child on the forehead, Murtagh on both cheeks, as she had done every night before.

She wondered if they would remember what her last words to each had been.

Worried what else they would remember, or choose to forget.

Dreaded the thought of them missing her, scared that they would not.

Hoped that they would understand, felt sick to know how impossible that might be.

Maeve walked to the boathouse without looking right or left at her neighbours' houses, her eyes following the narrow beam of yellow light from her torch as it traced a line down the lane before her.

With her right hand she clutched a heavy silver key inside the pocket of her coat; fingered the kangaroo keyring attached to it.

In her left, Murtagh's letter.

Both palms burned.

She tried not to think about the cold, how much colder it would get, as the wind flapped her dress around her legs.

The walk seemed so much shorter than it had ever seemed before, and all too soon she was standing before the currach inside the shed.

The boat was heavier than she remembered, and a layer of perspiration had settled on her skin by the time she'd dragged it to the shore, flinching as its heavy iron chain clanged against the wood.

She dabbed her face with the cuff of her sleeve and rested for a moment on the boat's edge.

The stones were waiting in a neat pile beside the boat-house door. She had been collecting them for three weeks now; building a little mound of those she found that were white, smooth, pure.

Inside the boathouse, she pierced the letter for Murtagh, sealed in a white parchment envelope, on a rusty nail that protruded from the back of the door.

She kissed her fingertips and touched it as she pulled the string to quench the light and shoved the door closed behind her.

One by one she filled her pockets with the stones and staggered back to the currach under their weight.

She rowed the boat as far out into the ocean as she could before the waves became too strong.

Maeve lay for a moment on her back, watching the stars above her, waiting for her mind to change.

The boat was damp, and she felt the chill seeping into her bones.

The mist in the air made her cough.

Without looking back at the island, resisting the lure of its lights calling her home, she sat up in the currach tentatively, balancing carefully to avoid it capsizing.

She wound the chain tight around her left foot, arranged it so it did not chafe her skin and stood up.

The currach rocked and she lowered her centre of gravity.

When it had grown still, she stood tall once again.

She held her arms out wide, shook her hair free behind her and stepped into the sea.

In the moment that the cold crashed into her body she saw the truth behind her eyes.

There was no regret. Only love.

THREE

As the Crow Flies

Inis Óg: January, 2006

Murtagh sat on the gravel at the foot of Maeve's lighthouse, his legs stretched out wide before him to form a perfect triangle.

At night the black that descended on the island was smothering; all his senses were heightened.

Red Christmas tinsel fluttered from the glass encasement of the beacon light in his peripheral vision.

The new bald patch at the crown of his curls rested against the dirty white paint; the damp placed a cold kiss on his scalp.

A smell of rubber burning in the distance smarted his eyes.

An inch of exposed leg below the hem of his grey tweed trousers bristled against the contrary wind that skated in off the Atlantic.

With just the protection of Birkenstock sandals, his feet were soaked, the toes of his mismatched socks turned black.

Murtagh squeezed them against the worn leather soles.

Squeeze and release.

Squeeze and release.

His shoulders collapsed inwards and his fingers clawed at the dirt as if he were trying to catch hold of the earth.

He howled but emitted no sound as his shoulders shook.

Holding his dirty hands to his face, he smelled the moist soil on his fingers.

It made him retch to think of her lying in the ground.

Convinced himself that this was all a cruel trick; a test of his faith; that she would appear on the doorstep once again, drinking milk straight from the bottle.

To catch sight of her toothbrush waiting on the bathroom shelf, the bristles brand new, was a blow.

Her dirty clothes in the laundry basket.

An unopened letter addressed to her from her mother.

His grief was bigger than the island, bigger than Ireland, bigger than the whole blue-and-green Earth; how could it fit inside his chest?

How could his heart keep stubbornly beating on against his will?

When its reason for beating was gone.

Why must he now be trapped in the too quiet house, with the too quiet children that he couldn't look at, couldn't touch.

He wished he could take her place in the ground, sea-water filling his lungs.

His grief was louder in his ears than the waves.

Louder than a million voices insisting time would heal.

Louder than every thought of survival his tired brain attempted: eat, sleep, remember to speak to the children.

But not as loud as her voice.

Her voice telling him to go on.

The whisper deep inside him that understood why she did it.

The hot, blinding light of grief seared in his mind, illuminating the shadows of his thoughts, exposing the streets of his mind which he sometimes joyrode through, sometimes crawled.

He turned a corner and bang! A truth was revealed to him.

A song played from the record player and became a revelation.

It seemed his heart was more mysterious than he had ever thought possible.

It was a relief. And a torment.

The interrogation light of his grief never dimmed; he walked the island feeling more overexposed than ever before.

Hated himself for understanding.

For not having prevented the thing he most feared.

All anger he felt was directed inward.

Never at his darkling.

His broken pot.

His Queen.

He scrambled up off the dirt, turning his ankle as he stood.

He limped towards home, loving the twinge that travelled up his left leg when he put weight on it.

When he reached the cottage he opened the door and listened inside the darkness.

For all of those years he had left the porch light on whenever Maeve went walking, always a beacon to guide her home along the lane. Since she was gone, he hated the sight of that glowing yellow bulb.

The washing machine churned.

The children were silent.

At the kitchen sink he washed the dirt from his hands, noticed the skin was broken in the fleshiest part of his palm.

And then he defrosted a fillet of halibut for tomorrow and

spritzed Maeve's cacti which stubbornly still sat on the windowsill.

He went on.

One morning, after several months had passed, it struck Murtagh that the howling inside his heart had stopped. Now he held his breath, waiting for some onslaught of feeling to hit him, but it refused to come. Every day he braced for impact, but felt nothing; his mind snowing softly as he lived inside its permanent chill. *Come back to me, Maeve.*

At his mother's funeral he had realised that all funerals from now on would be Maeve's once again; all coffins hers, all black mourning clothes forever worn in her honour. The persistence of her memory intruded upon all moments of his life. The assault of her absence endlessly new; his mind wouldn't release the image of her drenched on the beach. Every day it seemed to tighten its grip, bullying out all other memories, haunting his dreams at night, blinding him by day. It was hard to look at the children; to speak of her as they wanted to; as if all his words were buried with her. Life now was an exhausting game of cat and mouse, with the grief lingering always on the periphery, waiting to strike if for a moment he stopped hiding behind the ironing of school uniforms, hoovering and the mindless administrative tasks that he now luxuriated in.

Murtagh sat at his pottery station, in spotlessly clean overalls, as the wheel whirred in halting circles before him. He accelerated and decreased the speed with his left foot, gazing out of the window, a lump of clay left untouched. Without much enthusiasm, he had opened Makes of Moone that morning at dawn, as he somehow always managed to do, ignoring how the shelves had gradually emptied as tourists and islanders bought his last remaining porcelain ceramics and the deep-blue hand-built sculptures he was famous for. He made little new work. Who would photograph his pieces for him now Maeve was gone? Who would curate the window displays and christen the pots with names that captured their essence in her stead?

Murtagh lifted a perfect sphere of clay from the wheel and unceremoniously dumped it into the bucket by his feet. It made a satisfying thwack. On the few occasions he tried to pot, the results looked disfigured to him, and the glazes always came out black. Was his gift now lost at sea?

Sales reps from Brown Thomas in Dublin and Selfridges in London called to enquire about new collections. At first, he promised them, soon. Later, he stopped answering the telephone.

Nollaig updated the website she had built for him to say the shop was currently closed.

She told him that folks kept emailing asking for special orders, but he didn't want to know.

Murtagh knew eventually the time would come when he must find a way of working once again. When he could bear a little sunlight on his face once more.

But not yet.

His mind was too full of worries about the remaining Moones to care how his actions affected department stores. In the six slow months since they had buried their mother, Murtagh had watched each of his offspring wear her absence, and the circumstances that caused it, differently.

Mossy, Son Day, retreated further into the shyest part of himself, wearing away the soles of his heavy boots walking for miles in all weathers. Pilgrimages of mourning. Retracing Maeve's steps over the myriad craggy rocks of the island, regularly stopping to pick up small white pebbles that caught the light of his eye, working them between his fingers, before tossing them out to sea. He came home from university every weekend and hid in corners of the house that his long limbs defied physics to squeeze into. Escaped into one book after another. Mumbled poems aloud as he read – Patrick Kavanagh, Seamus Heaney, Emily Dickinson – and thumbed his mother's already over-thumbed volumes of Virginia Woolf with a reverence bordering on obsession. Would he find the answers he was looking for in those pages?

In contrast, Son Night's emotions were violently on display for anyone who came in contact with him. Barely six weeks after the funeral, Dillon had withdrawn all of his student grant from the bank, dropped out of his arts course at NUI Maynooth, bought a dilapidated Suzuki motorbike and caught the ferry to France. He survived on the odd jobs he picked up while racing around Europe, and though Murtagh couldn't imagine how this was possible, he was afraid to ask any questions; occasionally he overheard stories shared by Mossy involving haybarns, girls' hostels and living-room floors, but he didn't pry. He had learned, through great trial and error, that there was no mode of delivery that could present a question to Dillon in peace. Everything was an accusation, a reprimand or an insult. His mother had always known how to stroke the particularly wayward fur of Dillon, growing as it did in all directions, but Murtagh always caused him to bristle. Instead of bringing them closer together, Maeve's death seemed to snap any threads that still connected them. If it wasn't for the gentle persuasions of Mossy, he doubted Dillon would ever come home at all.

Within days of her mother's funeral, Nollaig had withdrawn from her midwifery studies in Galway and moved all her belongings from the nurses' halls back to her old bedroom.

It was never supposed to be a permanent arrangement.

In the beginning, she planned to stay until the twins were settled back into college and Sive had returned to secondary school on the mainland, but then she waited until the Month's Mind Mass had passed. Dónal had insisted on the ceremony. It wasn't just about the religious aspect, he'd said, but a moment for the community to come together in Maeve's name, to see the family and show their support. In the end, they were glad of it when the well-oiled grieving machinery of the island held them upright once again. Then suddenly, it was February, with Easter looming, so she thought it best to see them through that holiday. By then she had missed too many classes to fulfil her course requirements so she deferred until the following September. Committed to booking dental appointments, force-feeding the family vitamins and drawing up household chores lists that the others ignored, Nollaig was determined to offer stability where none was desired. And so, Nollaig's grief was harder to recognise; in her sense of duty she had found a purpose through which she could channel her mourning. When Sive failed most of her fifth-year exams, they decided she should finish her schooling at the small local school on the island, Coláiste Padraigín, instead of continuing on the mainland, and thus Nollaig's fate to serve as her unofficial chaperone was cemented.

It had surprised Murtagh when Sive agreed to the transfer from the city-centre school, where there were a hundred and eleven girls in her year, to the tiny island class of six, but she had grown to hate the ferry crossing and found changing schools to be the lesser of two evils.

Nollaig. Mossy. Dillon. Sive. His thoughts rotated between them in an endless cycle.

Murtagh stood up from the wheel and stamped his feet to eradicate the pins and needles that plagued him.

He turned off the light in the studio and sat for a moment in the darkness before facing the walk home.

His hands were numb, and he couldn't ever seem to warm them up.

No bread was baked.

No pots were thrown.

All Maeve's clothes still hung in the wardrobe.

The currach lay abandoned in the boatshed.

Murtagh was alone, lonely in the middle of what remained of his family.

Without courage to listen to the quiet bell of truth that sounded within him as he lay alone in the dark.

With no understanding, yet, of what other plans Maeve had for him.

Brooklyn: December, 2006

The first Christmas after Queen Maeve abdicated from her throne, the Moone family suffered through the anniversary of her death in Brooklyn with Grandpa Hank and Grandma June.

When they arrived on the twenty-first of December, dishevelled and bad-tempered as a bankrupt circus, Murtagh noticed immediately how much weight June had lost.

'Only a hundred and two pounds now,' Hank had whispered as he hugged him on arrival.

The first thing he said.

A necklace of chunky pearls looked too heavy for her kitten-like frame as she fussed around them. There was a faint stain of blue-black hair dye at the nape of her neck, exposed by the severe bun she had scraped her hair into with a white bow-tie clip.

In stark contrast, Hank was almost twice his former size, with half as many of his once-lustrous chestnut locks. 'Eating his feelings,' June in turn had whispered as Hank struggled up the stairs with Nollaig's suitcase, breathing heavily as he bumped it stubbornly from step to step, refusing help. Murtagh smiled when June leaned close; she still smelled like lemons.

It had been easy to rationalise not putting up a Christmas tree in Inis Óg when they would be away for most of the holiday.

No one sent them any cards, as was the custom in the year following a bereavement. In the sheltered environs of the cottage it was almost possible to pretend that nothing special should be happening. As for presents, well, no one wanted anything at all, it seemed. Murtagh put twenty-euro notes in red envelopes that Nollaig left on each child's dressing table.

To buy something they liked when they saw it.

Maybe in America.

He knew he should have done better but could not.

'If you don't try to have Christmas this year, I worry you'll never face it again,' Father Dónal warned as he handed Murtagh a Clarks shoebox filled with mince pies from the parish office. Murtagh nodded. 'Maybe next year,' he said, peering beneath the lid. 'Are these from Mrs Maguire?'

'Haven't you suffered enough, sir?' Dónal winked. 'They're Mrs Doyle's. I wouldn't part with them for anyone else.'

Murtagh shook his hand and Dónal held on for a moment. 'Your children, Murt. They can't lose both of you. You know that, don't you?'

'I do.'

June and Hank did their best to fill their cramped brownstone in Williamsburg with as much generic Christmas jolliness as they could muster but, despite the intensity of the living conditions, the house felt vacant. No one wanted to sit in Maeve's traditional seat at the table; her empty chair dominated the room. Nollaig perched on the edge once, but one look from Sive uprooted her.

The twins set up camp on the landing on the second floor in two reclining leather chairs that were earmarked for Goodwill; they plugged in Hank's mini-fridge from his man-shed and filled it with Kool-Aid at the front and bottles of Bud Light at the rear. A bowl of exotic American candy, Twizzlers, Reese's Pieces and Milk Duds sat on top and appeared to be self-replenishing. 'You can't beat Cadbury's, though, can you?' Dillon asked as he stuffed a handful of Milk Duds in his mouth. 'I'd murder a Golden Crisp.'

Grandpa Hank liked to join them sometimes and share the contraband. Mossy always offered up his chair and sat on the floor with his legs dangling between the bannisters, while Dillon and Hank talked over his head about wrestling, motorbikes and baseball, though the brothers had never seen a game.

Sometimes as Murtagh passed them en route to the bathroom he was tempted to take a seat on the top stair, but he never did. The conversation seemed to lull the closer he came, despite the friendly way Hank tilted his bottle of Bud at him, the condensation on the glass shimmering.

Nollaig seldom moved from the chaise longue in the kitchen, where June filled seconds, minutes, hours with busy work; Nollaig wanted to learn how to cook, how to bake, all the secrets of domesticity she believed would never be revealed to her now. June pored over recipe books with her and Nollaig diligently copied out family favourites into a hard-backed green notebook her father had given her for the purpose. 'Your mother had no interest in learning any of this, you know.' June smiled. 'She always said it was a waste of precious brain space as she didn't intend to ever put any of it to use.'

'I know. But I want to take care of them. Did I ever tell you how Mammy caused a scene at the school when they divided the class up so boys did technical drawing and girls did home economics? I was marched down to the workshop and presented to Mr O'Malley like some sort of prize.'

June laughed. 'That sounds like your mother. Always ready for a revolution. I don't know where she got it from.'

Nollaig turned to look at her.

'From you, Grandma. She always said you were a feminist but didn't even realise, that you encouraged her to be and do whatever she wanted, that you made her believe in *choices*.'

June stood up and fussed with her hair as she tidied away the books. 'Did she say that?' She gave a little cough to clear her throat. 'I always presumed she thought I was too old-fashioned, a bit embarrassing, maybe.'

Nollaig took her grandmother's hands.

'Oh no, no, no. The opposite. She said you were her hero and if you'd been born even five years later you probably would have had an amazing career as an astrophysicist or a politician or something, but that you were just a few years too early.'

'Well, now,' June said, pulling her shoulders back and straightening her spine. 'That is something.'

'You will still teach me how to cook, though, won't you?'

June laughed. 'A girl's gotta eat. But let's get those boys down here, too. I'm adamant they're gonna learn how to make something before the week is out.'

While her grandparents were monopolised by the other Moones, Sive was often found sitting on the porch steps, surreptitiously smoking and peering through neighbours' windows for glimpses of the sort of blissful domesticity she would loathe them for. One night, she crept from the house, a pink eiderdown pulled over her head as an impromptu umbrella, and kicked the life-size plastic reindeer that stood on the Andersons' steps into pieces. Afterwards she tried to piece it back together, but her fingers, rigid from the cold, struggled to coordinate the sticky tape and scissors, and it was too far gone. The next morning his remains had vanished. She jumped every time the doorbell rang, but no one came looking for her, and she was almost disappointed.

'Why are we even bothering with this charade?' Sive eventually screeched on Christmas Eve as the family sat in silence over lunch. 'It doesn't make it easier to pretend everything's normal!' Bing Crosby crooned 'White Christmas' from the CD player on the sideboard; Sive leaned over and yanked the plug from the wall.

Grandma June clutched at a string of rosary beads in her left hand and wiped crumbs from the tablecloth into a red paper napkin in her lap.

Grandpa Hank removed his thick brown spectacles and polished them with the stretched sleeve of his Christmas cardigan; elongated elves danced across his heaving chest as he hunched there. His colour reddened as the children's voices rose to attack each other.

Mossy and Dillon resorted to throwing torn-off pieces of bagel with increased aggression while Nollaig and Sive snapped at each other.

'You're so selfish, Si. Why can't you make an effort like everyone else?'

'To what, replace her? Like you, you mean?'

Murtagh stood and slammed his palms against the Formica tabletop. The dull smack was ineffective but the expression on his face was enough to silence the children. His arms were shaking as he looked each child in the eye in turn.

'That's enough! Remember who you are and where you've come from. Your mother would be ashamed of you.' He lowered himself back into his seat and slopped another spoon of potato salad on to his plate.

'You make *me* ashamed,' he mumbled, half under his breath.

'See?' Nollaig snarled at Sive and the table shook from the kick she received in response.

'Maybe *you* should feel ashamed,' Dillon sneered back, and Mossy jostled him in his seat.

Grandma June scuttled out to the kitchen, where she remained, scrubbing the already gleaming countertops, while the grandchildren dispersed throughout the house. Murtagh joined her, put an arm around her shoulder and leaned his back against the counter while she buried her face in the wool of his scratchy cardigan. He could feel the grooves of her ribcage through her cotton blouse.

'She was still my little girl,' she whispered.

'I know, June,' he answered. 'I'm so sorry I didn't look after her better for you. I'll never forgive myself for not saving her.'

June rubbed his back. 'I feel the same – wonder if I could have saved her, and honestly I don't know. Hank says no one knew Maeve's mind like Maeve.'

'But I was her husband!'

'And I was her mother, but she was still her own person. Murtagh, who could have loved her more than us? What she did wasn't done for lack of love, I do know that much.'

Murtagh lowered his voice in confession. 'I feel she tried to tell me so much that I just didn't want to hear. I look back now and distrust so many of my memories of her, like they're underwritten now by a truth I couldn't see then.'

June took his hands in hers. 'It's easy to rewrite history with coulda, woulda, shoulda, but you did your best. And so did Maeve. We all think there'll be more time to do better.'

'Until there's not.'

They were disturbed by Nollaig sidling in to find them. 'We want to go to Midnight Mass,' she announced. 'To hear the carols.'

June walked over and held her granddaughter's face in her hands. There was no glimpse of Maeve in her at all. 'That's a lovely idea, Nollaig, dear. We always used to take your mother.'

Nollaig nodded; she remembered her mam describing sitting between her parents each year, her hand inside the silky pocket of her father's winter coat. Mass was where she learned to sing. At least she got something out of it, she had liked to say.

When Murtagh and June were alone again, she asked him if he would join them. The last time he had set foot in a chapel was at his mother's funeral; the time before that was Maeve's. He was in no hurry to break that fast, but he nodded reluctantly. 'I worry about Nollaig, that she has no reprieve,' he said as he stood before the kitchen dresser, eyes lingering on the photos of Maeve; dressed up as the Statue of Liberty for a school concert; as a teenager on stage as Ophelia; on their wedding day.

'She's decided she will be the glue to hold us all together, but the harder she tries, the more the others are desperate to break free. Her siblings all have somewhere else to be, other people in their lives, but she's stuck in the house with me. And she lost her birthday, too. Christmas Eve will always be Maeve's anniversary now. Even her name is a constant reminder of this godforsaken time of year. What has she left at all?'

June came and stood beside him, picked up a framed photograph of her as a young woman holding baby Maeve in her arms. 'She has you, Murtagh, and in my book, that's a lot.'

Hank walked into the kitchen, glanced at the two of them huddled together and headed for the refrigerator. He slid a cheesecake out and found a space for it on the countertop beside a wire tray of cooling scones under a St Patrick's Day tea towel. He sliced a generous triangle free and scraped it on to a side plate which he grabbed from the draining board. Without a word to his wife or son-in-law, he carried it into the living room, a spoonful already in his mouth before he took his seat on the well-worn groove in his leather armchair.

'I'll go powder my nose,' said June, squeezing Murtagh's left arm as she passed where he stood, drinking in the gallery of Maeve. He picked up a photo of his wife from just before he knew her, standing between her parents in the departure hall at JFK.

It was 1978, the summer she arrived in Dublin, when their lives became so beautifully entangled.

When the foundations were laid for a love that proved evergreen.

When everything changed.

Inis Óg: July, 2008

A postcard from Sive lay on the doormat with a black-and-white photograph of Battersea's Albert Bridge on the front. Murtagh picked it up and squinted at her chicken-scratch handwriting.

Hi Dad,

I cycled across this bridge on Sunday morning at dawn.

We were on our way home, tired and hungry, but it looked so beautiful in the silvery light that I suddenly felt rejuvenated just to witness it.

Love,
Sive

PS I'm still alive, obviously.

He sighed, pinning it to the corkboard he'd hung in the hallway to display all of her postcards. Staring at the moody nightscape, he tried not to worry about where his youngest daughter had been until dawn, and who the *we* referred to. Was she a passenger on someone's crossbar, like her mother had been once? If so, he hoped they were happy. The thought struck him that, knowing her, she would probably be the one cycling, and it made him smile.

Sive had fled the island straight after she received her

acceptance to attend Camberwell College of Arts in London. On the evening she left Murtagh gently asked Nollaig if it might be time for her to consider returning to her own studies, but she resisted the idea. 'I've lost interest in midwifery completely,' she insisted. 'I think I'll stay a bit longer until I work out what I'd like to do instead. And besides, I can't leave you here all by yourself.'

She could have, of course, and there were times when Murtagh would in fact have welcomed the freedom that an empty nest may have awarded. He rearranged the postcards so that none were completely obscured and continued into the kitchen, where a pound of potatoes waited to be peeled.

The clock chimed five. Nollaig would close the shop soon and stroll home to eat dinner with him. In times past, their roles were reversed, when he had loved spending as many hours as he could in the studio, sometimes appearing only for meals. Now Nollaig was the one who devoted most of her time working for Makes of Moone, and in particular developing their online shop and social media presence. Her internet persona was much wittier than her real-life one and she enjoyed communicating with customers from all over the world. Murtagh knew he had his daughter to thank for the business surviving, for getting him to work again, but he often cursed his own inability to motivate her to want something more for herself. They were locked in a perpetual cycle that seemed impossible to break.

As for romance, an odd rumour had reached him from time to time of her carrying-on with Aindí O'Shea, the owner of the village post/tourist office, but both he, and presumably Aindí's wife, Úna, maintained a position of peaceful obliviousness. He had certainly never asked Nollaig about it but hoped that she wasn't suffering over him. What attracted his daughter to Aindí was decidedly unclear, allergic as Murtagh was to his saccharine sweetness and over-reliance on hair gel. He presumed that as a result of the limited choices in island men, Aindí's advances, through their novelty, had become welcome.

Murtagh's relationship with his daughter reminded him of those in Victorian novels; a sad widower and the unfortunate daughter who is encumbered by his sadness and her lack of suitor or independent profession. He hated the thought of it, and hoped that one day he would come home to find his daughter waiting to break the news that she was going backpacking in Australia, or had won a place at university, or secured a job in Dublin – anything that would project her forwards – but he worried his encouragement would be misinterpreted as lack of gratitude or heavy-handed interference. And so, he waited.

Nollaig, on the other hand, was relatively satisfied with her position. As Murtagh stood peeling potato skins into the compost bucket, she was locking the front door of the shop, content that she had finished boxing up all the orders in time to make the next ferry.

In the darkest part of her heart, in a secret spot of truth, lived a fear that her life on the island had simply saved her from a similar fate somewhere else, one without the easy excuse of her self-appointed responsibilities to explain her loneliness. At least on the island she could call it sacrifice. What would it be called out there?

It had never been easy for her to make friends; she seemed

unable to turn casual acquaintances from school or college or work into proper friendships in the way others managed to so easily. And when she did find someone to befriend, she seemed to care too much and ultimately always scared them away. Maybe it was because she didn't have a passion for anything of her own. She couldn't remember ever wanting to be anything in particular when she grew up, except maybe married with children. Sive was the creative one, the most like Mammy; Mossy had his books; and Dillon was passionate about music in a way that made her feel the loneliness of one without a tribe. She'd never had any special talents or shone in school at exams or sports or art. It didn't take much to make her happy; watching *Home and Away* and *Coronation Street* in peace, going to the pictures occasionally, using the expensive bubble bath every second Sunday for a good soak. She had tried to develop hobbies, but nothing stuck. Embroidery, baking, gardening – eventually they all became skills that she performed efficiently but without any flair. The only time she truly felt alive was when she was dancing at the céilí and her feet flew across the floor as if possessed. She was never short of a partner, though they were mostly married men in attendance. None of the wives saw her as a threat, and nearly all of them were right in that regard. Except for Úna O'Shea, of course, but what went on between Úna and Aindí was none of her business, although it was clear to her that Úna did not know how to make her husband happy. Occasionally she contemplated what her mother would have to say about the Aindí situation, but she chose not to dwell on that, like all the rest of the advice she was forced to imagine her mother might have given but could never know. She tortured herself worrying about the unreliability of the memories that she held of her mother; how slippery her identity seemed to be as time passed. It was difficult to know what was true, a genuine piece of history, and what was the collective narrative the family had all agreed on. They never told anyone how she had really died, for example, just that she had drowned. Without ever making the decision to, they all became complicit in the maintenance of that lie with new people. It was a heavy fiction for the heart.

At the front door, Nollaig noticed the paint was chipping and made a mental note to remind her father to top it up. She was excited to be home – it was the first Friday of the month, the July dance, and although it was too hot for her orange corduroy dress, it was the most flattering on her, so she planned to wear it anyway. She skipped up the stairs and wriggled into it, spraying on extra deodorant until the room was so smothered with the smell of chemical peaches that she started to cough. Her father passed along the hallway and she called out to him.

He swung the door open and then stepped back, waving the cloud of spray away; he was wearing just a vest and pyjama bottoms.

'Ah, Daddy,' she said. 'Why aren't you dressed? Will you not come with me?'

Murtagh shook his head and held his arms up.

'It's all right, love, you go ahead,' he said. 'There's a film on the BBC tonight I want to watch and I'm not in the mood for dancing.'

She released a dramatic sigh as she squeezed her feet into

white kitten-heel sandals that were half a size too small. Her frosted pink toenails looked as if they were gasping for air.

'You always say that,' she said. 'It's like you're determined not to have any fun.'

'It depends on what your idea of fun is,' he said, imitating an Irish dancer hopping on the spot.

She laughed at him as he danced down the hallway. Turning back to her reflection, she heard him rustling in the cupboards for her secret stash of contraband: she'd left a family pack of Maltesers for him that she'd scold him for later, but it made her happy to think of him having a treat, even a little one.

It never occurred to her to want a bigger type of happiness for him; maybe a new love, or a fresh start. When she looked at him, she didn't see Murtagh Moone, handsome at not-quite fifty and full of potential. She just saw her father, dependable and exactly where he'd always been. Her heart hadn't the imagination to dream of anything, or anyone, else for him. It was a flaw in her wiring that she wasn't even aware of; a silent killer, like carbon monoxide spreading through a sleeping house. She was utterly blind to him but believed she saw him in perfect vision.

As only a daughter can.

London: 2009

It was three years since Sive had last taken the ferry from the mainland to Inis Óg. She did always join her family for Christmas, but they never spent it on the island. In truth, she hated crossing the sea, had never made peace with the Atlantic since her mother had lost herself beneath its surface. The thought of the boat made her whole body prickle with anxiety.

Without anyone's intervention, her old bedroom remained an abandoned shrine to her adolescence. Murtagh opened the curtains every morning, aired the room, and closed them again each afternoon. He swept the floorboards that she had painted grey, and dusted the bookshelves, windowsill and dressing table. The candles she had made at school still stood on its surface, lined up in ascending height, alongside her skull-and-crossbones jewellery box and the giant red pencil sharpener that held her collection of Sharpies. Around the mirror, clumps of dehydrated Blu-Tack remained from where she had removed the Polaroid pictures of her friends to take along to London. 'In case I don't make any new ones,' she'd said. 'They will keep me company.' Sometimes on the nights when insomnia smothered Murtagh and whispered familiar worries in his ear, he would sit on the bed, pull her purple eiderdown over his legs and read one of her books by the light of the lime-green Anglepoise lamp that Grandma June had bought her as an eighteenth-birthday present. He had fallen a little bit in love with Joan Didion that way, for how she talked to Sive about mothers and mothering.

Sive's trips home had become shorter and shorter, until Murtagh finally accepted that if he was ever to learn anything of his youngest child's life, he would have to visit her in London. What little Jeremy told him suggested he either didn't see her often, or what he did witness wasn't suitable for her father's ears. It comforted him to know, though, that Jeremy could help Sive if she needed someone; she probably would reach out to his old friend if necessary. Especially as he knew how unlikely it was she would turn to her father, and not only because of the sea that flowed between them. Sive's problem wasn't just that she'd had less time with Maeve than the others; she'd had less time with the old him, too. The pre-grieving father that he still struggled to resuscitate even after all these years. *Could there be a new version of him that could learn the language of his children? Did they need that? As much as he did?*

Waiting on the platform at Heathrow Airport for the Tube to transport him to the centre of London, Murtagh filled his lungs with the warm, musky-blanket smell of the Underground.

He remembered his first visit to London with Maeve in 1980 for his interview at St Martin's School of Art; he had performed abysmally. When the young Brazilian interviewer asked his views on cultural appropriation by potters he was forced to confess that he didn't have any, that it wasn't something he'd even considered before that moment. Twenty-nine years later, he could still feel the judgement curling up his nostrils like a fog, winding down his throat to strangle any voice he had left. Maeve was waiting for him on the steps outside, still a smoker then, blowing perfect O's into the London footpath while she listened to the Sex Pistols too loudly on her headphones. 'Never mind,' she said when she saw his face, and physically shook off the disappointment he knew she felt as strongly as he did.

How would their lives have turned out if he'd been given that job?

If they had built their lives here instead of on that island on that wild edge of the world?

Would Maeve still be with him?

Or would London have taken her much sooner?

And what of their children?

Murtagh tore the Aer Lingus labels from his cabin bag and tossed them into the bin, rubbing his fingers together impatiently to lose the sticky residue. It was exhilarating to be here, although he was relieved to have missed the G20 protest riots the week before and that Sive hadn't chosen to exercise her democratic right as forcefully as he and Maeve had in the seventies. He scanned the platform, surveying the other waiting passengers, confident he could easily distinguish all the holidaymakers from the travellers who were coming home. He wondered if he was so easily categorised and stood up straighter, the way he thought a Londoner might.

The Tube pulled into the station, eerie with emptiness. Murtagh stood back to allow a Japanese family wearing matching tracksuits to board ahead of him. For a second, he wished he was one of their troop, focused and united. Sometimes he felt all he still had in common with his children was their shared grief and disappointment in him. He relaxed as a strangely comforting, although automated, female British voice told him to mind the gap, look after his belongings and move down inside the carriage. Through the nineteen stops to Leicester Square, he rocked in rhythm with the train's motion, his eyes growing heavy. He dozed off at Acton Town station surrounded by his Japanese travelling companions and woke at Green Park to discover they had been replaced by a group of schoolchildren with their faces painted like zombies. He had to change at Leicester Square for the Northern Line; it was tempting to exit the station and stand amid the neon signs and theatre revellers to compare it with his memories, but he resisted the temptation in lieu of getting to Sive's flat sooner.

Ten minutes later, he ascended from the Tube into Camden Town and felt assaulted by the cacophony and the electricity in the air. A teenager dressed as Lady Macbeth jostled him out of the way and he manoeuvred along the path to lean his back against the station's red-tiled wall. With his suitcase clenched tightly between his knees, he rustled in the pocket of his brown sheepskin jacket for the sheet of notepaper on which he'd scribbled directions to Sive's house. In the dim street light, the letters danced before his eyes as he was confounded by his own shorthand. As a mariachi band paraded past, he abandoned all hope of walking and slipped on the kerb in his haste to hail a taxi. The cabbie wound down the window to ask where he was going. 'You're only five minutes away,' he said. 'You'd be quicker walking.'

'You can take the scenic route,' Murtagh answered as he jumped in, relieved to slam the door on the smells, the sounds, the sights of the city. He shivered, despite the hot air pumping through the ventilator. It was a shock to find himself so discombobulated. To feel icy fingers poking through the safety blanket he surrounded himself so comfortably in at home. To feel anything at all. *What had become of the couple who thrived on the dangerous beauty of this borough once upon a time? Who had kissed in stairwells, up alleys, in car parks and pushed up against chain-link fences? Why had they stopped kissing as if the end of each kiss were a little death of its own?* Murtagh touched his lips with his fingertips and threw a kiss towards the sky.

Sive shared an ex-council flat off Delancey Street with two other members of her glam-punk band, Sylvia's Path – the drummer, Rose, and bass player, Gordon. The four flights of stairs leading up to it stank of urine and damp; plastic bags, broken glass and empty beer cans littered the stairwell. Angry graffiti shouted at him as he carefully picked his way up the stairs after her; the lift was out of order and the sockets where light bulbs once hung dangled like empty nooses. Wrought-iron bars covered the windows and door to number eleven. Inside, her self-selected prison cell was only a moderate improvement on the exterior. What would have been the living room had been converted into their rehearsal space, with amps and guitar cases crammed into its eight-foot by eight-foot dimensions. A dirty beige brocade curtain blocked a window that looked out on to the street; they couldn't risk someone spotting the equipment if they were smoking on the fire escape. A torn burgundy velvet chaise longue, stained, ripped and forlorn, half blocked the doorway to the kitchen. On a wobbly table laden with magazines sat wine bottles holding white dinner-table candles and a pint glass filled with plectrums. 'Gordon collects them,' Sive explained, giving it a shake.

Black-and-white prints of film noir classics were displayed behind frameless plates of glass: *Double Indemnity*, *The Maltese Falcon*, *Sunset Boulevard*, *Laura* and *The Postman Always Rings Twice*. White fairy-lights stretched in rows across the ceiling, secured with grey masking tape, and it improved the atmosphere a little. Murtagh longed to escape from this room; Camden High Street no longer felt so intimidating. It had been unclear what the exact sleeping arrangements would be, but Murtagh's heart sank to realise his daughter was giving up her own single bed to him. He offered to check into a hotel, but his daughter dismissed the idea, questioning if her flat wasn't good enough for him. He dared not say he thought it not good enough for her.

He followed Sive into the kitchen and twitched at the overpowering smell of bleach. She surprised him by tossing an orange in his direction and blushed when it hit him in the groin. A cardboard box filled with empty wine and beer bottles sat precariously on top of the bin. It was better not to think about what the little galley kitchen might have looked like a couple of hours before. A sandwich bar, with three high stools, looked out on to the square below. Father and daughter perched here, drinking Earl Grey from cracked china teacups, a sliver of space between them, and watched the shadowed courtyard for signs of life. A white HiAce van reversed around the perimeter at speed and then accelerated out on to the main street; a woman in a tiger-print fur coat walked a Persian cat on a lead; a boy with a blond ponytail in an Adidas tracksuit sprinted from one corner to the other, typing what they assumed must be his times into a mobile phone. From somewhere in the building, the screech of 'Old McDonald Had a Farm' played over and over again on a tortured violin. They didn't say much, but Murtagh liked sitting side by side with his daughter. It was easier than meeting her eyes; they always had this note of expectation, as if she were waiting for him to answer a question she hadn't asked.

Despite the utter chaos she lived in, it was clear that Sive loved her life there and thrived in the city. Sylvia's Path had even garnered something of a cult following and Sive always seemed to be exhibiting her angry paintings some-where; not usually in traditional galleries but on the walls of tattoo parlours, music venues and the hairdresser's where she experimented with the varying tones of blue that adorned her blunt bob haircut. Not that she told him any of this, of course. Nollaig showed him the highlights on the internet when he cautiously peered over her shoulder, ready to avert his eyes at any moment. There seemed to be a lot of happiness in her life, but Murtagh worried that her inspiration was driven by anger, bitterness and disappoint-ment. Losing Maeve had perhaps been the hardest for Sive, he thought, if it was possible to compare. Her already mel-ancholic disposition had been magnified in ways too subtle for an outsider to notice but flashed in neon bright to her father. Before the happening, the sad songs she listened to on repeat brought her joy. He remembered her asking him once why we take such perverse pleasure in hearing other people sing about pain and heartache? Did they make us feel less alone, less misunderstood? They were sitting in the garden at the rear of the cottage, listening to Elliott Smith, her great love at the time, while the rest of the Moones slept. Fireflies were fussing in the brambles and the moon was full. After the funeral, he found her Elliott Smith vinyl stuffed in the kitchen bin. He brushed off turnip peelings and rubbed away the stains of teabags, tomato ketchup and curry sauce, and hid the record in the bottom of his wardrobe, in case she ever changed her mind.

As they sipped their tea, Murtagh glanced at her stockinged feet. He remembered one evening back on the island when she had fallen asleep on the couch and her bare foot had slipped from beneath the blanket. The lines of fresh scars around her ankles had destroyed what was left of his heart. At the doctor's, she had promised to stop, scowling at them both from beneath her fringe, her arms folded around her knees, sleeves pulled over her hands. She had refused to talk to anyone. As his high stool shook a little from the beat she tapped with her feet, he hoped she had kept her word, that she hadn't just become better at hiding how she released pain from her flesh. Wished he could talk to her about her mother, ask her all the questions he regretted never asking Maeve.

It gave him comfort, though, to know that she resented her mother enough to lash out but respected her too much to ever let it go too far. Of that he was sure. She flirted with the line, but never crossed it. Jeremy reassured him all the time: the girl was going places.

A few minutes past midnight, she told him she was tired

and would see him in the morning. He leaned in to give her a kiss goodnight, but she had already turned her face away and it landed on the back of her head. She hesitated but then kept walking.

That night as he lay in her single bed, touched by the perfect creases in the blue duvet cover that exposed its brand-newness, he closed his eyes and listened to her quietly strumming the guitar next door.

She hummed along, but he didn't recognise the tune.

Later Sive staggered out to the kitchen in search of a glass of milk. The door to her bedroom stood ajar and she eased it open a touch more to peek around its edge. Her father was sitting upright in her bed, the case of her demo cassette in his hand, her tape deck on his lap and her yellow fuzzy headphones perched on top of his curls. His eyes were closed, and he rocked back and forth in time with the music, frowning, fist clenched. She saw tears gathering in the creases around his eyes and stepped back into the hallway.

She wanted to go to him but could not. Who was that man who looked like her father?

It frightened her to think of what lay beneath his quiet paternal care, what memories lingered of a life before her, before she and her siblings had come along, of what the reality of his life was now. She remembered sitting with Jeremy one night after he came to her gig in Spitalfields. Gordon and Rose's parents had surprised them by coming along, an embarrassing quartet dancing at the front of the stage that her bandmates were mortified by, but that sucker-punched her. 'You know every time you perform, every time you're

229

brave and brilliant and bold,' he'd said. 'that is your mother coming out in you. The older you get, the more you'll understand her.'

They sat on a fire escape, shivering in the bitter November frost, and Sive buried her head in his shoulder. 'But what if I do? And have to pay the same price?'

Jeremy lifted her chin to look her in the eye. 'You won't,' he said. 'These are the best of times and you are the best of her. And the best of your dad. Don't underestimate how much of him is in you, too. The genes you've inherited from both form an impeccable cocktail so that you can embody the best of both. A perfect combination. Just like they were. Although it took me a while to see that.'

Sive raised an eyebrow at him, 'Oh? I thought you three were always the best of friends?'

Jeremy shook his head and gazed at the traffic for a moment.

'It took me a while to accept her, because I felt like she was stealing your father away from me. And I had no one else back then.'

'So, what changed?'

Jeremy drained the dregs of his glass and waited a minute before continuing, as if considering whether to keep speaking at all.

'You know I lost my partner, Fintan?'

Sive nodded. 'But not much about it.'

'Well, in the late stages I was struggling on my own over here and your mam turned up on my doorstep. Without me ever asking for help. Your dad was working so hard at the time and couldn't leave the studio, and so, even though I'd always been pretty awful to her, she came. And she looked after me, while I looked after him. And brought me back to stay with you after he died. I don't think I'd be here now if it weren't for your folks.'

It was strange to think of the secret life of her parents. The interior world of Murtagh Moone remained a mystery to her; it seemed not somewhere for his daughter to tread. She wasn't ready to meet him, yet, but hoped she could one day. He had come all of this way to see her; that meant something. Didn't it?

With her glass of milk, she slunk back to bed, mortified to think of him listening to her lyrics.

She slipped into bed behind Rose and rested her cheek against her bare shoulder blade.

That night her dreams were full of the sea.

She woke up with her eyes sealed shut by salt; she had been crying in her sleep.

Dublin: 2011

'You don't need to tell me how big they are, but if you put them in the Olympia now, the next step is The Point and that's too much of a jump. Keep them in Whelan's and let the crowds mob Wexford Street. Roddy, Rod, can you hear me?'

Dillon looked at the screen of his phone; the photo of Roddy wearing a green cowboy hat was frozen on it. He slid his finger across the glass to clear the image and tossed it on to the bed, where Grace was still sleeping, or pretending to sleep. He knew she avoided him in the mornings so that he wouldn't ask what her plans were. She liked to start the day sipping espresso while diligently reading the emails and MSN messages on his computer for clues of other women. Not that he cared. There wasn't anyone else, not at the moment; he didn't have the energy. He wasn't sure how things had escalated so quickly with Grace from flirtation to this virtual co-habitation in only three months, but he needed to reverse-engineer that terrible lapse in concentration as soon as possible.

Dillon looked around his studio apartment, so recently the image of minimalistic virtue, and cringed at her clothes scattered around the bed, her tennis racquet lying on the sofa and the cardboard boxes containing the miscellaneous contents of her old life waiting impatiently by the door.

He didn't know which was worse, the sight of those boxes, or the thought of her unpacking them. A muffled snore wafted over from her pillow; she mumbled something about a tax return and rolled over on her back, her hair still secured in the silk turban she wore to stop it from knotting while she slept and a strip to clear her blocked pores stuck across her nose.

Her ballet company, Dance Theatre of Queens, was in hiatus since the managing partner had declared bankruptcy during their run at the Gaiety. Somehow the dancers were still getting paid, but once this contract finished in April Grace's plans seemed a little vague. Her visa ran out then, too, so maybe that would be an easy solution. He hated her accent; it reminded him too much of his mother, softened though her twang had become by her time in Ireland. Or at least it reminded him of what she sounded like on the VHS tape he had of her playing Desdemona. It was difficult to hear her voice any other way now in his head; he had accidentally recorded her Desdemona voice over his memory of how she had really spoken. Was she really only gone six years?

'Diiiilllllll,' Grace croaked from the bed, waving one long, muscular leg at him without opening her eyes. 'Waaaaaaattttteerrrr.'

He snapped his MacBook shut and pounded across to the kitchen, where he grudgingly filled her a glass. The pristine chrome fittings pleased him as he turned the tap. That cleaner was worth every euro he paid him. He plonked the glass down on the hardwood floor beside the mattress where Grace lay. Her hand reached out to find it and knocked it across the shining surface. Dillon cursed and started to mop it up with the towel he had draped over the radiator earlier. 'You can get it yourself this time. I'm late for work.'

Grace sat up in bed, kohl eyeliner smudged around her eyes, and prodded her forehead gently with her fingertips. 'Don't be mad, Dilly. It's only water.' She reached out to ruffle his hair, but he snapped his head back and retreated to the bathroom to toss the towel in the laundry basket.

'What time will you be home this evening? Will I cook us something?' She sat with her legs crossed, watching him as he packed his Alexander McQueen leather satchel.

'Don't bother. I have a show at Vicar Street, and I'll need to take the band on somewhere afterwards.' He filled a second glass of water and brought it back to her. She gulped it down in two big, thirsty mouthfuls, her teeth chattering from the cold.

'Will I come down? Who is it?'

'No one you'd have heard of. Electro-stuff. Why don't you meet the girls and see if there's any news? You shouldn't just hang around here all the time.'

Grace flopped back down on to the mattress and pulled a pillow over her face. Dillon crouched beside her for a moment, hesitated, then kissed her on her exposed hip bone. 'I'll call you later,' he said, lifting his fixie bike down from its rack to escape from his own home.

His phone vibrated in his pocket and he grimaced to see his father's name flash up; he had no photo saved for him, but he stared at the stock-image silhouette until the call disconnected. He could picture his father standing in the hallway at home waiting for him to answer but felt no desire to speak to him. His new life in Dublin was at such odds with his roots on the island. Sometimes he wondered how he had scrambled his way into this quasi-glamorous job as a promoter for the biggest entertainment agency in the country, booking talent for nightclub appearances and convincing international bands to include Ireland on their European tours. It certainly hadn't been discussed as a career option back in his Christian Brothers school in Galway, but the best advice he ever received had come from his mother: don't wait for someone else to offer you the life or job you want; you need to make it happen for yourself. He didn't like to think about how his mother had learned that lesson, what she'd sacrificed for that piece of wisdom. Mossy told him their father was impressed by his career, that he would love to hear more about his job, to share stories of his own adventures in music in Dublin in the seventies, but Dillon wasn't interested.

On the rare occasions he visited the island, his cashmere jumpers, Italian leather boots and luxurious winter coat made him look more like a tourist than a native. It was hard to picture him ever having been a boy there and he fully embraced his new identity as stranger when he was in the company of his father. It wasn't *just* that he blamed him for not saving his mother, although that certainly was enough to fuel his resentment; Dillon also struggled to forgive his father for how he had shut down after she was gone. Was it his responsibility to try to connect with his only remaining parent? He thought not. It made him feel like an orphan, and by the time Murtagh was revived enough to notice how long it had been since he'd last hugged his son, Dillon was out of reach.

Dillon strode through Temple Bar, trying to decide if he

should wait things out with Grace or finish it now. He was composing the perfect exit speech in his head when a figure ran out of the Irish Film Centre and knocked him into the street.

'What the hell?' he shouted as he regained his balance.

'Dillon? Mother Mary of God. Is that you, Dillon Moone?'

He looked up to see a woman with auburn hair tied in a bun on top of her head staring at him with big green eyes; she was wearing a white chef's coat and black-and-white chequered trousers; on her feet were pink Converse trainers.

It took him a second to place her and then he spluttered out a nervous laugh that surprised him with its force.

'Molly Bracken? What are you doing here?' he asked. 'Trying to finish me off after all these years?'

She held her arms out for a hug and he planted an awkward kiss on her ear before pulling away. His phone rang again but he muted it and shoved it back in his pocket.

'I didn't know you were living in Dublin,' he said. 'You finished cookery school, then?'

'Nothing gets past you, eh?' she said, smiling. 'Only the past six weeks, but I'm designing a new menu for the IFI in there. All local produce, nice organic ingredients. You should come in some evening.'

Dillon stepped back to allow a man pushing a vintage pram to squeeze between them on the narrow path.

'Well, I work in the evenings a –'

'It's grand,' she said. 'I was just being polite, don't look so worried. I wasn't proposing marriage or anything.'

He snorted and spontaneously leaned in for another hug, surprising both of them.

'Do you get back to the island much?' he asked.

'More than you do, I hear.' She smiled. 'My mam hasn't been well, so I go every second weekend now. My little sister, Sinéad, and I alternate. Do you remember her?'

'Sort of,' he said, frowning. 'I'm sorry about your mam. Wow, it must be years since I've seen you.'

She stepped away from him. 'Not since your twenty-first, when you dumped me and then got off with Sorcha Clarke in the middle of the dancefloor.'

He stood perfectly still, hands in pockets, and focused on a point over her head.

'Yeah, that wasn't my finest moment. I'm sorry, Moll,' he said. 'You didn't deserve that.'

She put her hands on her hips and chased his eyes with hers.

'I didn't,' she said, 'but it doesn't matter now. I hope you've found a better philosophy.'

'Philosophy?' he asked, waving at a friend as he sped past on a moped.

'Hurt first,' she said. 'That's what you told me – hurt first.'

Dillon grimaced, shoving back thoughts of Grace as he met Molly's eye.

'Well, my heart's still intact, if that's what you're asking?' he said. 'No damage done.'

'It wasn't, but I guess, good for you!' She gave him a little wave and carried on, calling back over her shoulder, 'See you around, Son Night.'

The past colliding with his carefully curated present was unsettling.

He dreaded to think what Molly thought of his abstinence from the island.

And how much it might mirror how his mother would feel to see him rejecting his father.

Maeve had always liked Molly, called her 'a good egg', his mother's favourite term of endearment.

He watched Molly walking away; the memory of her walking ahead of him up the pier road on the island made his stomach flip.

He opened his mouth to call her name but swallowed it.

His phone was ringing.

He answered it and strode onwards up Crow Lane.

Hurt first.

Galway: March, 2012

Someday soon, Tomás vowed, he would empty the basement of the university's flotsam and jetsam: the crates of damaged folders stacked imperfectly; the unsealed cardboard boxes with crumpled paperwork erupting through torn seams and inefficient brown sticking tape. The magnolia floor tiles were sticky underfoot, the original colour revealed only when an old filing cabinet was shoved into a new position. A fluorescent blue liquid congealed beneath the boiler, snaking in ominous streams beneath a tower of wicker waste-paper baskets.

Mossy peeled his trainers from the floor with each tread, edging around the obstacles in his path so as not to disrupt a single item and trigger an avalanche of chaos. The dust tickled his nose, already antagonised by hay fever, and he released three epic sneezes. He scanned the room, his eyes flitting over a red crate of lost umbrellas, broken chairs, venetian blinds rolled and tied with their own cords; cracked blackboards leaning at an angle against the dirty window, burst purple velvet cushions with their insides showing, a black plastic bag tied with Christmas tinsel. All fallen soldiers of administration abandoned here and illuminated by a solitary swinging yellow bulb. It hummed. Attracting a moth that circled it relentlessly. A surge of students trampled past the window, singing along to The Lumineers' 'Hey

Ho', which blasted through tinny speakers. He smiled to think of Kalindi in the kitchen that morning, dancing with the kids to that same song while trying to pack her briefcase, simultaneously eating a slice of dry toast and brushing her hair. He remembered how he and Dillon had often danced with their mother in much the same way.

It was for Kalindi he had braved the basement, hunting for a unicycle she wanted for reasons undisclosed. Convinced one was down here somewhere, he continued his hunt with more enthusiasm and tried to ignore the faint scratching noises he could discern in the corner of the room.

While he hunted, Kalindi was leaving a slice of carrot cake in a Styrofoam container on his desk in the research library. She scribbled 'Don't forget to eat' on a pink Post-it note and stuck it on top. As usual, his desk was perfectly tidy: three photo frames all lined up in descending height – the black-and-white print of him and Dillon on the beach with their mother, Sive crawling towards them; their twin babies, Maya Maeve and Ajay Deepinder, sitting on either side of Murtagh wearing Galway football jerseys and nappies; their wedding day at Chelsea Registry Office in London.

Kalindi picked up their wedding photo and grimaced. She hated that dress now, how frumpy it made her appear. They looked relaxed and happy, but she knew it belied the anxiety she felt as the photo was taken. Their wedding hadn't been spontaneous, but it had been extremely small. Just her Aunt Rupi and Dillon as witnesses, and a Polaroid photo shipped with a long letter back to her parents in Bengal. The children were two now and had still not met their naana and nanee, although she held them up to the camera on her computer whenever they attempted to Skype. At least they had Murtagh, and he doted on them as if he knew he had to compensate for all the other missing grandparents.

It was little surprise to anyone Mossy had chosen to become a librarian; no one expected much chit-chat in a library, and it allowed him to spend time with his best of friends, Flannery O'Connor, Jane Austen, Hemingway and the Brontës. It was, however, a great delight for his father when he discovered that the security of his sanctuary had been invaded by Kalindi, the kindest of girls, fiercely intelligent, who took pleasure in walking across acres with him, equally comfortable in deep conversation or companionable silence. She understood the homesickness that filled his heart; his for a home that could never exist again; hers for one that continued on in her absence. Mossy, or Tomás, as Kalindi always called him, had the good sense to marry her as soon as he possibly could. When Murtagh had heard about the wedding, he decided not to be hurt by his own absence. He understood; it was easier to have few people there than suffer the acute pain of just one missing person.

Kalindi returned to her office in the art history department; she wiped a smudge from the brass plaque on her door with a handkerchief, lingering over her name, Dr Kalindi Aguri Moone, and nodded. On her desk lay a present for Murtagh: prints from the kintsugi exhibition she'd visited in Tokyo. She felt a tug, remembering his look of longing when she told him she was attending; 'the art of precious scars,' he'd said. She spread the images across her desk in a fan, examining the glossy coloured photographs of the ceramic pots, once broken, now pieced back together, their

cracks filled with lacquer mixed with gold and silver powder. Their fractured history celebrated and not hidden.
Illuminated. She gathered the prints together and sealed
them in a brown envelope and placed it on top of two heavy
pouches of the kintsugi powder wrapped in white paper
inside a corrugated cardboard box. They would bring it to
him on Sunday, with the unicycle he'd mentioned in passing
he'd always wanted to try. His fifty-fourth birthday seemed
as good a time as any.

She heard squealing from the marble corridor outside her
door and looked up to see Mossy wobbling through the
door on the unicycle. 'It appears I am something of a natural,' he said, before crashing into her bookshelves.

'Aagggh! Be careful!' she shouted, rushing forward to steady
him.

'You know something, darling,' he said. 'I'm not sure, if our
house burned down, I'd be the first thing you'd save.' She
helped him dismount and patted him on the bottom. 'But you
wouldn't need saving,' she said. 'You've got legs of your own.
The books, however, can't help themselves.'

He stood over her desk and poked the squidgy parcel with
his forefinger. 'Is that the stuff for Dad?'

'It is,' she said. 'And the unicycle!'

'Oh no! Is that why you wanted it? Where do you even
get these ideas?'

'From listening,' she said, and yanked his ear.

'What is it?' he asked. 'Your worry vein is protruding.'

She rubbed between her eyebrows with her right knuckle.

'It's just your dad, the studio, his work. I wish he would
try some new things; those sculptures he used to make, they

were so, so powerful – and now, he's happy reproducing the same things over and over again. It's so sad.'

Mossy shrugged. 'His heart's not in it.'

She closed the box and neatly secured it with tape.

'But after all this time?'

'It doesn't feel so long ago to me.'

Kalindi stopped what she was doing, watched her husband pretend to read the spines of books on her shelves.

'I'm sorry, hon, I didn't mean it like that. I just don't understand how he can shut off that side of himself. He has a gift, and instead he acts like a factory worker on an assembly line.'

'I feel bad that we don't visit more often. When we were in school we made the trip from the island to here five days a week, and now it feels like such an expedition to go once a month.'

Kalindi nodded. 'And we should make more excuses for him to come to us. Your dad loves a good project. I'll have a think about it.'

Mossy sneezed, three times, and she passed him a handkerchief plucked from amidst the clutter on her desk. 'Are you picking up the kids today?' he asked.

'You know I am.' She sighed. 'Every Tuesday. I only forgot them once, you know.'

'That's not what I was suggesting.' He tossed the handkerchief into her overflowing waste-paper basket. 'I'd better go. There's a tour coming through at three.'

He dipped her into a Hollywood kiss, and she laughed, pushing him away.

'Don't forget to eat something,' she said, and started

sizing up the unicycle for wrapping paper. He was humming 'Hey Ho' as he left the room, and she picked up the tune.

Kalindi wasn't sure she believed in luck, but she knew she believed in him.

Was that why Murtagh was so stuck?

The person who had believed in him most was gone.

She thought of the Cure song Sive had sung at her birthday and realised 'Just Like Heaven' could have been written for Murtagh.

The only girl he'd ever loved was drowned deep inside of him.

And now he was still lost.

And so lonely.

How could she help him believe in himself again?

As he had inspired her after the babies were born, when she was wracked with guilt and felt she was failing both at home and at work. He had taken her aside and said, 'Kalindi, you have a chance now to set your daughter free – break the chain of guilt you've inherited from your mother – and her from her mother before that. Let Maya see you loving your work, and taking time for you, and so one day she will feel okay to claim that for herself. There's probably fewer greater gifts you can give her.'

How could she help him honour Maeve's memory but still find a way to move forward?

To let go just enough.

So, the scars became precious cracks, instead.

Cracks that let the light in.

Dublin: February, 2013

Murtagh sat in the window on the first floor of Cornucopia restaurant on Wexford Street.

He fiddled with the gold sash curtains that brushed against the back of his chair. It annoyed him, feeling the presence of them there, the glance of colour in his peripheral vision, but he couldn't change tables again. This was his third attempt to settle; his first seat rejected as the table rocked a little when he leaned his elbows on it; the second because it was in the direct path of the door so it was impossible not to look up at everyone as they flounced through as if arriving on stage. This conversation was going to be difficult enough without the constant distraction of unwitting intruders. He should have chosen somewhere quieter, but at least they'd be by the window now. Awkward silences, should there be any, could be so much more subtly negated by people-watching through a window than by being trapped in the centre of a room.

Even though the watery February sunlight blasted through the windows, a yellow tealight burned defiantly in a glass holder. He nudged it forward with two fingers across the wooden table, testing how close he could push it to the brink without it falling over. A waitress wearing a long hemp dress that covered her feet shuffled over to him with his chai latte and the wheatgrass shot he had accidentally also ordered, but he accepted both, worrying as she moved away that her skirt would trip her on the stairs. Downing the wheatgrass shot in one swift movement, he grimaced as it slid down his throat, beating his chest with his fist to expedite its passage, then surreptitiously placed the empty glass on the windowsill behind the curtains.

With every creak of the floorboards he glanced towards the door, willing a familiar face to appear while simultaneously dreading it. If this thread remained unpulled, wouldn't everything be simpler? But that wasn't what he wanted. His life had become so neat that he barely impacted upon the world at all; he was desperate to colour outside the lines. There was room in his life for one more dream, maybe.

And then, feeling as if he had received no warning at all, Murtagh saw him.

There he stood, across the street, waiting for a break in the traffic. As if he were an ordinary person conducting his business in Dublin that day. As if the Earth hadn't been quietly rotating towards this moment for decades; the truth his grief had illuminated.

Murtagh watched him waiting as the restaurant dissolved around him. He wished himself invisible, so he could observe forever, prolonging this moment of anticipation before he confronted whatever reality would offer instead.

Fionn looked physically different and yet essentially unchanged.

His dreadlocks were gone, replaced now by a close crop. It made his cheekbones appear more prominent, his jawline more severe.

Silver-rimmed spectacles and a full beard gave him an air of sophistication that Murtagh couldn't recall from before. He was forced to admit how much time had truly passed – of course Fionn would have abandoned his khaki shorts and tie-dyed T-shirts by now. He just hadn't expected the slim-fitting dark slacks and crisp white buttoned-down shirt or a silk turquoise scarf.

Murtagh glanced down at his navy corduroys, seeing with new eyes how old his good trousers had become. He sucked in his stomach and tucked in his blue-and-white check shirt before pulling it back outside and sighed.

It was all he could do not to attempt an escape, but it was too late.

Fionn looked up and saw him.

Stared directly into his eyes.

Raised his hand to wave, but Murtagh detected no smile.

If anything, confusion creased his face.

Shock, even.

Was that at his appearance?

Murtagh leaned back behind the curtains.

Gripped the white rail that bordered the window.

Later Fionn would tell him, yes, he had been shocked, not by how Murtagh looked, but rather by the realisation he was sitting there at all. A physical human, flesh and muscle, wearing clothes, hair and nails growing, heart beating and blood flowing. As if he suddenly understood that for all these years he hadn't been frozen exactly as Fionn had remembered him. As if time hadn't stood still on the island ever since the moment he had left on the ferry with no one there to wave him goodbye.

Murtagh heard a stumble at the door and braced himself for impact, but Fionn didn't appear as quickly as he'd expected.

He forced himself to stare at the laminated red-and-white menu centred on the table.

To read it slowly and not watch the door.

His lips silently mouthed the words: *Sweet potato and butter-bean soup, garlic potatoes with roasted hazelnuts, baked tofu with beetroot, pear and rocket.* The text blurred before his eyes when he felt a hand on his shoulder.

The firm grip steadied him and he placed his own hand on top of Fionn's.

It was cool to his touch, the softness of his skin now familiar in a way that he'd forgotten, but that brought him immediate comfort.

Without meeting his eyes, he stood and enveloped Fionn with his arms. Breathed in the soapy cleanliness of him, the hint of lemongrass, a note of something muskier. They sat, their knees touching so gently under the table that Murtagh wasn't sure if he was imagining the sensation of it.

Fionn spoke first.

'Maeve – I'm so sorry, Murtagh. I –'

Murtagh shook his head. 'I know,' he said. 'I know.'

Fionn watched him, absorbing what could not be said but lived in his eyes. 'When I got your letter. I couldn't believe it. I'd given up waiting for you to reply.'

'I posted it in Eyre Square five years to the day since I got yours,' Murtagh explained. 'On the eleventh of January, 2013.'

Fionn bit his thumbnail then visibly flinched, joining his hands together on the table as if in prayer. 'What took you so long?' he asked. 'Your letter didn't explain why now, after all this time.'

Through the window, Murtagh watched a child run out in front of a pizza-delivery man on a bicycle, who swerved to avoid him. The boy dropped a doughnut on the street and started to cry as his mother yanked him away by the sleeve of his bottle-green school-uniform jumper.

'It felt like it was the right time.' He stopped, and Fionn nodded at him to go on. 'No, that's not true,' he continued. 'It was more like I suddenly realised that it would never be the right time. Not for someone like me. And I was tired of waiting for some great sign that would never come. I still can't believe she wrote to you. She left no letter for the kids, you know? That was hard for them, very hard.'

'Why do you think she chose not to?'

Murtagh smoothed his hair away from his face. 'Because there would never be the right words? So they wouldn't fix-ate on it? So they'd remember her and not just what she said in a letter? I'm not sure, but Maeve would have had her rea-sons, and they would have been good ones.'

Fionn leaned back in his chair and looked up at the wait-ress, who was beaming at him, twisting her ginger ponytail between her fingers while she waited for his order. Murtagh didn't like the way he smiled back, as if they shared a secret that would never be known to him.

Fionn ordered a peppermint tea then called her back to upgrade to an espresso instead.

'You know I didn't get it until much later. Maeve's letter, I mean,' he said. 'I was teaching in Sri Lanka at the time, when it happened, and it was nearly two years before I was back at my mum's. I might never have found it at all if I hadn't gone home to clear out her flat when she died.'

'Oh, I'm sorry, Fionn. I didn't realise . . . I know how close you and your mother were.'

Fionn pulled back his shoulders, sat straighter in his chair.

'If she meant that much to me,' he said, 'maybe I should have been there looking after her instead of gallivanting around the world sending her postcards.'

Murtagh moved the menus out of the way and touched Fionn's hand tentatively before recoiling again.

'You can't think like that. All parents want is for their children to be happy, trust me. You have to live your own life – and it must have been sudden?'

Fionn nodded. 'Pneumonia. It shouldn't have killed her, but it did. It was complicated.'

'Had you told her . . . about . . . you? Before she died?'

Fionn smiled. 'Yes, she laughed at me. Thought it hysterical that I imagined it was news.'

He looked relieved to see the waitress arrive, and Murtagh waited for him to speak again.

'Do you want to read it?' Fionn paused. 'Maeve's letter?'

Murtagh leaned back in his chair, moved it a little away from the table.

'You brought it?'

Fionn reached inside his blazer and fumbled to open a small red wooden button that secured a pocket there. From inside he retrieved one of the powder-blue envelopes that Maeve had loved so much. It was creased, frayed at the corners, the stamp curling away from its place. Murtagh stared at Maeve's handwriting, feeling the stroke of the letters curling up from the page like vines to wind around his wrists and bind him. *Oh, Maeve.*

Fionn placed it on the table before him but Murtagh looked away.

'Not now, Fionn. Not now.' His hand hovered over the envelope, but he didn't touch it.

Fionn buttoned it back inside his blazer.

'I understand how you feel about your mother,' Murtagh continued, cupping his coffee in both palms. 'The absence of action can feel terribly violent in the end – aggressive passivity. I feel with Maeve, I was too . . . too hands off, maybe, when I should have been grabbing on. Stronger than her. I feel the person I am now can see what needed to be done, but the me back then was incapable. Did she want me to intervene? Could I have helped her?'

Fionn took his glasses off and wiped the lenses with Murtagh's untouched napkin.

'You did help her, Murtagh,' he said. 'No one could have loved her more. It's so easy to look back and imagine a different way of being, but you both did the best you could with who you were then. We can't resent our past selves for not knowing or thinking what we know and think now. We had to live through all of that history to be able to reach that understanding.'

'But Maeve never got the chance.'

'No,' he said quietly, 'but you did.'

His cup clattered into its saucer and Murtagh pressed his fingers over his eyes, taking deep breaths.

'Do you feel like a walk?' Fionn asked, squeezing his knee under the table.

Murtagh smiled weakly. 'Didn't I always?'

Following Fionn down the stairs, he wondered what kind of pair they made.

He reached out to lift a single brown hair from Fionn's shoulder and let his hand, this time, rest upon him for a moment.

With each step, his boots felt a tiny bit lighter and something within him began to unravel.

He let the threads go and they rolled out from his fingertips into the street below, guiding him on.

Inis Óg: 20 September, 2014

Not many people were expected to arrive from the mainland for Nollaig's thirtieth-birthday party. It would be Christmas week, after all, and the crossing perilous, as the Atlantic raged against who knew what. It made it easier to explain an absence of friends; the guest list consisted mostly of islanders. There was no need for official invitations; word had spread, along with news of Pegeen O'Flaherty expecting again and the trouble the Clancy brothers had found for themselves after the match in Cork against Skibbereen. Everything was set for Saturday night; the function room of Tigh Ned's reserved, unnecessarily, since July.

'Of course, I can't celebrate my birthday on the actual day,' she'd said to Ned as he scribbled her name across the page in a battered blue diary from 1998 that the ESB had sent with his electricity bill sixteen years before. It was helpfully marked each month with the day the payment was due.

'The maaynest thing I ever got,' he'd said, and repeated again now as Nollaig watched him misspell her name with a stubby pencil. She ignored him. 'As usual, people want to be with their own families that day.'

Ned coughed and closed the cover of the diary with a slap, rolling the pencil along the top of the bar. 'Aye,' he answered as he watched the pencil stall in a circle of sticky red lemonade. 'Some people are fierce selfish all right.'

In the nine years since Maeve had died, the Moone family had avoided spending Christmas together on the island. Any mention of even the possibility of it happening arose only when immovable plans were already fixed. On this policy of passive aggression, they were resolutely, if silently, bound. So when, in September 2014, Nollaig called each of her siblings to request their presence at home for her birthday that year, she was met with varying degrees of enthusiasm. The first thing Dillon said was that he wasn't staying for Christmas. 'I'll swim back to Galway if I have to.'

'I don't care about Christmas,' she said. 'Just promise me you'll be there for the party.'

This was the big test, she had decided. Having never pushed them to come home before, if they didn't show up for her this time – well, they'd better.

After the plans were set, Murtagh announced he, too, had something important to discuss with them while they were all together. Speculation as to what he would say was rife, but he held his counsel. Nollaig, still living with their father, was particularly peeved by her own lack of insider information; Murtagh's intentions remained unfathomable to her, despite her persistent needling away as she tidied up around him, or sat on the garden wall, her heels beating a rhythm against the stone as she watched him prune the roses.

'You're not sick, are you? Because you can't nurse that secret for another three months if you are,' she said one evening as he cursed the *Irish Times* crossword and grimaced at how cold his coffee had become since he'd started it. 'And it would ruin the party, you know?'

'No, love,' he answered, without shifting his gaze from the black-and-white print. 'I'm no sicker than any man of fifty-six could expect to be. Now, can you think of a *nymph who loves to dance in Trinidad*, seven letters, ending in O?'

Nollaig bit her lip while she chased the answer around in her mind. 'Calypso? She was a nymph who loved Odysseus, but I don't know where Trinidad comes in.'

Murtagh tapped the newspaper with his pen in victory. '*Maith an cailín*! Good girl! That's it!'

He folded the newspaper and tucked his fountain pen into the breast pocket of his shirt, after checking once, and then twice, that the lid was secure. Leaning slightly back on the hind legs of his chair, he saw waves of worry ebbing and flowing across his eldest daughter's face.

'I promise I'm fine, Noll. There's something I need to discuss with you all, and I want everyone to hear it at the same time. And straight from this old horse's mouth. I know it's hard on you, but try to be patient.'

'The others don't believe me. They think I must be in on it and won't stop interrogating me,' she said, half-heartedly flicking through the *Irish Times*.

'Well, they will have to be patient, too. Shall we have fish and chips for supper? I have a real hankering on me for a nice piece of mackerel. Would you be tempted?'

'Okay, I'll go,' she sighed, and messily shuffled the newspaper closed. 'You get the fire going while I'm gone.'

Murtagh listened as his daughter wrestled her bicycle down the hallway with more clanging than should have been necessary and held his breath until the front door slammed behind her. Of all his children, he worried about Nollaig the most. *Would Aindí be coming to the party? And his wife?*

As much as a father could mean to a daughter, he knew he wasn't enough. That he should not be enough. And he hoped it wasn't too late for her. *His news would give her a push all right, if the shock didn't kill her first.*

And what about the other three? Would they take it any better?

It was a daily torment to fantasise about what each of their reactions would be; self-flagellation to prepare himself for the worst.

Meeting the war halfway, Maeve would have said, were she here, although if she were still here, there would be nothing for her to comment on. Would there?

Am I really ready for this?

He knew they held a fixed idea of who their father was; could easily picture how the fabric of his life was sewn together, imagine him working in the studio, looking out over the island from his long-suffering leather stool, or nursing a hot whiskey in the snug of Ned's as he held his toes up to the fire, or fishing off the furthest point on the island that the real fisherman insisted was the Bermuda Triangle for fish and where one would never be caught. He hadn't proved the islanders wrong yet, but he loved it there, where the island felt adrift and the sky and sea merged into one. Maeve and he had often sat there, melting into one shadow, while the light dissolved. He was sure his children felt confident enough to anticipate his every move.

What will the fall-out be when I shatter that illusion?

Will I become a stranger to them? A liar? A coward? A fraud?

In the dusk light he opened a parcel containing a present he had bought for Nollaig and placed it on Maeve's old desk. A sewing machine. It was back in fashion, it seemed, to make your own clothes. He wondered what made young women hanker after older lifestyles that were so much more difficult than their own. Maybe they pined for the physical artefacts of life that the digital age had squandered: hand-written letters, vinyl records, that which was made by hand, slowly, with care. *Maybe less had proved more, after all, for some.*

He heard Nollaig burst back into the hallway, a fog of Aindí O'Shea mingled in her hair that was just tousled on one side. She didn't meet his eye as she unpacked the fish and chips on the kitchen table and poured them two glasses of milk. He knew it wasn't his place to comment and swallowed the instinct he always had to tell his daughter to leave that married man be.

'We don't need plates, do we, Daddy?'

'No, love, they're grand as they are. Turn on *The Late Late Show* there and we'll have them in front of the fire.'

Normally she objected to eating in the living room but said nothing as she passed him the two soggy bundles of salt-and-vinegar paper. She followed after Murtagh, a pint glass of milk in each hand and a jar of Heinz tomato ketchup tucked under her arm. Father and daughter sat in their usual spots in front of the television, feigning rapt attention at the screen.

They were both glad the other could not read their thoughts.

Inis Óg: 20 December, 2014

The morning of the party

At nine o'clock in the morning, Nollaig was banging on the door of Tigh Ned's for access, two boxes of decorations at her feet and a denim rucksack covered in embroidery patches on her back with rolls of paper sticking out of the top. Ned didn't look surprised to see her, even though he answered the door in his vest and long-johns, his face still covered in shaving foam. He waved her in and tiptoed in his bare feet back behind the bar and through the grey velvet curtain that might have once been cream and which separated his work and home life.

Nollaig struggled into the back room with her paraphernalia and dropped it on the wooden floor, raising a cloud of dust. With a heavy sigh, she stomped to the bar and found a dustpan and brush, returning to attack the floor with vigour. In truth, she mostly moved dust around, but the effort pleased her. She turned on all the radiators, smug to think of Ned's face if he knew, and listened in satisfaction as the pipes creaked into awakening for the first time in months. A smell of burning tickled her nose as the dust resting on the pipes singed, so she spritzed the room with jasmine air freshener and hoped for the best. Through a little speaker connected to her smartphone, Janis Ian kept her company while she worked.

Between each dark green window frame she hung one of

her home-made posters. They were covered with dozens of photos of herself dating from when she was a baby up until recent times, and scrawled happy-birthday messages, the sort friends made to embarrass each other at parties. She hoped no one would guess she'd written them all herself. It hadn't been easy to find enough pictures of her looking as if she was having fun. Most of the photos on her phone were selfies, or pictures of Mossy's twins, or her neighbours' cats, or snaps of recipes from cookbooks she was too mean to buy in Charlie Byrne's Bookshop in Galway. She stood back to survey her work and nodded in satisfaction. Her eyes lingered over the one photo she had of herself and her mother when she was a baby. Black and white. Herself, a few months old, lying on her belly as she laughed at Maeve, who was pointing at something in the sky.

'Probably calling out clouds to me,' her father had said, but he couldn't remember the exact day. 'There were so many lazy days like that.'

Nollaig smiled.

She couldn't remember even one.

From the cardboard boxes she lifted pink crystal tealight holders. Pink wasn't her colour, but she'd won a hundred of them in an auction on eBay. From a wedding that was cancelled, apparently. Was that bad luck? No, you needed prospects of a wedding first to worry about it being called off. She snaked them across the windowsills, white seashells scattered between them like a trail of breadcrumbs. Only the balloons were left. Inflating them impatiently with a warped bicycle pump, she persevered until a cluster of three was taped to the end of every bench and a solo balloon stuck to the back of all the wooden chairs that lined the walls. She covered the trestle tables at the back with white tablecloths and lined the edges up perfectly so they sat two inches above the ground. Liamie Beag would be bringing in the food at seven. 'One pot of vegetable curry for the *vegetarians*,' he'd said. 'And one of beef stew. A few baskets of chips, a couple of plates of salad and plenty of crisps in bowls, and you're done. I'll even throw in a few goujons. Happy out.'

'What about a cake?' she'd asked.

'Will you be ordering that yourself now?'

'I will.'

'Chocolate gateau or carrot cake with icing?'

'Carrot.'

'And the message, *Happy Birthday, Nollaig*?'

'I suppose so,' she said, her humiliation complete as she handed him euros and watched as they vanished inside his breast pocket like a magic trick.

'I'll keep it in the pub fridge. Give me a nod when you want it and I'll bring it in.'

Nollaig hoped everyone would turn up on time. Hated to think of the food going cold.

She stood at the door of the function room and decided she'd done the best she could. There was no point wondering how different things might have been if her mother had been here. She had spent too long walking that road already, and it only led to more loneliness.

The afternoon

Mossy arrived first, Maya in her Spiderman costume on his back as together they stepped on to the pier, Kalindi walking behind them, holding Ajay's hand as he struggled to steer a scooter. Murtagh crouched down, with Packie the koala bear perched on his shoulders, and held his arms out wide enough to enfold two giddy four-year-olds. Kalindi leaned over and kissed him on the top of his head while Mossy assembled all their belongings into a bundle he could carry. He watched the easy way his family embraced his father, so full of the affection now that he, too, remembered receiving as a boy and then had so keenly felt the absence of after his mother died. His father, well, it took his grandchildren to unlock that part of him again. Mossy rubbed his back and Murtagh smiled up at him.

'*Fáilte romhaibh*,' he said. 'Welcome home, Son Day.'

'Where's the birthday girl?'

'She's in Galway having her hair done. Herself and Sive are getting the next boat. Si flew in last night and stayed with one of the girls from school – Aisling, I think. Was Dillon not coming with you?'

'He was, but he must have missed the boat.' Kalindi's eyes met Mossy's but he shook his head at her. 'He'll probably come on the next one with the girls.'

Murtagh stood up and searched his son's face.

'He *will* come, though, won't he? If he doesn't, we'll never hear the end of it. Your sister is up to ninety and –'

Mossy held out his hands to Ajay and Maya, who each grabbed on. Maya, always on the left, Ajay always on the right. 'He'll be here, Dad,' he said. 'He promised.'

Nollaig burst through the door while Murtagh was dishing up pancakes with blueberries and honey to Mossy and his clan. 'Sive's staying at the hotel, can you believe it?' she shouted from the hallway before the front door had even closed. 'And she's brought some eejit from London with her. *Luka*. If that's his real name. Twice her age and half the cop-on. He has an *asymmetrical haircut*. And is wearing black nail polish. Does he think that makes him edgy? Please. He looks like an extra from a Joy Division video.'

Murtagh took off his glasses and rubbed his eyes in an attempt to alleviate the pressure headache that was building behind them. Kalindi stood and fetched another plate from the cupboard, squeezing his shoulders as she passed by. Whenever she looked at him, all she saw was Tomás of the future, although she hoped life would go a lot easier on her husband.

Nollaig strode into the kitchen, and the sight of the twins softened her. 'It's my two best pals,' she said, hugging each in turn, holding her face away at an angle so as not to smudge the make-up Tracy in Brown Thomas had applied so enthusiastically.

'Is it not a bit much?' she had asked Tracy as she puzzled at her own face in the mirror. 'I don't even look like me.'

'You do, doll. It's just *glam* you. You can totally pull it off. What are you doing with your hair?'

Nollaig's face fell. 'This is it. I've already been to the hair-dresser's. It's meant to be an up-do, but it looks a bit –'

'Scrooged up? Tight? Old-fashioned?' Tracy offered, hand on her hip. 'Do you mind if I . . . ?'

Nollaig nodded.

Tracy unpicked all the hairpins holding Nollaig's do together and told her to turn her head upside down and give it a shake. Starting at the nape of her neck, Tracy teased out the curls and back-combed them to add volume. 'Now, give it another good shake.'

When Nollaig looked in the mirror she screamed. 'It's massive – what have you done? I've spent the last thirty years trying to stop my hair looking like this.'

'Hon, that's where you've been going wrong. Your hair is bleedin' deadly. It's time to set it free. You're leaving here a new woman.'

Nollaig raised her hand to touch her new do, but Tracy slapped her hand away.

'Don't you dare try to flatten it. Trust me. You look a picture.'

'A picture of what?' Nollaig smiled at herself self-consciously in the mirror. She did look different, and that had to be a good thing, didn't it? She slipped Tracy an extra ten euros before she left, stealing another glance at her reflection in the window on the way out.

Kalindi walked around the table to hug her sister-in-law. 'Noll, you look like a film star. Where did you get all that hair from?'

Nollaig laughed and blushed as she kissed the air between their faces. 'I felt like a change. Hiya, Moss. Where's Dillon?'

The atmosphere shifted as she glanced around the table.

'He's not here yet. Come here, sis, and give your little brother a hug. Should we give you your presents now or at the party?'

'Where is he? Have you tried his mobile? There's only one ferry left and, even if he catches that, he'll be late. Did you text him?'

She pulled out her mobile phone and tried to call him, but it wouldn't connect.

'His phone's off, or out of coverage,' Mossy explained, 'but don't worry about him. He knows he has to be here.'

'Has to? Does he not want to? It's not like I'm dragging him here kicking and screaming.'

Mossy looked away and spooned another pile of blueberries on to his plate. Nollaig stared at him, red lipstick staining her teeth. 'Is that it? You're all here under duress?'

Kalindi pulled out the kitchen chair beside her and lowered Nollaig into it by the elbow.

'Of course not,' she said. 'You know Dillon finds it hard to come home at this time of year.'

'At any time of year,' Murtagh mumbled under his breath, still reeling from the shock of Nollaig's makeover and the news of Sive's guest. He turned to his eldest daughter. 'When you say *twice her age*, you're exaggerating, I presume?' She slammed a silver spoon against the table, where it bounced into the sugar bowl with a clatter.

'Dad, can you focus? I'm worried about Dillon.'

'I'm sorry, love. Listen, don't upset yourself. Tell me, is Sive coming home before the party?'

Nollaig scraped the hind legs of her chair across the floor tiles and stormed out of the room. Kalindi shook her head at the two men, watching her leave while she folded her napkin into a perfect square. 'I'll go,' she said. 'Tomás, can you give these two their bath and try to get them settled down a bit before the sitter gets here? We'll never get out of the house later otherwise.'

'I will,' he said. 'Thanks, Kal. Go work your magic.'

After she left, father and son sat together eating cold pancakes for a few minutes longer before Mossy started to navigate the twins towards the downstairs bathroom.

'Do you need any help at all? Shall I fill the tub?' Murtagh asked.

'I'm grand, Dad, we'll –' Mossy looked up and saw his father properly for what felt like the first time in years. When had he turned so grey? 'Actually, that would be brilliant. We'll be there in a sec.'

Murtagh jumped up and rushed to gather warm towels from the hot press on his way to the bathroom. Mossy heard him humming a tune over the sound of the water gushing into the tub, but he didn't know the song. It sounded like a happy one.

The evening

Nollaig wasn't much of a drinker but decided that a few glasses of Prosecco would help to steady her nerves and lift her spirits. She had barely allowed herself to celebrate a birthday at all since her mother had died, but she needed to face her third decade with a different attitude. She wasn't sure what her new philosophy would be yet, or what she might have in her, but wanted to at least take part in the world a bit more. Not by abandoning her father, though; that was inconceivable; she was looking more for something to add on than to take away.

In the post-Prosecco fizzy glow she was swimming in, her cocktail dress from Coast looked perfect. A purple velvet bodice and taffeta skirt; she knew it was perhaps more fitting for a wedding than a birthday party, but this dress was compensating for all the years of doing without. She came downstairs, and her father was waiting for her, sombre in a black tweed suit and white cotton collarless shirt. 'You'd have made a lovely priest, Daddy,' she said, and he threw his eyes up to Heaven.

'You wouldn't wish that on your ould father now, would you? You look lovely, Noll. Are you ready?'

She stopped in front of the hallway mirror to gently pat her curls and pull them outside the collar of her coat.

'Have the others left? I don't want to be the first to arrive.'

'Mossy and Kalindi are gone ahead of us and they were going to collect Si and, er, *Luka* on the way. I presume Dillon will turn up eventually.'

'Do you think we should wait a bit longer? Give the place a chance to fill up a bit?'

'Noll, let's go.'

Nollaig didn't know that Mossy and Kalindi had left two hours before to knock into all the neighbours along the way to chivvy them along, telephoning those further afield to make sure they were leaving soon.

They walked to Tigh Ned's, Nollaig gripping her father's arm to steady herself in black patent stilettos that were never intended for the craggy roads of the island. 'It's almost like we're walking down the aisle,' she said, and laughed wryly.

'It's better,' her father answered. 'Because you've still got all that to look forward to, if you want it. Life isn't just about getting married, you know. Or staying married. Much as the world tells you so. There are so many ways to find happiness.'

She snorted. 'Like you do, you mean?' Her remorse was immediate. 'I'm sorry, Daddy. That wasn't fair. But you've had your great love affair. Even if it's behind you, at least you had it once. Isn't that better than never at all?'

They continued in silence until they reached the front door of Tigh Ned's.

'Ready?'

'You go first and come out and tell me if there's anyone there.'

'Nollaig, would you get a grip. Get in there, girl.'

He opened the door wide and she stepped into the pub. Only Jimmy Severin sat on a high stool, watching a repeat of the Laois v Kerry match on the television. Ned wasn't even serving behind the bar.

'Oh no, where is everyone?'

'Keep going! Sure, isn't the party in the back?'

Her heel caught in the gap between the floorboards as she proceeded slowly to the rear of the pub. She hopped on one foot, holding on to her father for balance, as he wrestled her shoe free, cursing under his breath.

Back on two feet, she paused, gathering herself as she approached the function-room door.

Disco lights flickered in its frosted glass panels and she could hear the muffled sound of a Blondie track and, best of all, the beautiful chorus of voices chattering – lots of voices chattering. She flung the door back and was overwhelmed to see half the inhabitants of the island crammed into every available inch. A great cheer went up when they saw she'd arrived and Nollaig was propelled through the crowd, passed from hugging arm to arm until she was standing on a little stage, just two feet off the ground, where Seanie O'Shea had set up his DJ box. A table full of presents was set up beside him and in the centre a giant birthday cake in the shape of an N covered in chocolate buttons, with 'Happy Birthday' spelled out in miniature vanilla cupcakes. 'That's not the cake I ordered,' she whispered to Kalindi, who laughed at her. 'Of course not, you daft woman. Did you think we wouldn't get you a cake? Have you no faith in us at all? Brace yourself, I think your father's going to say a few words.'

'But is everyone here? Where's Dillon?'

'Did you not see him? Look, he's in the corner over there with Si's boyfriend. That's his punishment for coming so late.'

Nollaig saw her little brother, backed into the corner of the room, while Luka towered over him, arms gesticulating wildly as he waxed lyrical on something dull enough to drain all the colour from Dillon's face. When Dillon saw Nollaig watching, he waved and used the intervention as an excuse to break free.

'Documentary-maker,' he said. 'Don't ask. I mean it. Never, ever, ask him about what.'

She laughed and squeezed him hard. 'I was so afraid you wouldn't come.'

'You needn't have been.'

She raised an eyebrow at him.

'Stop it,' he said. 'I'm here now.'

Seanie faded down the Arctic Monkeys and Murtagh tapped the microphone as he picked it up, thus filling the room with an ear-shattering squeal. '*Testing*,' he boomed so loudly that his own head snapped back. 'Hello,' he whispered, much too quietly this time.

'C'mon, Goldilocks,' someone shouted from the back. 'Next time, you'll be just right.'

A laugh rose around the room as Murtagh cleared his throat and beckoned Nollaig to join him on the stage. Nollaig half walked, half skipped towards her father. A white bra strap, stained with orange fake tan, slipped off her shoulder and dangled against her bare arm. Kalindi caught Nollaig's eye and gestured to her to pull it up, but the mime confused her. She thought it was an encouragement to strut with some attitude, which, unfortunately, she tried to do.

Murtagh put his arm around his daughter and she rested her head on his shoulder as she scanned all the familiar faces before her. She wasn't sure who she was looking for, someone just hers, perhaps, where a gaze could linger a little longer. Instead, her eyes eventually found the chipped plum nail polish on her big toe.

Her father cleared his throat and began again.

'I'd like to say *go raibh míle maith agaibh*, a huge thanks, to you all for coming out tonight to celebrate my wonderful daughter's thirtieth birthday. I can't bear to think how old that must make me but, thankfully, those sums are too hard for me.'

The crowd laughed gently, and Nollaig elbowed him.

'It gives me so much pleasure to have all my children gathered together under one roof, and to see so many old friends and neighbours here to celebrate Nollaig's milestone. There is no one more selfless, more caring, no one kinder than my eldest daughter, and I'm incredibly proud of her. If only I could train her to turn off the immersion when she's finished, my work would be complete.'

The crowd laughed again as Nollaig rolled her eyes and gave him a little shove.

'Of course, I wish her mother could be with us this evening, as we do every day, but I only have to look at my four children to know that she is still with us, in so many ways. Every time they shine, any day they speak a difficult truth, all righteous paths they walk, each noble task they perform, that is Maeve coming through. And I know she would want you all to have a riot tonight, as I do. Friends and family, please join me in raising a glass in honour of Nollaig. To Nollaig.'

'To Nollaig!'

'Do you want to say something?' Murtagh whispered to his daughter, but she shook her head, blowing her nose in a crumbling tissue he handed her from his pocket. Attention shifted from them as the DJ faded the music back up, 'Sultans of Swing' this time, and people began to shuffle their feet in time to the beat as the hum of voices rose again. The party cast a new glamour on the islanders, elevated them from their usual perfunctory exchanges and practical attire. It was amazing what a bow-tie here, a pair of pearl earrings there, could do to lift their spirits. Murtagh sat on the windowsill, nursing a tumbler of Jameson, diluted by the ice cubes that melted before he had time to drink it. The heat of a radiator burned through the backs of his trouser legs where they rested against it. Borne of habits long established, he found himself checking the room for the whereabouts of each of his children.

Mossy was propped against a speaker, flinching at the

pounding bass drum, while Father Dónal pointed out some-thing of great interest to him in the parish newsletter. Too polite to break away, he looked resigned to his fate as he watched Dillon spinning Kalindi under his arm, where they danced in front of the DJ box. They made a handsome couple and Murtagh felt a pang for Mossy, who must have been aware of it, too. Mossy had never been one for dancing. Murtagh remembered once overhearing a heated row between them, rare though they seemed to be, when Kalindi asked Mossy if she would have to borrow someone else's husband for the rest of her life every time she wanted a dance. Murtagh noticed that young Bracken girl watching Dillon, too, out of the corner of her eye, and remembered how she and Dillon had circled each other in their teens. There was hurt there, he remembered, but couldn't recall the details. That could get interesting later, he thought.

Sive and *the boyfriend* were in an animated debate where they sat on the windowsill opposite him, but it looked more passionate and electric than angry or hurtful. He could see that from the way Luka tapped out a point on his daughter's knee with his forefinger. Why was he wearing white finger-less gloves? Sive reached up to swipe his lopsided fringe behind his ear and their noses touched. Murtagh looked away. This man reminded him of too many of his old class-mates; still clinging on with their painted fingernails to the dream the seventies had promised them of something more revolutionary while what had once made them unique iden-tified them now as figures of fun. *What did Sive see in him? Was he somehow to blame?* He could only imagine the fish food Maeve would have turned him into. *If she were still here, though, would Sive still be attached to this eejit?* He dismissed the thought – it was unfair to assume every poor decision his children made was as a result of her absence. Murtagh stole a glance back at them but quickly regretted it as Luka began nibbling Sive's ear as she leaned closer into him.

Twice his eyes scanned the room for Nollaig, but he couldn't place her. It seemed too long since he'd last seen her, but before the niggle of doubt could prompt him to search properly he was struck by the sight of someone else appearing through the function-room doors. Dressed in a manner more fitting to a Milanese sidewalk café than Inis Óg, Fionn slunk into the room like a cat, shoulders bent to duck under the low ceiling. He clutched a silver gift bag tightly in his hand, his shoulders tense. Murtagh saw Síle McGrath look him up and down as Fionn leaned against the back wall to acclimatise to the room; she nudged Mary O'Loughlin and winked in delight towards him. Murtagh's heart skipped but before he could corral his courage a blood-curdling scream cut through the party din from outside. He pressed his forehead against the windowpane, his hands cupping his eyes, but couldn't see anything in the pitch-black exterior. Heads turned as those who'd heard the shriek pushed towards the exit to see what was happening. Murtagh followed, pausing only for a moment, to give the sleeve of Fionn's black cashmere pullover a gentle squeeze as he passed. 'Welcome back,' he whispered, rolling his eyes in anticipation of whatever awaited him outside.

Nollaig was lying on her back in the long grass, her skirt bunched around her waist, Aindí's wife, Úna, straddling her in a gold strapless dress that had slipped to expose her right breast. Úna was shaking Nollaig's shoulders like a rag doll while Nollaig kicked her legs in vain to be free of her. 'You couldn't leave him alone, not for one night, could you? While I'm sitting inside holding his pint like an eejit? Well, it's all over now, you brazen slut. You're going to get what's been coming to you.'

Dillon shouted at her to let Nollaig go and ran towards them. Úna raised a fist into the air but, before she could deliver the blow, Aindí had gripped her wrist and began pulling his wife off Nollaig, who stayed lying where she was. Úna turned her aggression towards Aindí now, beating her fist against his chest as he tried to drag her further away while she hoisted back up her dress. Dillon pushed past his father, frozen where he stood, and helped his sister up from the ground. She stood shaking in his arms and he turned his back to shield her from the gaze of the miniature mob that had gathered.

'All right, folks, let's give them all a minute to calm down. Go on inside with ye!' Father Dónal shepherded the islanders back into the pub.

They reluctantly moved in a slow procession, craning their necks to look behind them as they walked. Murtagh felt a hand on the small of his back and instinctively took a step forward. 'Is everything okay?' Fionn asked. 'What's been going on?'

'Too much, by the looks of things. Would you mind – would you maybe head back in? I'll see you inside in a minute.'

A shadow fell across Fionn's face but he did as he was asked, catching Dillon's eye before flicking his gaze away and returning inside. Murtagh could see the O'Sheas staggering along the pier, Aindí dragging his wife along, her pausing every few feet to curse at him again. Her words carried on the breeze, turning the air blue. Murtagh walked over to Dillon and Nollaig. She was a little calmer now, emitting big hiccups. Black mascara spread across her face, giving her panda eyes, and her nose was running. 'I'm so sorry, Daddy,' she said. 'I've made a total show of myself. Ruined it all.'

He pulled her under his arm, the same place she had stood at the start of the evening as he had made his speech. 'Shush, love,' he said, smoothing her hair. 'It doesn't matter. None of it matters.'

'Who was that man you were talking to?' Dillon asked, nodding in the direction of where Fionn had been standing. 'What man?' Nollaig asked, looking up at her father.

He avoided their eyes as he stared out into the inky-black abyss of the sea.

'Do you not recognise him?' he asked, his voice catching a little as he spoke. 'That was Fionn!'

Nollaig leaned away from him, searching his face for answers. 'Fionn? What's he doing back here?'

Murtagh took off his blazer and wrapped it around his daughter's shoulders. 'Just visiting. Don't worry about him. Now, what do you want to do? Are you going back inside or . . . ?'

'God, no, look at the state of me.' She held her skirt out in front of her, ripped and covered in grass stains. Her tights were torn to shreds. 'I don't know how I'll ever face any of them again.' She buried her head in her hands.

Dillon gave her a playful shove. 'Aindí O'Shea? Really, sis? Of all people? I remember he had terrible athlete's foot and had to wear these gross antibacterial socks in the school locker room. Once, we —'

'Not helpful, Dillon, thank you,' his father cut him off.

Sive crunched across the gravel towards them, a champagne flute dangling from her hand. 'What the hell has been going on out here? The whole place is alight in there with one story more outrageous than the next. Noll, what have you been up to?'

Murtagh caught her by the elbow and steered her back towards the door, appealing for her just to go inside.

'Okay, okay, I'm going,' she said, shaking the dregs of her glass into a heather bush.

'Dillon, why don't you two start walking, and I'll follow with your things?' Murtagh said. 'Go on, you'll catch your death out here.'

He watched his two children follow the path the O'Sheas had taken, but they were a much more subdued couple as they strolled along, Dillon's arm slung around his sister's shoulders.

Murtagh walked back through the pub to the function room, ignoring how the conversation halted as he approached, noticing that the television was muted over the bar. He couldn't help but wonder if folks had been pressing glasses up to the window to eavesdrop on the events outside but continued walking through to the party with as much dignified aplomb as he could muster. Fionn was waiting inside for him, a hot whiskey ready in his hand. Murtagh took it gratefully, drank it in one long gulp that burned his throat. He felt the liquor fizz through his veins and begin to thaw the shock from his skin. 'Nollaig's gone home,' he said. 'I think maybe it might be best if you slip away. There's been enough drama for one evening.'

Fionn clicked his tongue. 'If that's the way you feel.' He waited a moment and then continued. 'I'm not sure this was such a good idea any more. Perhaps we should try again another time?'

Murtagh manoeuvred him further away from possible prying ears.

'I'm sorry, Fionn, you know I'm delighted you're here, but my nerves are gone. Why don't you come over for breakfast in the morning? Things will have calmed down by then, I promise. Let's just leave things for tonight, okay?' Fionn nodded and left the room without another word.

Murtagh swallowed hard as he watched his back leave and then faced what remained of the party. Sive came towards him with Luka in tow, both their arms full of presents, two handbags dangling from her shoulder; the studs on her vintage suede jacket stopped the straps slipping down her arm. Luka nodded as he passed by but Murtagh was relieved that he didn't say anything. He saw Mossy on the stage cutting the cake. Kalindi passed it around on green paper plates, the picture of smiling serenity as she moved through the room. Murtagh wove his way through the crowd to her and leaned in to speak in her ear. 'We're slipping away. Can you wind things down here and I'll see you back at the house?'

'This is the last song,' she said. 'Just the national anthem to go and the lights will be going up.'

He kissed her on the forehead. 'Thanks, my dear. I'm sorry to leave you two here on your own. What a mess.'

She shook her head at him while passing a slice of cake over his shoulder to Father Dónal, who was eyeing it wolfishly. 'We're grand. I just hope she's okay.'

Murtagh shrugged. 'I think she'll be fine.'

He waved at Mossy, who gave him a big thumbs-up from the stage, as if he hadn't a care in the world, and managed to snake his way back outside without stopping to speak to anyone else.

A prickling frost was settling on the island. Murtagh brushed past a gorse bush as he squeezed through Ned's gate and shivered as the cold, damp air penetrated his trouser legs. He felt as if his very life force was draining from him with each numbing step. And yet, his pace was slow. Not even the prospect of the open fire at home could motivate him to move faster as he considered tonight and what the following morning would bring. Little could Nollaig know; her affair was the least of his worries. Soon the island would have a whole new story to obsess over, and one they would not be so easily distracted from. All the hopeful excitement he had allowed himself to build in recent weeks ebbed away with each step.

After the party

The red ember of Sive's cigarette glowed in the endless black, moving slowly as she rotated her wrist like a firefly circling in the dark.

Murtagh peered into the shadows of the doorway, attempting to discern if she was sitting there alone. He was confused by his own sense of dread; was it worse to creep across the cracking ice beneath their feet with his daughter unaccompanied? Or to have that boyfriend of hers bear witness to their awkward side-shuffles?

The hot ash drew an arc over a rose bush like a half-hearted firework and fizzled away.

Sive turned her head towards him, her face a bowl of milk in the light, and her resemblance to Maeve gave him a chill. She smiled at him in that wry way she had, with only one corner of her mouth turned upwards and the effect never quite reaching her eyes. When was the last time he had seen her happy? Heard her laughing from her belly? Not since Maeve had gone, he was sure of it.

When he reached the doorstep she held out her hand from under Maeve's hound's-tooth shawl so he could help her stand up. She toppled forward, but he caught her in his arms, held her there for a moment before she gently pushed him away.

'And there was I thinking Nollaig never did a bold thing her whole life,' she said, while he blew into his hands to warm them.

Murtagh snorted. 'You could take a little less satisfaction in it. Speaking of which, where's your *gentleman friend*, eh? Fled the island, has he?'

'He's gone back to the hotel. He'd had enough Moone exposure for one night but you'll see him in the morning for breakfast.'

'Oh goody,' he replied, rubbing his hands together, and his daughter whacked him on the arm. 'How is your sister doing?'

Sive sighed and pushed in the front door. 'Hysterical, of course. They're all in the kitchen. Every bottle in the house is open on the table and Dillon is making medicinal punch.'

Murtagh paused for a moment at the threshold. 'I think I'll stay with you at the hotel, Si. Himself won't mind, will he? I'm sure you have your own rooms anyway, no doubt?'

She rolled her eyes and pushed him down the hallway in front of her. 'They're your children, you can sort them out!'

'You say that like I ever had the power to do such a thing.'

'You always did,' she said, her voice softer. 'Even if you chose not to use it.'

Murtagh spun around to face her but she slipped under his arm and through the kitchen door, where the radio hummed in the background. Everyone was speaking at once, but no one was listening to anybody else, which was probably for the best.

'Do you think everyone knows?'

'There's only orange juice as a mixer, that'll have to do.'

'The trick to punch is you need to be able to taste the alcohol or you don't realise how drunk you're getting.'

'It was all a big misunderstanding.'

'Did someone bring the cake?'

'Will you open the back door? It's boiling in here.'

'I'm freezing. Pass me my scarf there.'

Kalindi stood at the kitchen counter, buttering slices of toast that Mossy piled to her right. She restacked them on a cracked ceramic plate, midnight blue with white roses, the first piece Murtagh had made in his studio, and placed it in the middle of the table with an open packet of sliced ham and a block of Cheddar cheese. Mossy made her a sandwich first and rested it on a sheet of kitchen towel before her. She smiled at him as he stood up to make an optimistic pot of coffee as Dillon ladled punch with a soup spoon into the polka-dot glass tumblers Sive had sent home from Spitalfields Market.

'I can never show my face again,' Nollaig wailed as she dragged the make-up from her face with cotton-wool balls drenched in cleansing milk. The used wool, stained orange, formed an untidy mound before her. 'I can't believe she ruined my party. She so did it deliberately, that –'

Murtagh cut her off as he hung his coat on the back of her chair. 'Now, Nollaig, I think, of all those involved, Mrs O'Shea is hardly the most at fault here, is she?'

'Daddy!' she shouted, the sound wet in her throat. 'You could try being on my side, you know. I'm the one who has been assaulted, made a laughing stock of in front of the whole island. She was jumping to conclusions anyway, we were only talking, not even . . .'

'Not this time, eh, sis? But it wasn't for the want of trying, I'm sure. That Aindí was always a total creep. I can't believe you went anywhere near him. You'd think Úna would be delighted with a night off.' Sive kicked off her military boots and crossed her feet on the edge of the table as she nudged Nollaig with her foot.

Nollaig stood up and threw a clump of the used cotton wool at Sive.

'Shut up, you. You don't know anything about it, and it's not like you've won any prize yourself with that Tim Burton wannabe. You had the whole of London to find someone and *that's* who you get lumbered with?'

Sive flicked the cotton wool from her lap on to the floor and glared at her sister as everyone tuned into how quickly things were escalating between them. Dillon topped up Nollaig's glass and swiped Sive's feet off the table. 'Now, ladies, we've had enough drama for one night. Let's have a toast, shall we?'

Nollaig looked relieved, but Sive's face remained unchanged as she stood up.

'Yes, a toast,' she said. 'I'd like to raise a toast to my big sister. Thirty years old and not a friend in the world. Reduced to stealing another woman's depraved husband. May the next thirty years be less miserable.'

'Sive, that's enough,' her father snapped, but he was too late to stop Nollaig from reaching across the table to slap Sive hard across the face. Her hand left a red sting on her sister's cheek.

'How could I have a life?' Nollaig shouted. 'When *I* was the one stuck here trying to keep the pieces together? *I* was the one who stayed behind so ye would have some semblance of a normal life and still have somewhere to come home to.'

'Do you still not get it?' Sive shouted back, shaking her head. 'No one wanted you to do that. You made it *worse*. Trying to replace her, acting the martyr. You. Made. It. Worse. Why do you think we hate coming home here?'

Murtagh stood between his daughters, his eyes glassy, colour deepening, but he couldn't get past a stammer. Mossy pulled him away by the elbow. 'Leave it, Dad,' he said. 'Let them have it out. It's a long time coming.'

Dillon sat down and held his head in his hands.

'She's right, Noll,' he said. 'I'm sorry, but it's true. This place. It's like, it's like you've tried to keep everything the same, so we're stuck in that Christmas Eve for ever. You couldn't move on, so this place is this awful shrine.' He looked around the kitchen. 'The wallpaper in here has never even been changed – it's all just stuck.' Kalindi rubbed his back and said, 'I don't think that's fair, Dillon. It's always harder for the ones who stay behind to make the changes. They don't get such an easy fresh start.'

Sive turned to her. 'But they haven't even tried, Lin! Do you know all Mammy's clothes are still in the wardrobe? Her things still sitting on the dresser the way she left them? That's not right. I hate even passing the room in case I catch a glimpse of something.'

Kalindi glanced at Murtagh, who nodded sadly.

'I couldn't in the beginning. Wasn't able to give her stuff away. And then it became too important, like whenever I did it would mean I was over it, and that day could never come.'

'But you're never going to be over it,' Sive said, throwing her hands in the air. 'None of us will. Don't you get it? The stuff won't change that. It just makes everything worse.'

Mossy poured black coffee into a mug and handed it to his father. 'Maybe we can do it for you, Dad. I think it would be good for you. For all of us.'

Nollaig sat on the floor, squeezing cotton wool against her eyes.

Sive's voice dropped low. 'What about the boat?'

They all looked towards her, but her father spoke first. 'What about it?'

'It's still in the boatshed, isn't it? I dream about that bloody thing.' She shuddered. 'Can picture it in there in the dark every time I walk on the pier. I feel like she's still in there inside it. I can't even look towards the door. Why did you keep it, Daddy?'

He lowered his head into his hands. 'I don't know. What was I supposed to do with it?'

'You were supposed to get rid of it, *obviously*, like any normal person would.'

Dillon spoke again, 'That's what I thought you wanted to talk to us all about. To see if we wanted any of her stuff before you finally let it all go.'

Murtagh looked confused, upset that this conversation would happen now, when he was prepared for something so different.

'So, what *did* you want to tell us?' Nollaig asked. 'Daddy?'

Sive stood up and started wrestling her boots back on, losing her balance and grabbing her father's arm to steady herself. 'Come on, let's go. We're doing this now. Right now.'

'What are you talking about?' Murtagh shouted, his temper finally lost. 'No one's going anywhere except bed.'

Sive darted from the kitchen, her boots pounding on the stairs like muffled cannon fire in the distance. 'Daddy, stop her!' Nollaig cried. 'What's she doing?'

'No,' Dillon said. 'I'll go.'

They heard her footsteps run along the landing and into her father's bedroom. Dillon ran up the stairs after her while the remaining Moones huddled in the hallway, straining to discern meaning from their muffled voices.

'I think I should go up there,' Murtagh said. 'I don't like this.' They listened to the approach of four feet on the landing, stumbling a little, and then the brother and sister appeared at the top of the stairs. Sive's dark eye make-up was smudged, Dillon's face pale but determined. Between them they wrestled a white bedspread filled with a disturbing softness. Nollaig made for the stairs. 'They're Mammy's clothes! Leave them alone. I swear to God I'll kill you if you don't.'

Her father pulled her back as he started up the stairs. 'Dillon Moone, Sive Moone, put that down. Right now.'

Sive was calm now, but her cheeks were flushed. 'Nollaig, listen to me. Dad, it's time.'

'What are you going to do with them? You can't dump them in the street?' Nollaig wailed. 'Not all Mammy's things.'

Sive tightened her grip on the sheet and wiped her eyes with the corner.

'I know exactly what we're going to do,' she said. 'We're going to get the boat, push it out into the water and put Mammy's things inside. And then we're going to cremate it.'

Nollaig started sobbing. 'Are you mad? Daddy, tell them they're mad.'

Mossy stepped forward from the doorway to the kitchen and reached for his raincoat, which was hanging on the bannister. 'A pyre. She's right. I feel like I've been holding my breath waiting for something like this since Mam died.'

He looked towards his father, who stared back at him helplessly. It was as if with each passing minute he aged another year.

'Mossy! I expect you to be the voice of reason. Well, I'm having no part of it,' Nollaig shouted. 'And in the morning when you sober up, you'll all hate yourselves for this.'

Without saying another word, Murtagh reached for his duffel coat and walked towards the front door, leaving it open behind him.

Kalindi followed Murtagh and waited with him at the gate while Mossy helped Dillon and Sive navigate their bundle down the rest of the stairs, through the hallway and into the lane.

They made a silent procession towards the pier, each refusing to acknowledge how much it looked as if they were parading a funereal shroud across the island.

The moon hid behind a cloud as if to award them some privacy and the easterly wind stalled to a hush.

At the boathouse, the children hesitated and Sive looked to her father to somehow propel them onwards. He pulled the hood on his duffel coat up and it gave him the look of a monk as he moved quietly to shake the padlock free. The clatter of metal was offensive to their silence and Sive nudged forward to stand between her brothers. The door swung open and Murtagh was swallowed by the cave-like interior. He didn't pull the cord to turn on the light, so no one could see anything; instead they heard the horrible drag of the currach along the gravelly ground towards them. Murtagh backed out of the shed, his arms hugging the bow, and Mossy and Kalindi stepped forward to lift from each side. Sive and Dillon picked up the rear and the Moone family carried the black crescent of the currach on their shoulders towards the strand, the way the islanders had once carried Maeve's coffin before.

They rested it on the sand and stood around it, their eyes meeting, locking and breaking away while they contemplated what would happen next.

Sive moved first and walked back to the boathouse, where Maeve's clothes lay in a crumpled pile. She kneeled in the sand and buried her nose in the fabric, but she could not smell her mother there. Kalindi crouched beside her and they gathered the bundle into their arms and slowly skidded across the sand to where the three Moone men waited. An arm of peacock-blue silk trailed in the sand, like a hand clawing the earth. They tipped the contents into the boat and spread the cloth taut across them; Mossy tied it to the edges with the sailor knots he had learned in Boy Scouts.

Murtagh cleared his throat, but no words came as each told themselves the story of what was happening in a way they could understand, in a manner they could bear to remember. A voice carried from along the headland – 'Wait, wait for me!' – and they saw Nollaig running along the harbour wall towards them, waving her hands above her head with no coat on, and still wearing her ruined party frock. The skin of her back was cold as marble when Sive hugged her; the sisters clung to each other for a moment, a lifetime of distance resolved in one embrace.

Dillon stepped forward, kneeled beside the boat and wriggled a box of matches from the pocket of his leather jacket. He lit one, and then another. A third.

A fourth.

None would catch; each extinguished by the damp air before even a smoulder caught the bedspread.

'We'll need kindling,' Nollaig said, gulping. 'Or petrol.' She paused for a moment before offering to check the boatshed.

A few minutes later she walked across the sand towards them, a blue petrol cannister in her hand. She'd already twisted the cap off, and handed the can to Dillon, who handed it to Mossy. Mossy clenched his jaw and walked the length of the currach, shaking the can as he dripped petrol across the fabric like molasses. He shoved the empty container in the bow of the boat and Dillon lit one final match, holding it close to the petrol-soaked fabric. This time it caught, and the flames whooshed across the glowing white bedspread, roaring at the Moones as if to say, *Is this what you wanted? You can't stop me now.* They stood watching the fire burn, trying to ignore the smell that curdled up their nose. Then Dillon began to push the boat towards the water.

While Murtagh sat on the damp sand, clenching it in white fists to steady himself, his children waded waist-high into the water to set the boat adrift.

Wet. Exhausted. Frightened. Relieved. Grieving.

They splashed back out of the water and collapsed beside their father in the sand and watched the fire feed. The flames spread and found the petrol cannister. It exploded, lighting the sky in an amplification of Sive's cigarette from a few hours before.

Nollaig broke the silence first. 'Do you remember the last time you saw her?' she asked. 'I do. She sat behind me at my bedroom mirror, brushing my hair, even though I protested I was too old for that, but I was delighted, really. And then she told me she loved me.'

Sive turned to look at her sister, 'Her last words to you were *I love you*?'

Nollaig nodded.

'Me, too,' Sive croaked. 'I was lying on my bed listening to Suede and she came in and lay down beside me. She asked me to play the song she'd loved from the concert we went to, 'The 2 of Us', and we listened to it together on my iPod, sharing headphones. I haven't been able to listen to it since. And then she told me that she loved me and stayed with me until I fell asleep.'

Dillon's voice shook when he spoke. 'The last time we saw her she brought us to Tigh Ned's and we tried gin and tonics for the first time.'

'And then,' Mossy continued, 'we walked home, the three of us linking arms, with her in the middle, doing the Monkees walk. She seemed so happy that night. Talked to us about what being a Moone man meant.'

'When we got home, she kissed us both goodnight, and told us she loved us, too,' Dillon finished.

Murtagh reached out and his four grown-up children found their way into his arms and shook out grief that had been trying to break free for so long.

As the dawn began to break, Murtagh and his children sat side by side on the sand, each alone with their own thoughts but united with new understanding. Every so often they heard voices drawing closer from the pub; a few stragglers had been enticed by the flames, but when they saw who was sitting on the shore, and realised what was burning, they slunk back into the night and left the Moones in peace.

All except one solitary figure who sat on the harbour wall and hoped his love would emanate from him to wrap around the body so beloved that sat before him in the distance. Fionn watched over the Moone family while they watched the currach burn.

He waited until they began their slow walk home, until they dissolved into shadows, before he turned away, his eyes stinging, his heart that had always been lost to them afraid of what must come next.

Inis Óg: 21 December, 2014

The smell of fresh loaves baking woke Nollaig first; familiar but almost forgotten.

She staggered down the stairs in the fluffy peach dressing gown that she wore like a second skin; squinting into the light, as her stomach churned. Her father sat at the kitchen table with his back to her as he dried cutlery with a red-and-white checked tea towel. When he turned, she screamed – his bushy grey beard was gone, exposing fresh pink cheeks. He looked ten years younger; he looked like a stranger.

'Daddy!' she shouted. 'What happened? I can't believe it.'

He shyly patted his face with both hands and smiled at his daughter's shock.

'Oh, it was time for a change,' he chuckled. 'I barely recognise myself in the mirror. Ajay started crying when he saw me this morning.'

Nollaig came closer and leaned towards him. 'I don't blame him. You could've warned us!'

He returned to the cutlery, gathering it together and carrying it to the open drawer under the sink. 'I didn't know myself until this morning.'

Nollaig looked around the gleaming kitchen. 'I'm sorry you had to do all the tidying up. Did you get any sleep at all?'

'No.' He smiled at her. 'But I feel fine. I didn't want to face more chaos this morning. And Mossy helped me. He's gone to the shop with Kalindi and the twins.'

She glanced at the clock over the stove. 'It's only half eight – what time were they all up?'

'Maya appeared first, about seven,' he said. 'Not everyone stayed up until dawn, you know.'

Nollaig shuddered. 'I feel like I should still be in bed.' She held up her phone and took a picture of her father as he poured himself some orange juice.

He shook the carton at her. 'What are you at, Noll?'

'I'm sending it to the others. They won't believe this!'

Murtagh sighed. 'They'll believe it time enough. Go get dressed. Everyone will be here soon. And don't go plastering me all across the internet either.'

The front door slammed shut and Sive appeared with Luka in tow; their hair still wet, chattering with the cold.

'We went for a swim,' she said. 'Big mistake.'

Luka looked as if he might be about to enter cardiac arrest, his lips blue and trembling.

Murtagh rushed to the hot press and grabbed armfuls of towels. 'What were you thinking, Si?' he said. 'And no wetsuits?'

She took a warm towel from him and wrapped it around her hair before looking at her father properly for the first time. 'Oh my God,' she said. 'Your face! It's so weird. I don't think I've ever seen it before.'

'Never mind that,' he said. 'Here, stand in front of the range. I'll put the kettle on.'

'Looking good, Murtagh,' Luka mumbled at him as he dried his face in a towel. 'Very smooth.'

'Well, thank you, er, Luka,' he said, catching Nollaig's eye as she smirked.

Nollaig's phone beeped and she burst out laughing. 'That's Dillon,' she said. 'He says you look like a toddler, Dad. He's on his way. Just walking Molly home, he said. Molly? Where did she come from?'

Sive grabbed the phone to read his message. 'So, that's who he was calling last night. Well now, that escalated fast.'

The back door swung open and the twins ran in, dressed in matching yellow tracksuits and red wellington boots. Mossy followed, his arms full with two damp brown-paper bags that looked about to disintegrate. Kalindi stood on the doorstep, shaking the raindrops from an umbrella. 'We passed Dillon on the way,' she said. 'He'll be along in a minute. Said to start without him. He was in high spirits, I must say.'

Sive smirked at her and began plunging the coffee pot, breathing in deep lungfuls of its heady aroma and sighing with contentment.

The front doorbell chimed and Murtagh dropped a saucepan into the sink with a clatter.

'Why is he ringing the doorbell?' Mossy asked, idling down the hallway, his mouth already full of croissant, straight from the bag.

Nollaig heated oil in the pan to start frying sausages and bacon while Sive whined at having to endure the smell of flesh cooking. They heard Mossy's voice booming from the front door, his laughter, but couldn't discern what he was saying. He bounced back into the kitchen, beaming at them as he called out. 'It's Fionn!' he said. 'Fionn is here! And I don't have my uke, damn it.'

Sive hung back while Nollaig came forward to hug him, tightening her dressing gown and taking her fingers through her sticky hair. 'Dad said you were here, but I wasn't expecting you this morning,' she said. 'It's so great to see you – I can't believe it.'

Fionn looked overwhelmed as his eyes flew about the room; so much looked the same, but who were all these adults where once children had been? He touched Murtagh on the arm, and held his hand for a second before reaching out to Sive.

She placed her coffee cup on the kitchen counter and kissed him on the cheek. 'I've heard so much about you,' she said, 'but I have to say I don't think I remember you properly. More like I've just inherited memories from the others. Mam and Dad often spoke about you, kept all your letters.'

Before he could answer, Luka stepped forward and held out his hand. 'I'm her boyfriend,' he rushed, 'Luka, I make documentaries about –'

Mossy jumped in: 'And this is my wife, Kalindi, and our twins Maya and Ajay.' The children stood shyly on either side of their father, hiding their faces, while Kalindi kissed Fionn on both cheeks.

Fionn smiled at them. 'It's so strange. In my mind's eye, that's closer to what I expect you and Dillon to be like.' Mossy laughed as Dillon appeared from the hallway, still in last night's clothes, dark circles under his eyes.

'I saw you last night,' he said, punching Fionn gently on the shoulder. 'What the hell brings you back to this godforsaken place?'

Murtagh handed him a pile of plates. 'Here, son, set the table while I start dishing out.'

Dillon laid the plates while they all bumped into each other, passing cups and glasses, plates of ham, pastries, sugar bowls, orange juice, apple juice, the teapot and coffee pot, a bowl with boiled eggs, two punnets of strawberries and a saucepan of boiling hot porridge. Finally they were all sitting, all eating, and for a moment all quiet.

Murtagh cleared his throat and Nollaig looked up, a slice of toast with strawberry jam halfway to her mouth. 'Oh no,' she said. 'This is it. He's going to tell us his news.'

The clatter of breakfast stilled; only the noise of Ajay making fire-engine-siren noises broke through their silence. Kalindi popped a strawberry in his mouth to keep it busy for a moment.

Murtagh stood up, then sat back down, wiping the corners of his mouth with a yellow paper napkin. 'The thing is,' he said. 'What I've been meaning to tell you . . .'

He stopped to take a deep slug of his orange juice.

Sive's leg bounced up, and down under the table, making the cloth shake, until Nollaig grabbed it and held her still.

Dillon stared into his coffee cup and met no one's eye.

Mossy moved his arm closer to Kalindi's and she took his hand.

Murtagh stood again, looked around the table, and sat back down.

Nollaig groaned. 'Dad, you're killing us,' she said. 'Just spit it out. It can't be that bad.'

'It's not bad at all,' Fionn burst out. 'It's a good thing.'

Dillon looked at him. 'What do you know about it? He's not going off with you to save the whales or something, is he?' He started laughing but it trailed away as he saw Fionn reach out and squeeze his father's hand.

'That's quite close actually, son,' his father said, then continued in a rush. 'You see, the thing is, I've met someone – or rather, I've re-met someone.'

Nollaig pushed her plate away from her, her eyes already flooding. 'What are you talking about?' she said. 'How could you meet someone without me knowing? Who is she? And what's that got to do with Fionn?'

For a moment no one spoke and then Luka piped up, 'Doesn't he mean Fionn? Is that not who he re-met? Or am I missing something here?'

Nollaig snorted. 'Don't be daft, Luka. Are you joking?'

Sive watched her father and Fionn steal a glance then burst out laughing.

'Oh my God, he's right,' she said. 'Daddy, what's going on? How did this happen? Am I having some kind of psychotic break here?'

Fionn's eyes passed over each Moone in turn while Murtagh struggled to begin. Eventually he spoke himself. 'Well, your mother wrote to me, before . . .'

Dillon stood up, knocking his chair over. 'I'm not sitting here and listening to this,' he shouted. 'Have you all lost your minds?' He stormed over to his father and grabbed fistfuls of his jumper. 'Was this going on the whole time?' he spat in his face. 'Is that why Mam did it? Because she knew about you and him?'

Fionn stood up and tried to pull Dillon away, but Dillon shoved him. 'Don't touch me, you creep. All the time you were hanging around here, were you two getting it on behind my mam's back?' He squared up to Fionn but Fionn held his ground.

'Nothing happened back then,' he said. 'Not. One. Thing. What Maeve did had nothing to do with this.'

Dillon pushed him hard and he lost his footing for a moment. '*How would you know anything about her?*' he shouted. 'Don't you say her name, don't you ever say her name,' he snarled, pushing him again.

Mossy stood up, placed himself between his brother and Fionn. 'Sit down, bro,' he said. 'That's enough.'

Maya started crying and Kalindi took both the children by the hand and hurried them out of the room, closing the kitchen door behind her and throwing Mossy a look of apology.

Murtagh sat at the table with his eyes closed, head in hands, his face ashen.

Patti Smith broke through the heavy silence from the radio on the windowsill, but Sive turned it off as Dillon pushed past his brother and flung the back door open. 'I'm not sticking around to hear any more of this.' The half-door slammed behind him and they heard him stamping away down the gravel path.

'I'm sorry,' Murtagh whispered. 'I'm sorry. I know this is a terrible shock.'

Fionn filled a glass of water from the tap and gulped it down.

Nollaig's head was buried in her dressing gown, but her muffled sobbing was clear. Sive whispered something to Luka and he, too, retreated through the back door, a towel still draped around his shoulders.

'Daddy,' she said, moving along the bench to sit beside him. 'Can you help us understand a bit? What does this mean about Mam? Did she know? About you, I mean? When did all this happen?'

Murtagh took a deep breath, 'You have to understand,' he began, 'what your mother and I had was all real. We loved each other so much, and this has nothing to do with that.'

Sive interrupted him. 'So, you're *bi*? Is that what you're saying?'

Murtagh frowned. 'I don't think I'm anything. All I know is I've loved two people this way in my whole life – your mother, and Fionn. That's it.'

Nollaig poked her head out, wiping her nose on her sleeve. 'But when did you realise about Fionn? Mam was still here then.'

Fionn sat back down at the table. 'Nothing happened when I was on the island,' he said, 'but I think we all knew deep down that your father and I had a connection that was more than just friendship – or that could be more. Your mother saw it. I think she understood before your father or I did. I'd only just come out that summer and never expected to meet the love of my life there. Or that he would already be happily married. And to a woman.'

Murtagh let out a sad little laugh. 'It only hit me after your mother died. When my heart cracked open with grief

I was surprised what I found there, this truth I'd been oblivious to.'

Fionn continued. 'A few days before she died,' he said, 'she wrote to me, told me what was going to happen, asked me to come find your father.'

Nollaig snapped, 'She wrote to *you*? You make it sound like she gave you her blessing.'

Fionn looked at her. 'I know it's hard.' He hesitated. 'But that's exactly what it felt like.'

Sive leaned across the table and nudged Mossy's shoulder. 'You're suspiciously quiet over there.'

Mossy sat back, sighed. 'It just doesn't shock me. I mean, it does, but it doesn't. I feel like I always sort of knew.'

Nollaig stood up. 'How could you know?' she shrieked. 'I've been living with him all this time and I didn't know!'

Mossy held his hands up. 'I think I saw something once, when we were little. I didn't understand it, but the memory stayed with me. We went swimming and when we came out of the water, Fionn, you dried Dad's back with your towel.'

Murtagh gasped. 'I don't even remember that,' he said.

Fionn looked at him. 'I do.'

Sive leaned back in her chair and put her feet up against the table, 'So, what happens now?' she asked, watching her father's hands tremble.

'Well,' he said. 'I want to move to the city, with Fionn.' the paused. 'Maybe sell the house.'

Nollaig was pacing up and down the kitchen, the soles of her fluffy slippers slapping against the tiles. 'So what about me?' she shouted. 'Am I to be homeless?'

Murtagh walked over to her, put his hands on her shoulders. 'Of course not, love,' he said. 'This home will be yours for as long as you want it.'

She allowed him to pull her in for a hug; her nose tickled at the smell of his shaving foam.

'But there's nothing here for me without you,' she mumbled into his shoulder.

'Maybe your life's waiting out there,' he said. 'Perhaps this is the new start we both need.'

She pushed him away. 'No, I'm sorry,' she said. 'Don't pretend this is good news for me. It's too much.' She shuddered. 'I need to lie down.'

Nollaig slunk out of the room and they listened to her slow, laboured ascent up the stairs. Mossy went to find Kalindi. 'Thank you,' Fionn said to Sive, as she turned the radio back on. 'For trying to understand.'

She started clearing the breakfast things away. 'I don't think it's hit me, to be honest,' she said. 'I feel like we've suddenly met our father for the first time, so where's our old dad gone? How do we reconcile the two men, our old and our new dad? This will take everyone a long time to get our hands around.'

Murtagh took the dirty plates from her hands. 'I'll always be your old dad, love,' he said. 'I'm figuring all of this out, too, but I'm still the same me. I haven't been pretending all these years.'

She gave him a squeeze. 'I believe you,' she said. 'Like Mam always said, love is a big tent.'

Tears filled her father's eyes. 'Yes,' he said, 'but I'm not sure I ever knew how big.'

Phuket,
13 February, 2015

Dear Daddy,

Greetings from Phuket. I'm sitting under the shade of a proper palm tree, drinking water straight from coconuts – can you believe it? Trust me, I am making GREAT use of my inheritance.

It is so hot here that my hair stands three feet off my head in all directions but, unbelievably, my skin is finally turning from pink to brown – I'm not sure you'd recognise me!

It was strange at first, travelling alone, but I've been following the itinerary Fionn suggested and he's right – the hostels have been a great way to meet other lone travellers. Sometimes we spend a few days together if we're heading in the same direction and then we go our separate ways. Meeting people without expectations has made it easier for me to make friends, and guess what? I'm fun here! I even did karaoke last night!!

I've been thinking a lot about how I behaved over Christmas and in the weeks before I left, and I'm mortified. Some of the things I said were unforgivable and, even though you pretended not to be hurt, I know you were. I'm so sorry, Daddy. I was so shocked at how fast things were changing, scared of what would happen to me. But I should have been happy for you. I hope you know it wasn't because it was

Fionn – I think I would've behaved equally as badly if it had been a new woman. The shock factor of Fionn just seemed to give me a licence to behave like a brat in a way a thirty-year-old woman should be ashamed of.

I've decided that it's okay for you to sell the house, so you can move your studio to Dublin. It was wrong of me to stand in your way, especially when I'll be living in Galway myself from September when I go back to college. For what it's worth, I think I'll be a better midwife now than I would have been when I first began; those chips on my shoulder would've weighed me down on the wards. I'm so happy that I'll finally be able to use the nurse's fob watch Mam gave me; I've always felt guilty about that. Can I ask you one thing, though? Can we have one last Christmas on the island before we go? And then we can put it up for sale in January and start the new year fresh. I'd appreciate that, if we could.

I hope you haven't run the business into the ground while I've been away. Please don't ignore your inbox – there are orders there!!!

I'll sign off now before I lose the light. Please give Fionn a hug from me and tell him he's taking care of precious cargo for me now.

All my love,
Noll Xx

Dublin: 24 May, 2015

Dillon sat in the grounds of Dublin Castle, drinking cava from the bottle with a rainbow-striped straw while Molly took pictures on her phone of the Taoiseach, Leo Varadkar, hugging Panti, Ireland's new undisputed Queen and the public face of the country's LGBTQ community. The exit polls for the marriage referendum had all but guaranteed a Yes vote, but when the official result was announced, revealing that sixty-two per cent of the country had voted in favour of same-sex marriage, the city exploded. Rainbow flags dangled from apartment blocks, flew from lamp posts and were waved in the air by the thousands of people who spilled out into the streets in celebration. Strangers hugged, recognising a friend from the YES badge they wore. It felt as if the whole country had woken up to a new Ireland.

The only person in the crowd who looked dispirited was Dillon, despite the YES badge on the lapel of his denim jacket. Molly put her arm around his shoulder. 'You should call him,' she said. 'Imagine how he must be feeling now.'

Dillon shrugged her off. 'I can't. I haven't spoken to him since the party, and he's probably with *him*.'

She sighed, sipped from his straw and took his face in her hand. 'Dillon, my love. Look around you. See what love can do? Your father is so brave, and you want to be on the right side of this.'

He stretched his neck away from her. 'This isn't about the marriage referendum,' he said. 'I voted yes – it's not that that he's suddenly supposedly gay that has upset me. I can't believe he lied to us all these years. He's a fraud.'

She stood up and swung her handbag over her shoulder.

'You tell yourself whatever you want,' she said, 'but you know it's not that simple. This vote means nothing if men like your father can't get even a *bit* of empathy from their own children. Look at you sitting there, with your YES badge. *You're* the only fraud I see.'

She turned on her heel and vanished into the mob before he could stop her. He felt his phone vibrating and slid his finger across the screen to answer the call from Sive. 'Don't you start,' he said.

'Dillon?' she said. 'Hang on, I'm here with Mossy.'

'What are you doing in Galway?' he asked.

The line was bad, muffling Sive's voice. He pressed the phone hard against his ear while ducking into a derelict telephone box to try to hear better.

His father's voice came down the line. 'Hello, son.'

Dillon could hear his voice cracking, feel the others listening. He rested his forehead against the dirty glass of the phone box and disconnected the call. A better part of himself knew he should call back, but he couldn't force himself to do it. He pushed through the crowds to get back to his flat, where he closed the curtains, turned off the lights and slid a video cassette into the VHS player he still kept connected to the television. He sat on the floor in front of the couch, Molly's coat draped over his knees, and watched the old tape of his mother playing Desdemona. He knew she would want him to make peace with his father, but she hadn't stuck around long enough to show him how. Molly found him there later that night, asleep at an awkward angle, the television set crackling with black-and-white fuzz. He woke up and saw her standing there, flushed and tipsy from too much alcohol.

'I'm sorry,' he said, reaching out for her.

'It's not me you should be apologising to,' she said, ruffling his hair. 'But tomorrow is another day. In the morning we wake up in a new Ireland. Don't start it on the wrong foot, love.'

'I don't believe it can be this easy for the others to accept it.'

'It's not,' she said, smiling at him. 'But they're trying to. Because you've all suffered enough and they want to at least try to be happy for him. Can't you do the same?'

He turned off the television and followed her into bed, disappointed to find that there were no more missed calls on his phone.

Were the others all celebrating with his father now?

Lying in the dark, Molly softly snoring beside him, he couldn't sleep.

Who was all this punishing, really?

He crept back to the sitting room, rewound the tape and sat on the floor in front of the television. But this time he didn't press play.

Instead he quietly lifted a battered briefcase down from the top shelf of the closet and spilled a pile of unopened letters across the carpet.

Dozens of letters that had been arriving since Christmas and that he had never read.

With his name and address written by the hand of someone who loved him.

His father.

He started to read.

Date: 9 June, 2015
To: Nollaig, Tomás, Dillon, Sive
Cc: Kalindi, Fionn
From: Makes of Moone
Subject: From your father

My dear children,

For the second time in less than a year I want to tell you all something at the same time but, unfortunately, on this occasion it's not possible to gather you all together, for many reasons.

I have started and deleted this email a dozen times and you all know how slow I am at typing, so my two forefingers are almost blunt from banging on the keys. As a result, in this final attempt, I am going to try and say simply what feels so complicated.

On the eve of the marriage referendum, Fionn asked me to marry him. He said he wanted to propose before the result so, no matter which way the vote went, I knew how he felt regardless.

I said yes.

And I hoped that when the results came through, I would feel that Ireland accepted our decision. Now, we know the country supports us, or at least two thirds of it, I hope my children can, too.

Some would say it would have been easier for me to continue on as I was without causing all this drama – to them I say, what sort of man would I be if I watched all those brave folks campaign for my freedom and then pretended that I didn't want it?

Here comes the sentimental bit. I have denied a part of myself for so many years since we lost your mother, flattened any seed of hope before it could blossom into even the idea of an idea, and now I want to give myself a chance to bloom.

I have been given a second chance of happiness that I never thought would come. I know this may not be what you imagined happiness would look like for me, but here it is. And, as much as you might struggle with it sometimes, I think I would be a poor parent if I didn't seize a chance of happiness when it was offered to me, even if the circumstances were difficult, even if it was hard to explain.

What sort of parent would I be if I taught you to run away from love?

We have decided to get married on the island on Christmas Eve. You must believe me when I say I truly believe that this would make your mother happy – it is time that Christmas became an occasion we can celebrate again. And we will celebrate her, too, on the day, and Nollaig's birthday, and thank her for bringing us together.

I hope that you will all be there for us, but we will understand if it is too difficult. Please remember, sometimes we have to endure the difficult parts to get to the good place again, and happy endings don't always look like we expect them to, if there even is such a thing.

I will speak to you all soon, I hope, but wanted to give you time to absorb this news before I do.

I send it with all my love, and a heart full of hope.

Dad

Inis Óg: Morning, 19 December, 2015

Murtagh was surprised to see the blue door of Makes of Moone swaying open in the wind as he turned the bend on the pier road. *Was Nollaig working already?* He was sure he'd heard her on the telephone when he left the house. *Did I not close the door last night when I left?* The possibility that an intruder could have broken in and left the door swinging in their wake never even occurred to him. Not until he saw the glass glittering on the windowsill and the ugly words spray-painted in red across his whitewashed wall. He rushed forward and started rubbing at the graffiti with the sleeve of his duffel coat, but only the original white paint flaked away. *Is that what they call me behind my back? The islanders? Someone I know?*

He crunched through the broken glass and stood in the doorway, flicked the light switch, but the bulb had been smashed, so he pulled the curtains to let the weak winter sunlight illuminate the damage. The red paint was sprawled over each wall, some of the words not even spelled correctly. He tried not to look at them.

The last shipments due to leave the shop before he moved to Dublin were no longer stacked in neat white cardboard boxes along the back wall but strewn about the floor, the boxes shredded, contents shattered.

Murtagh steadied himself and entered the back room; all of the glazes he'd stored there were spilled across the floor, puddles of terracotta, golden yellow and sea green mingling unhappily and smearing across the tiles.

On his desk, the midnight-blue porcelain vase he had made as a wedding present for Fionn lay in seven pieces like a three-dimensional jigsaw puzzle. He moaned, a deep, low noise, as he traced his fingers along the edges, remembering the hours he had spent moulding it into the perfect shape, engraving symbols from their life together into the clay, mixing the exact shade of the sea under moonlight. Weeks of work destroyed, irreplaceable.

'Dad?' A voice made him jump and he turned to see Dillon standing at the doorway, a suitcase in his hand, his face pale.

'Dillon' – his father held out his arms to him – 'Dillon, I'm – I'm so –' But his knees gave way and he crumpled to the floor among the broken pots and started to shake.

Dillon dropped his case and came towards him. 'Be careful, Dad,' he said. 'Don't cut yourself. Come on, let's get out of here.'

He helped his father stand and steered him from the studio by his elbow. Outside, they both sat on a bench, facing the ocean in silence.

'Who would do such a thing?' Dillon asked, looking back at the studio and turning his face away in disgust. 'It must be someone we know.'

Murtagh stood up. 'I should try and clean it up before folks come along,' he said. 'Maya and Ajay are here this afternoon. I don't want them to see that.'

Dillon took his father's arm again and navigated him towards home. 'Don't worry about it. Let's go home and I'll get some things to take care of it. You're not going back there.' His breathing was heavy as he walked, shock now being overtaken by anger.

'I'll find out who did this, Dad, and when I do –'

His father cut him off with a hand on his wrist.

'When you do, you'll do nothing,' he said. 'You can't beat hate with hate. That just fuels their fire.'

Murtagh opened the front door and interrupted Fionn and Nollaig sorting through the contents of the hall cupboard.

'How long is it since we did this?' she asked. 'Because I've found Sive's Leaving Cert results and – Dillon! Dillon, you're here – oh my God, what's happened?'

Inis Óg: Midnight, 19 December, 2015

Murtagh slipped out of the house while everyone else was sleeping and gathered together a few things from the shed, before returning to his studio. It was comforting to find the door firmly locked and the walls freshly painted white again. Offering some silent thanks for his children, he touched the plastic that covered the window with his fingertips as he passed and let himself in. The paint fumes were potent, the white walls blinding when he turned on the light. His studio was almost completely empty now; all the shards had been swept away, the cardboard boxes removed. The floor had been mopped almost completely clean of the glazes, but there were still faint traces of colour between the grout on the tiles that would never be erased.

On his workstation, the remains of Fionn's vase lay on top of newspaper. Murtagh sighed in relief that it had not been thrown away. He spread out the contents of his bag, propped himself on his old stool, and set to work mixing lacquer with the powdered silver that Kalindi had brought him from Tokyo. When instinct told him that the mixture was the right consistency he began to piece the porcelain vase back together again. The fragments were sewn together in silver, and slowly it became whole once again. As dawn was breaking Murtagh lifted the repaired vase with its silvery veins and turned it towards the light flooding in from the east.

It was more beautiful than before.

Art made of precious scars.

Kintsugi.

Inis Óg: 20 December, 2015

Father Dónal raced through Mass, barely leaving enough time for the islanders to give their responses before slamming the Bible shut and leaving the pulpit to begin his sermon. He stepped down from the altar, his colour rising, and for the first time in all his years as the island's parish priest he paraded up and down the aisle as he spoke. He was not so much delivering a sermon as summoning all the wrath of the heavens down upon them. The congregation watched aghast, swivelling their heads to watch him striding past with his black cassock flapping about his legs.

'I have lived on this island for thirty-five years,' he began, 'and always thought being appointed here was a gift from God Himself. These islanders are good people, I thought. Kind, Christian people, I thought, who support one another, live in peace, and would do each other no harm. It seems *I was wrong*. For an ugly thing has happened and shocked me to my core.

'A great man of this island, whose family has lived amongst us for over three decades, who I know has been a good friend to everyone sitting here, has been the victim of a terrible and cruel act of malice. You all know what I speak of; the rumours have been buzzing across the island all day like a swarm of angry wasps. But *who*, may I ask, offered a hand of help to rectify this maleficent deed? *Who* sought him out to express their sorrow that such a thing should happen here on our beloved island? *Not one of those kind Christian people of my parish.* You may not have picked up the hammer, or kicked in his door, but if you know who did and you say nothing, your sin of omission is a terrible one.

'On the twenty-second of May this year, we as a country voted to allow people of the same sex to marry each other. I know there were many priests across the land who told their congregations to vote no, but I tell you here and now, my conscience was clear when I put a big giant X in the box that said yes. And I'll tell you why. I know I can stand in front of my God and tell him I didn't prevent two people who loved each other from being happy, and I don't believe any loving God would want me to. Now, we are going to sit here in silence for ten minutes. *Ten minutes*, and I want you all to think about what has happened on this island and decide if you are okay with that, or if you are going to stand up and support one of our own whose only mistake, as far as I can see, was trusting us with his truth.

'In the name of the Father, and the Son, and the Holy Spirit.'

For the next ten minutes, Father Dónal stood at the altar, resting his eyes on each person along every pew in turn.

When they were eventually released into the night, the freedom felt like a storm finally breaking after a heatwave.

The islanders were broken, and desperate for repair.

FOUR

Kintsugi

Inis Óg: 24 December, 2015

It was Christmas Eve.

Murtagh wore brown brogues, shiny as chestnuts, as he paced to and fro along the well-worn floorboards in the hallway of the Moone family home.

Standing before the looking glass, he smoothed his silver curls. He wore a new suit, cut from navy-blue tweed, slim fitting, with a white shirt and a dark green velvet bow-tie that kept coming undone.

Nollaig stood before him, wearing a black silk dress that trailed the ground and a crown of lilac anemone flowers in her hair, which hung loose.

'Are you ready?' she asked him, re-tying his bow once again and holding him at arm's length. 'You look ready,' she said, and kissed him on the forehead.

The door to the living room was open.

Christmas waited inside.

A fir tree from Gallagher's field was adorned in white lights and the decorations made by Nollaig, Mossy, Dillon and Sive as children. Traditions that had not been outgrown, after all.

Nollaig and her father were the last to leave the house. As they closed the front door behind them, the cuckoo from Maeve's clock chirped four times and Murtagh exhaled a deep breath.

'Just a minute,' he hesitated, opening the door once again and turning the porch light on.

They linked arms as they walked down the lane together, reminiscent of so many walks they had taken before, but this time the air crackled around them. 'I remember the first time you were allowed to walk to Siopa Síle on your own,' he said. 'Your mother followed you all the way, trying to hide so you wouldn't see her.'

Nollaig laughed. 'Oh, I knew she was there but pretended not to see her. I was relieved, to be honest.'

The rain had held off all day and the evening was drawing in, clean, crisp and black. 'I hope it won't be too dark,' he said. 'At the castle. We don't want anyone stumbling.'

'It's fine. Mossy hung the fairy-lights, remember? Pól gave us his generator,' she said. 'You should worry more about folks hearing you over the noise of that thing.'

He stopped and looked at her. 'Should I?'

She laughed at him. 'I'm only joking, Daddy. Don't look so worried.'

They started walking again, their pace picking up.

'It's not like we're expecting many people,' he said. 'It's just ourselves, Jeremy, Dónal, and maybe one or two from the island will show. Probably for the best.'

As they marched a beat down the long, narrow lane towards the pier, Murtagh trailed his hand along the stony wall covered in moss and repeated his mantra.

Give me courage, Maeve. Give me courage.

In their companionable silence, Nollaig ran through the lines of the speech she'd written in her head. 'What's funny this time?' he asked her, stopping to shake a pebble from his shoe.

'Nothing,' she said. 'Nearly there now.'

Soon they would turn right at the chapel and follow the road until they reached the hilly path that led to the ancient ruins where the ceremony would take place.

The sea was calm tonight, lapping at the shore like a kitten's tongue in her milk bowl. Murtagh slowed down to breathe in the sea air when his attention was caught by the glitter of lights up ahead.

'What's all that?' he said. 'Mossy hasn't dragged lights all the way down here, has he?'

'Come on,' Nollaig said, pushing him forward. 'You'll see.'

As they drew closer, Murtagh squeezed her hand and said:

'Oh Noll, is that −?

'What are they all −?

'Is that . . . ?'

Along the winding lane to the castle, every man, woman and child from the island lined the path holding a flickering candle inside a pint glass, jam jar or tumbler.

Their faces glowed in gold as he passed, each one smiling at him as he fought back tears, reaching out to shake his hand or give him a quick little hug.

As he moved along the lane the islanders fell in step behind him, so a parade of lights followed him to the crumbling fortress wall of the castle.

In the grass before it, a patchwork quilt of dozens of blankets lay spread across the grass.

An aisle was marked by oars adorned in yellow ribbons and ivy.

At the end of the aisle stood Fionn, handsome in a black

tuxedo, complete with a white silk pocket square sent to him by Maeve's mother June.

He waited with Jeremy, who had acquired his marriage licence especially for them.

Over his shoulder, Murtagh saw Mossy, Dillon, Sive, Kalindi and the twins clustered together on two wooden pallets, just like the stage the Moones had used when they were children. Mairtin Higgins played the fiddle quietly while the islanders spread themselves around on the blankets, a few of the older folks propped on fold-out deckchairs at the back. Father Dónal was the last to take his seat, and then Sive gave Mairtin the nod. He let the last notes of his tune fade away, waited for a moment and then with gusto launched into the melody for 'Moon River'.

Sive started singing, and the rest of the Moones joined her as Nollaig walked her father down the aisle.

Murtagh and Fionn stood in front of a tall ebony pedestal that displayed the matrimonial kintsugi vase full of the mistletoe, so rare in Ireland, that grew in the island cemetery around the bark of an old apple tree. Beside it sat a photograph of Maeve, Murtagh and Fionn sitting on the beach at Inis Óg with the four Moone children scattered around them.

The good people of the island joined in for the second chorus of the song.

Everyone joined in, even those who didn't believe they were singers.

In fact, theirs were the loudest voices of all, as, with each verse, the light grew brighter.

It was Christmas Eve.

Inis Óg: 24 December, 2005

My dearest Murtagh,

I feel as if I have been writing this letter in my head for twenty years or more, but now, when it comes to finally doing it, I am lost for words.

I know on some level you've been expecting it all this time, too, hoping it was lost forever in the post, but always on the alert.

I am sorry for that, and for so many other things.

I am sorry that this terrible illness has dogged our lives, teasing us with good times and then punishing us for enjoying life without it, storming back in, petulant and unforgiving.

I am sorry that our children have borne witness to it, and learned to handle me with care, like one of your fragile pots.

I am sorry that I can't stand up to it any more, but I've had glimpses of how bad things could get, and you have, too. I don't want either of us to see how that version of life ends, and want to give you all a happier ending, impossible as that may be to believe in now. I am scared of who I will become, scared that the good that still remains in me will be completely destroyed. If I leave now, there may still be more good than bad for them to remember.

Please believe me when I say there is nothing you could have said or done to change this outcome. You could not have saved me, because, and you need to hear this, my love, this seizing of control is in truth the only way I can be saved. You know I've never lied to you.

I am so sorry that I couldn't always be a better mother to our children, but I take comfort in knowing that by leaving earlier than we all might have hoped, I have stopped myself becoming a worse one.

It is so much easier to love a dead mother than a mad one.

To grieve a dead wife than a sad one.

My truth is not a universal one, I know, but I recognise it as my own. One that has crept up on me so gradually but now leaves me dazzled by its beauty. And I know the hot light of truth will revive you, too, when you are ready.

When we met, Murtagh, we were such untethered spirits floating through the world, as if one of us might drift away if we didn't hold hands tightly. We were imperfect people, who fitted perfectly together.

You have made me so happy.

When I think back on our life together, I am filled with gratitude.

I am illuminated by your love.

For so long now I have been filled with dread and worry about the future, about what this illness would do to me, to the children, to you, but now for the first time in such a long time I think of your future and I am filled with hope.

I am sorry that you will have to tell the children, to answer impossible questions, and help them to make sense of all of this. I must accept that it may never make sense to them; it is all but impossible for them to separate me as a woman from their mother. That is how it has always been for mothers since the dawn of time so who can blame our lovely children for the same?

And one more thing, my darling man in the moon, love will come for you again, and when it does you must throw your arms open wide to it. You deserve someone to take care of you, to love you, and you must know I would want that for you.

Please tell the children again and again how much I love them, share with them stories from the good times, and when they are ready, maybe you can help them understand the bad times that led me here.

I hope I have laid the foundations in their heart for understanding, and have taught them how to love, and to be loved.

I leave them, I leave you, because I love you, and because I want you to always be able to love me, too.

I am rambling now. It is hard to finish this letter.

Darkling I listen; and, for many a time
I have been half in love with easeful Death,
Call'd him soft names in many a mused rhyme,
To take into the air my quiet breath.

My darling, wherever I go, my heart stays with you.

Please leave a light on now for yourself, a light to guide you home.

All my love,
Your Maeve

Acknowledgements

The title for this novel was drawn from the poem *Tell all the truth but tell it slant* by Emily Dickinson.

The song 'Dublin Saunter', sung by Maeve and Murtagh in Dublin was written by Leo Maguire with lyrics reproduced here with the kind permission of Waltons Music Ltd.

I would like to sincerely thank all of the following people for their endless support and encouragement while I was writing this book:

- Peter Straus, my incomparable agent, and the amazing team at Rogers, Coleridge and White.
- Jessica Leeke, Clio Cornish and all the brilliant folks at Michael Joseph, Penguin Random House.
- My American agent, Kimberly Witherspoon and all at Inkwell Management.
- Melanie Fried and the Graydon House team.
- My mentor and friend, Michèle Roberts.
- My writing group comrades, Marc Lee and Natalie Burge.
- Niall Williams and Christine Breen Williams.
- My parents, Frank and Margaret Cullen.
- Gaby and Hans Wieland.
- All of my loved ones, my family and friends, for their love and inspiration.
- Demian Wieland, to whom this book is dedicated.

Q&A with Helen Cullen

The novel has the Japanese concept of kintsugi running through it. In what way did this art form inspire the novel?

I was really inspired by kintsugi – the practise of repairing broken pottery with powdered gold, silver or platinum. The breakage and the repair remain visible to show the history of an object, rather than being something to be disguised, and so the pots become even more beautiful than before they were broken. As any family spans decades, both hairline fractures and critical breaks can occur. Some tragedies seem insurmountable; we can't go on, and yet we do. Some cracks feel irreparable, but then often reveal themselves to be the gap we squeeze through so that we can find a way to keep moving.

Telling the Moone's story, I was inspired by the power of the truth – how it can give power to your legs to keep walking. Writing the book forced me to consider how our personal truths may not always chime with those that are felt to be universal, and how sometimes that realisation creeps up on us gradually, and leaves us dazzled by its beauty. As the great Leonard Cohen said, '*There is a crack in everything, that's how the light gets in.*'

The complex challenges of motherhood are an important theme in the book. Do you feel the voice of the mother has been neglected in Irish literature?

In general the accounts of women's experiences are routinely missing from historical records and, in literature, mothers have often been neglected as potential protagonists. In contemporary times many writers, especially women writers, have worked hard to address the cultural silence that still often prevails surrounding motherhood and women's lives. When I started writing *The Truth Must Dazzle Gradually,* I was ready to write about Ireland and wanted to bear witness to the societal changes we've experienced through the lens of one family. Inevitably I found myself writing about motherhood – it seems strange to me that anyone could write about Irish society and not interrogate the cultural meaning of the Irish Mammy to some degree, and yet Irish mothers, as subjects with agency and autonomy rather than a symbolic role, have historically been largely absent from our literature. Maeve is not Irish but she embodied the role of the Irish Mammy to her children and so her outsider status allowed me to observe the Mammy as an Irish cultural phenomenon – to consider how much of the plight of the mother was universal, and what was specific to our own tiny island.

The island of Inis Óg is a fictional one, but is it based upon somewhere real?

Yes, Inis Óg was inspired by Inis Oírr, the smallest of the Aran Islands, which are located off the west coast of Ireland.

It is probably my favourite place in the world, but I chose the creative freedom of inventing a fictional island rather than setting the book on the real one. I felt that otherwise I would have become too shackled by an obsession to get every detail perfectly right, and that the restrictions would have impeded my ability to let the narrative flow. Instead, I was able to luxuriate in the feeling of the island without stressing about misrepresenting it. I spent many summers as a teenager there at the Gaeltacht and it's a very important place to me.

Music features greatly in both of your novels. Is choosing the music an important part of the writing process for you?

It definitely is. One of my favourite elements of building the world of a book is creating a soundtrack to accompany the narrative. Curating a book's playlist allows me to indulge in the perfect intersection of my two great loves, music and literature. Scoring a scene with the perfect song to reflect and reinforce its mood helped me to have faith in the emotional truth of those scenes, and deepened my connection with them. Every day, before I begin to write, I choose a song to listen to that encapsulates for me the energy or the feeling of the scene I want to work on. Sinking into the music, the physical world around me slips away, and I am able to cross the bridge from reality to the wonderland of the imagination. For *The Truth Must Dazzle Gradually,* I listened to a vinyl record of 'Moon River' performed by Henry Mancini and his orchestra most days before I began writing, and it will forever be associated with it now.

What advice would you give to other people who would like to write their own novel?

Just keep going – word by word, day by day. Don't let perfection be the enemy of finishing your work – anything can be fixed in a later draft, but you need to reach the end first. If you do, you'll have a better understanding of what your novel is about and be better placed to edit and finesse it then. The only thing all the writers that I know have in common is that they finished their books, so persevere!

Reading Group Questions

1. The concept of kintsugi is a significant metaphor in the book. It comes from the Japanese art of repairing broken pots with gold and silver filament so the breakages become part of the object's history, making them more beautiful than before. How did you feel this theme resonated through the novel?

2. How important do you feel the island setting was in creating the atmosphere of the book?

3. Maeve's diary entries provide insight into her interior world, which often clashed with her public self. Did they change your understanding of her as a character? Were you surprised by what they revealed?

4. The novel touches on some sensitive topics, including the impact of mental health problems on the entire family. Discuss how you feel Maeve's struggles affected Murtagh and the children.

5. How did Maeve's final letter, which concludes the book, alter your understanding of her?

6. When Fionn arrived on the island, it was clear his presence was going to be significant to the Moones. Were you surprised by what he came to mean to the family in the end?

7. The notion of personal truth is central to the novel – how our personal truths may not always align with the public perception of who we are. Discuss how this idea was expressed in the novel and whether it resonated with you in your own life.

If you loved this novel, don't miss out on

The Lost Letters of William Woolf,

available to buy now

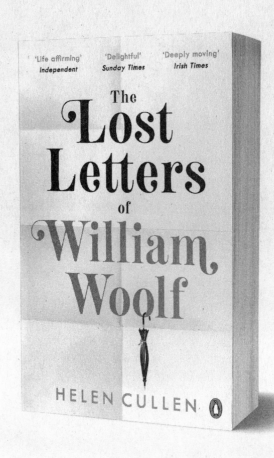

Read on for an extract...

I.

Lost letters have only one hope for survival. If they are caught between two worlds, with an unclear destination and no address of sender, the lucky ones are redirected to the Dead Letters Depot in East London for a final chance of redemption. Inside the damp-rising walls of a converted tea factory, letter detectives spend their days solving mysteries. Missing postcodes, illegible handwriting, rain-smudged ink, lost address labels, torn packages, forgotten street names: they are all culprits in the occurrence of missed birthdays, unknown test results, bruised hearts, unaccepted invitations, silenced confessions, unpaid bills and unanswered prayers. Instead of longed-for missives, disappointment floods post boxes from Land's End to Dunnet Head. Hope fades a little more every day, when doorbells don't chime and doormats don't thud.

William Woolf had worked as a letter detective for eleven years. He was one of an army of thirty, having inherited his position from his beloved uncle, Archie. Almost every Friday throughout William's childhood, Archie, clad in a lime-green leather jacket, rode his yellow Honda Dream 305 over for tea, eager to share fish and chips doused in salt and vinegar served with a garlic dip, and tales of the treasures rescued that day. Listening to Archie opened William's mind to the myriad extraordinary stories that were unfolding every day in the lives of ordinary people. In a blue-lined copybook, he wrote his favourites and unwittingly began what would become a lifelong obsession with storytelling, domestic mysteries and the secrets strangers nurse. What surprised William most when he started working there himself was how little Archie had exaggerated. People send the strangest paraphernalia through the post: incomprehensible and indefensible, sentimental and valuable, erotic and bizarre, alive and expired. In fact, it was the dead animals that so frequently found their way to this inner sanctum of the postal system that had inspired the Dead Letters Depot's name. A photo taken in 1937, the year it had opened, showed the original postmaster, Mr Frank Oliphant, holding a pheasant and hare aloft, with three rabbits stretched out on the table before him. By the time William joined in 1979, it was a much more irregular occurrence, of course, but the name still endured. He still felt Archie's presence amid the exposed red-brick walls of the depot, and some of the older detectives sometimes called William by his uncle's name. Their physical similarities were striking: muddy brown curls, chestnut beards flecked with rust, the almond-shaped hazel eyes that flickered between shades of emerald green and cocoa, the bump in the nose of all Woolf men.

In a vault of football-field proportions hidden below Shoreditch High Street, row upon row of the peculiar flotsam and jetsam of life awaited salvation: pre-war toy soldiers, vinyl records, military memorabilia, astrology charts, paintings, pounds and pennies, wigs, musical instruments, fireworks, soap, cough mixture, uniforms, fur coats, boxes of buttons, chocolates, photo albums, porcelain teacups and saucers, teddy bears, medical samples, seedlings, weapons, lingerie, fossils, dentures, feathers, gardening tools, books, books, books. Copious myths and legends passed from one colleague to another; stories of the once lost but now found.

Each detective cultivated their own private collection of the most remarkable discoveries they had made. For William, there was a suit of armour dismantled in a tarnished silver sea-chest, an ebony-and-glass case housing two red admiral butterflies, each wing secured by a tiny pearl pin, and a miniature grandfather clock only three feet tall. 'More of a grandson clock, really,' he always joked.

There were still some deeply unpleasant discoveries to be made. The detectives harboured daily fears of strange stenches, soggy parcels and departed creatures; mostly, white mice, cockroaches and bugs originally destined to feed pet lizards, snakes and rats. At least William hoped that's what they had originally been intended for, before they met another, equally unpleasant end in 'The Furnace', the final destination for contaminated goods, the unrecyclable and unsalvageable. It sat shoulder to shoulder with the gnashing, monster shredder where lost letters became dead letters and all hope was vanquished.

Every day, the detectives opened letter after letter, parcel after parcel, searching for clues. The satisfaction of solving a mystery never faded. The joy of knowing that something so anticipated could find its way after a lengthy

3

diversion remained exquisite. It was the thousands of unsolvable conundrums that wearied bones and wasted skin on paper cuts. Sometimes, there just wasn't enough evidence to trace, no clue to worry over until the blessed eureka moment. Over the years, William had learned not to fret over the truly lost, to let them go and to invest his time instead in those that presented greater hope of a solution. Every week, hundreds of new puzzles arrived, so the mountain of mail in the depot seemed self-replenishing. A pessimist could find much to confirm a bleak worldview in this museum of missed messages. Only a quarter of the post that passed through the depot ever found its way home, but just one very special victory could sustain a detective for weeks in their endeavours.

William had recently reunited a battered Milk Tray chocolate box brimful of wedding photos from 1944 with the bride, Delilah Broccoli. The son of her maid of honour had found them when executing his mother's estate and tried to post the box back to the last known address, but the street, never mind the individual house, no longer existed. When items discovered lost in the post held considerable monetary or sentimental value, or had been missing in action for an exceptionally long time, the letter detectives would courier them to their rightful home rather than send them off into the cavernous postal system once again. A still-breathing tortoise, a crystal chandelier and a silver pendant hanging from a garland of rubies were among some of the undeliverables William had elevated to his personal care. In some very exceptional cases, the letter detectives went one step further and delivered items in person, out of fear that something so precious may become lost once again. On this most recent occasion, William had successfully traced Delilah to the nursing home in East Anglia where she now lived and decided this should be one of those exceptions.

When William entered Delilah's bedroom, she looked confused as she tried to place him. 'We haven't met before, Mrs Broccoli,' he reassured her. 'I work for the post office, and wanted to deliver a parcel to you that went astray.'

He moved a pink plastic cup of water from the table-top tray that lay on her lap and placed the world-weary chocolate box before her. It was the same shade of purple as her dressing gown; velvet with a white lace collar. Delilah's eyes flitted from William's to the box and back again. She tried to speak, but the words caught in a raspy net in her throat. Her silver curls were flattened on the right side of her head from where they were crushed against the pillow. He moved closer and laid his hand gently on her arm.

'It's all right, nothing to be frightened of. Here, let me help you.'

He prised the lid from the chocolate box and placed the crinkled photographs before her one by one. Delilah traced a finger beneath the row of sepia and a look of recognition spread across her face. She picked up one with a trembling hand and held it close to her nose. William watched as a shy smile illuminated her expression and her eyes grew misty.

'I'll leave you in peace now, Mrs Broccoli,' he said.

She reached out and grabbed his sleeve with her

papery grip and held on tight for a second. It was days like those that kept his faith alive.

Lately, William had retreated more and more into the soft silence of the post delivery room, away from the chatter and bustle of the shared office space where the letter detectives worked. He had never been very good at rising above his moods and found it increasingly hard to shake off the melancholia he brought from home in order to join in the collegiate banter. In the solitude of the delivery room, he rummaged deep into postbags, a shirtsleeve rolled up to his pointy elbow, to extract what he hoped would be something special. Each time, he closed his eyes and forced his breath to grow slow and deep. His ribcage expanded like the bellows of old, his lungs paused at their fullest expansion, before he slowly exhaled, with a gentle whoosh. He hunched over the slate-grey canvas bag, with his left hand supporting the small of his back, and wriggled the fingers of his right hand inside. His thirty-seven years didn't command this posture; it was more an affectation that had evolved as part of his hunting regime. With great concentration, he would linger over the folds of the envelopes, squeeze parcels tentatively between forefinger and thumb, until, instinctively, he would clasp one, tugging it gently free and drawing it to the surface. He imagined he was like the mechanical arm of a teddy-bear machine, retrieving a soft toy. These rescue missions were different from the piles of post left indiscriminately on his desk every morning at six by the night-owl team who accepted the midnight deliveries. The letters that he found this way, he believed were destined for him. Over ten years of flirting with coincidence, defying the odds and witnessing serendipity had left him superstitious and more inclined to believe in a divine intervention he would have mocked in his days before the depot. He now was convinced that some letters found him because only he, with his particular personal collection of experiences and insights, could crack their code. Other letters depended upon different detectives, of that he was sure, but some were searching specifically for him.

He just wanted a decent book to read ...

Not too much to ask, is it? It was in 1935 when Allen Lane, Managing
Director of Bodley Head Publishers, stood on a platform at Exeter railway
station looking for something good to read on his journey back to London.
His choice was limited to popular magazines and poor-quality paperbacks –
the same choice faced every day by the vast majority of readers, few of
whom could afford hardbacks. Lane's disappointment and subsequent anger
at the range of books generally available led him to found a company – and
change the world.

*'We believed in the existence in this country of a vast reading public for intelligent
books at a low price, and staked everything on it'*
Sir Allen Lane, 1902–1970, founder of Penguin Books

The quality paperback had arrived – and not just in bookshops. Lane was
adamant that his Penguins should appear in chain stores and tobacconists,
and should cost no more than a packet of cigarettes.

Reading habits (and cigarette prices) have changed since 1935, but
Penguin still believes in publishing the best books for everybody to
enjoy. We still believe that good design costs no more than bad design,
and we still believe that quality books published passionately and responsibly
make the world a better place.

So wherever you see the little bird – whether it's on a piece of
prize-winning literary fiction or a celebrity autobiography, political tour
de force or historical masterpiece, a serial-killer thriller, reference book,
world classic or a piece of pure escapism – you can bet that it represents
the very best that the genre has to offer.

Whatever you like to read – trust Penguin.